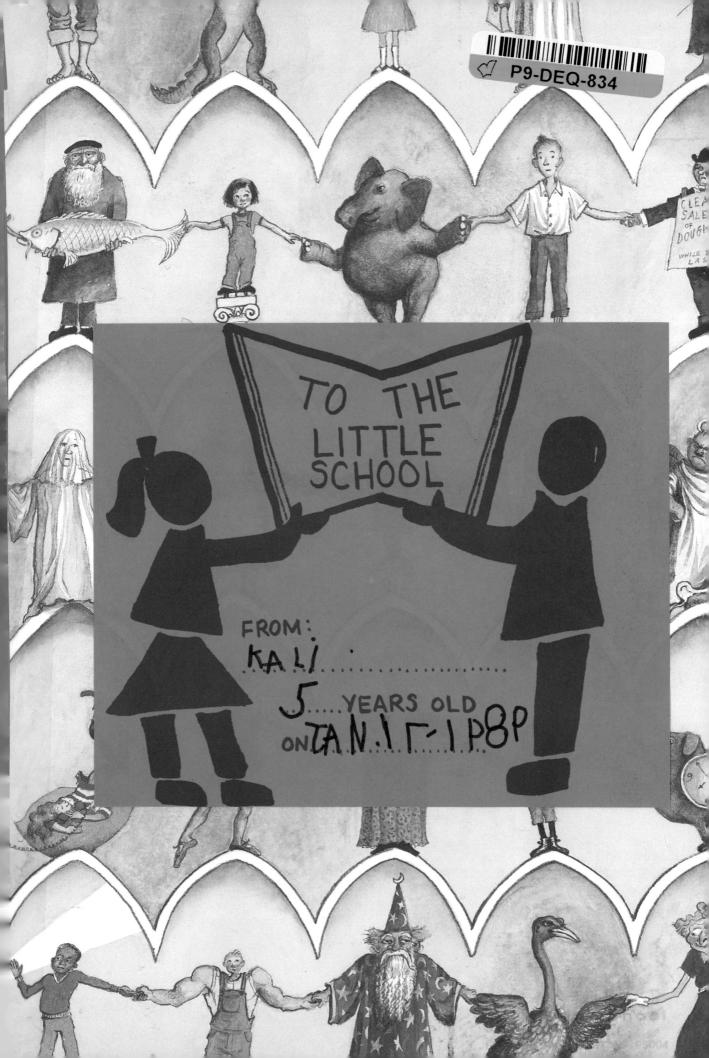

TO THE
LITTLE
SCHOOL

FROM:
KALI
5 YEARS OLD
ON TAN. 1 Γ - 1 P8P

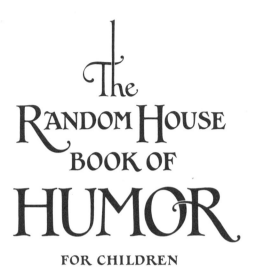

The
RANDOM HOUSE
BOOK OF
HUMOR

FOR CHILDREN

The Random House Book of HUMOR

FOR CHILDREN

Selected by
PAMELA POLLACK

Illustrated by
PAUL O. ZELINSKY

Random House · New York

For Oz, who knows the way to make me laugh
—P.P.

With love, for Rachel, who got here first
—P.O.Z.

Compilation copyright © 1988 by Random House, Inc.
Illustrations copyright © 1988 by Paul O. Zelinsky.
All rights reserved under International and Pan-American Copyright Conventions.
Published in the United States by Random House, Inc., New York,
and simultaneously in Canada by Random House of Canada Limited, Toronto.

Library of Congress Cataloging-in-Publication Data:

The Random House book of humor for children.
SUMMARY: A humor collection for middle graders composed of thirty-four prose selections—
short stories and "chunks" from novels.
1. Wit and humor, Juvenile.   2. Humorous stories. [1. Humorous stories]
I. Pollack, Pamela. II. Zelinsky, Paul O., ill.
III. Title: Book of humor for children.
PN6153.R36 1987 [Fic] 86-31478
ISBN: 0-394-88049-8 (trade); 0-394-98049-2 (lib. bdg.)

Manufactured in the United States of America   1 2 3 4 5 6 7 8 9 0

Copyright and acknowledgments are continued on page 307.

Contents

CONTENTS

A NOTE TO THE READER

Laughing is a good way to spend time. I laughed a lot at these stories. Each one came from a different book. Some are short stories, and some are chapters or selections from longer books. I've chosen pieces that stand on their own. You don't need to have read what came before. You can enjoy each selection all by itself. After you finish these, you may want to find out where your favorite pieces came from. You can do that by turning to the Acknowledgments (pages 307–310), which lists each piece in the book alphabetically by the author's name. This list tells the title of the book that the piece came from and the name of the publisher. Read and have fun!

—*Pamela Pollack*

JUDY BLUME
Tales of a
Fourth Grade Nothing

I will never forget Friday, May tenth. It's the most important day of my life. It didn't start out that way. It started out ordinary. I went to school. I ate my lunch. I had gym. And then I walked home from school with Jimmy Fargo. We planned to meet at our special rock in the park as soon as we changed our clothes.

In the elevator I told Henry I was glad summer was coming. Henry said he was too. When I got out at my floor I walked down the hall and opened the door to my apartment. I took off my jacket and hung it in the closet. I put my books on the hall table next to my mother's purse. I went straight to my room to change my clothes and check my turtle, Dribble.

The first thing I noticed was my chain latch. It was unhooked. My bedroom door was open. And there was a chair smack in the middle of my doorway. I nearly tumbled over it. I ran to my dresser to check Dribble. He wasn't there! His bowl with the rocks and water was there—but Dribble was gone.

I got really scared. I thought, *Maybe he died while I was at school and I didn't know about it.* So I rushed into the kitchen and hollered, "Mom . . . where's Dribble?" My mother was baking something. My brother sat on the kitchen floor, banging pots and pans together. "Be quiet!" I yelled at Fudge. "I can't hear anything with all that noise."

"What did you say, Peter?" my mother asked me.

"I said I can't find Dribble. Where is he?"

"You mean he's not in his bowl?" my mother asked.

I shook my head.

"Oh dear!" my mother said. "I hope he's not crawling around somewhere. You know I don't like the way he smells. I'm going to have a look in the bedrooms. You check in here, Peter."

My mother hurried off. I looked at my brother. He was smiling. "Fudge, do you know where Dribble is?" I asked calmly.

Fudge kept smiling.

"Did you take him? Did you, Fudge?" I asked not so calmly.

Fudge giggled and covered his mouth with his hands.

I yelled, "Where is he? What did you do with my turtle?"

No answer from Fudge. He banged his pots and pans to-gether again. I yanked the pots out of his hand. I tried to speak softly. "Now tell me where Dribble is. Just tell me where my turtle is. I won't be mad if you tell me. Come on, Fudge . . . please."

Fudge looked up at me. "In tummy," he said.

"What do you mean, in tummy?" I asked, narrowing my eyes.

"Dribble in tummy!" he repeated.

"What tummy?" I shouted at my brother.

"This one," Fudge said, rubbing his stomach. "Dribble in this tummy! Right here!"

I decided to go along with his game. "Okay. How did he get in there, Fudge?" I asked.

Fudge stood up. He jumped up and down and sang out, "I ATE HIM . . . ATE HIM . . . ATE HIM!" Then he ran out of the room.

My mother came back into the kitchen. "Well, I just can't find him anywhere," she said. "I looked in all the dresser drawers and the bathroom cabinets and the shower and the tub and . . ."

"Mom," I said, shaking my head. "How could you?"

"How could I what, Peter?" Mom asked.

"How could you let him do it?"

"Let who do what, Peter?" Mom asked.

"LET FUDGE EAT DRIBBLE!" I screamed.

My mother started to mix whatever she was baking. "Don't be silly, Peter," she said. "Dribble is a turtle."

"HE ATE DRIBBLE!" I insisted.

"*Peter Warren Hatcher!* STOP SAYING THAT!" Mom hollered.

"Well, ask him. Go ahead and ask him," I told her.

Fudge was standing in the kitchen doorway with a big grin on his face. My mother picked him up and patted his head. "Fudgie," she said to him, "tell Mommy where brother's turtle is."

"In tummy," Fudge said.

"What tummy?" Mom asked.

"MINE!" Fudge laughed.

My mother put Fudge down on the kitchen counter where he couldn't get away from her. "Oh, you're fooling Mommy . . . right?"

"No fool!" Fudge said.

My mother turned very pale. "You really ate your brother's turtle?"

Big smile from Fudge.

"YOU MEAN THAT YOU PUT HIM IN YOUR MOUTH AND CHEWED HIM UP . . . LIKE THIS?" Mom made believe she was chewing.

"No," Fudge said.

A smile of relief crossed my mother's face. "Of course you didn't. It's just a joke." She put Fudge down on the floor and gave me a *look*.

Fudge babbled. "No chew. No chew. Gulp . . . gulp . . . all gone turtle. Down Fudge's tummy."

Me and my mother stared at Fudge.

"You didn't!" Mom said.

"Did so!" Fudge said.

"No!" Mom shouted.

"Yes!" Fudge shouted back.

"Yes?" Mom asked weakly, holding on to a chair with both hands.

"Yes!" Fudge beamed.

My mother moaned and picked up my brother. "Oh no! My angel! My precious little baby! OH . . . NO. . . ."

My mother didn't stop to think about my turtle. She didn't

even give Dribble a thought. She didn't even stop to wonder how my turtle liked being swallowed by my brother. She ran to the phone with Fudge tucked under one arm. I followed. Mom dialed the operator and cried, "Oh help! This is an emergency. My baby ate a turtle . . . STOP THAT LAUGHING," my mother told the operator. "Send an ambulance right away; 25 West 68th Street."

Mom hung up. She didn't look too well. Tears were running down her face. She put Fudge down on the floor. I couldn't understand why she was so upset. Fudge seemed just fine.

"Help me, Peter," Mom begged. "Get me blankets."

I ran into my brother's room. I grabbed two blankets from Fudge's bed. He was following me around with that silly grin on his face. I felt like giving him a pinch. How could he stand there looking so happy when he had my turtle inside him?

I delivered the blankets to my mother. She wrapped Fudge up in them and ran to the front door. I followed and grabbed her purse from the hall table. I figured she'd be glad I thought of that.

Out in the hall I pressed the elevator buzzer. We had to wait a few minutes. Mom paced up and down in front of the elevator. Fudge was cradled in her arms. He sucked his fingers and made that slurping noise I like. But all I could think of was Dribble.

Finally, the elevator got to our floor. There were three people in it besides Henry. "This is an emergency," Mom wailed. "The ambulance is waiting downstairs. Please hurry!"

"Yes, Mrs. Hatcher. Of course," Henry said. "I'll run her down just as fast as I can. No other stops."

Someone poked me in the back. I turned around. It was Mrs. Rudder. "What's the matter?" she whispered.

"It's my brother," I whispered back. "He ate my turtle."

Mrs. Rudder whispered *that* to the man next to her and *he* whispered it to the lady next to *him* who whispered it to Henry. I faced front and pretended I didn't hear anything.

My mother turned around with Fudge in her arms and said, "That's not funny. Not funny at all!"

But Fudge said, "Funny, funny, funny Fudgie!"

Everybody laughed. Everybody except my mother.

The elevator door opened. Two men, dressed in white, were waiting with a stretcher. "This the baby?" one of them asked.

"Yes. Yes, it is," Mom sobbed.

"Don't worry, lady. We'll be to the hospital in no time."

"Come, Peter," my mother said, tugging at my sleeve. "We're going to ride in the ambulance with Fudge."

My mother and I climbed into the back of the blue ambulance. I was never in one before. It was neat. Fudge kneeled on a cot and peered out through the window. He waved at the crowd of people that had gathered on the sidewalk.

One of the attendants sat in back with us. The other one

was driving. "What seems to be the trouble, lady?" the attendant asked. "This kid looks pretty healthy to me."

"He swallowed a turtle," my mother whispered.

"He did WHAT?" the attendant asked.

"Ate my turtle. That's what!" I told him.

My mother covered her face with her hanky and started to cry again.

"Hey, Joe!" the attendant called to the driver. "Make it snappy . . . *this* one swallowed a turtle!"

"That's not funny!" Mom insisted. I didn't think so either, considering it was my turtle!

We arrived at the back door of the hospital. Fudge was whisked away by two nurses. My mother ran after him. "You wait here, young man," another nurse called to me, pointing to a bench.

I sat down on the hard, wooden bench. I didn't have anything to do. There weren't any books or magazines spread out, like when I go to Dr. Cone's office. So I watched the clock and read all the signs on the walls. I found out I was in the emergency section of the hospital.

After a while the nurse came back. She gave me some paper and crayons. "Here you are. Be a good boy and draw some pictures. Your mother will be out soon."

I wondered if she knew about Dribble and that's why she was trying to be nice to me. I didn't feel like drawing any pictures. I wondered what they were doing to Fudge in there. Maybe he wasn't such a bad little guy after all. I remembered that Jimmy Fargo's little cousin once swallowed the most valuable rock from Jimmy's collection. And my mother told me that when I was a little kid I swallowed a quarter. Still . . . a quarter's not like a turtle!

I watched the clock on the wall for an hour and ten minutes. Then a door opened and my mother stepped out with Dr. Cone. I was surprised to see him. I didn't know he worked in the hospital.

"Hello, Peter," he said.

"Hello, Dr. Cone. Did you get my turtle?"

"Not yet, Peter," he said. "But I do have something to show you. Here are some X-rays of your brother."

I studied the X-rays as Dr. Cone pointed things out to me.

"You see," he said. "There's your turtle . . . right there."

I looked hard. "Will Dribble be in there forever?" I asked.

"No. Definitely not! We'll get him out. We gave Fudge some medicine already. That should do the trick nicely."

"What kind of medicine?" I asked. "What trick?"

"Castor oil, Peter," my mother said. "Fudge took castor oil. And milk of magnesia. And prune juice too. Lots of that. All those things will help to get Dribble out of Fudge's tummy."

"We just have to wait," Dr. Cone said. "Probably until tomorrow or the day after. Fudge will have to spend the night here. But I don't think he's going to be swallowing anything that he isn't supposed to be swallowing from now on."

"How about Dribble?" I asked. "Will Dribble be all right?" My mother and Dr. Cone looked at each other. I knew the answer before he shook his head and said, "I think you may have to get a new turtle, Peter."

"I don't want a new turtle!" I said. Tears came to my eyes. I was embarrassed and wiped them away with the back of my hand. Then my nose started to run and I had to sniffle. "I want Dribble," I said. "That's the only turtle I want."

My mother took me home in a taxi. She told me my father was on his way to the hospital to be with Fudge. When we got home she made me lamb chops for dinner, but I wasn't very hungry.

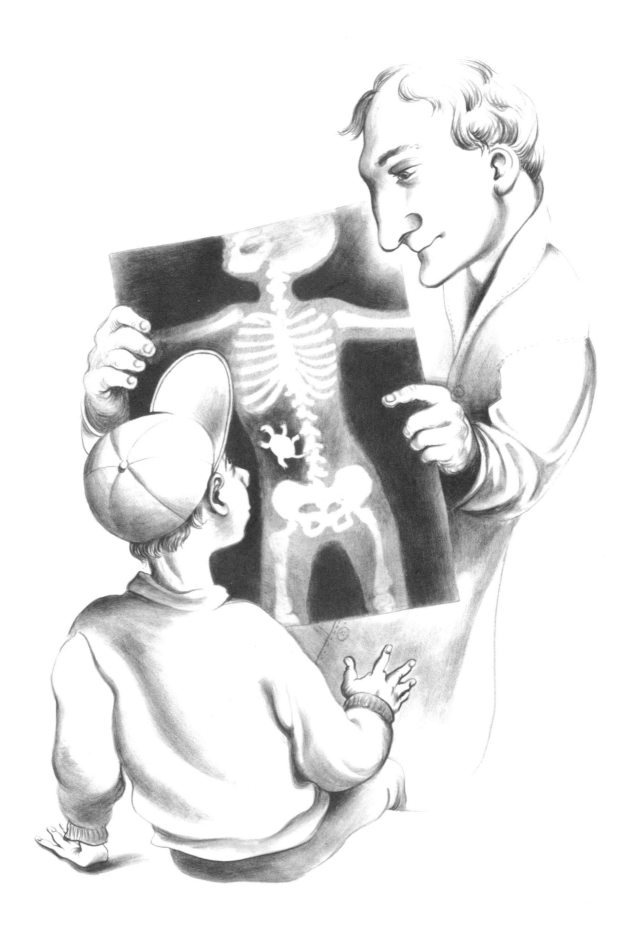

My father came home late that night. I was still up. My father looked gloomy. He whispered to my mother, "Not yet . . . nothing yet."

The next day was Saturday. No school. I spent the whole day in the hospital waiting room. There were plenty of people around. And magazines and books too. It wasn't like the hard bench in the emergency hallway. It was more like a living room. I told everybody that my brother ate my turtle. They looked at me kind of funny. But nobody ever said they were sorry to hear about my turtle. Never once.

My mother joined me for supper in the hospital coffee shop. I ordered a hamburger but I left most of it. Because right in the middle of supper my mother told me that if the medicine didn't work soon Fudge might have to have an operation to get Dribble out of him. My mother didn't eat anything.

That night my grandmother came to stay with me. My mother and father stayed at the hospital with Fudge. Things were pretty dreary at home. Every hour the phone rang. It was my mother calling from the hospital with a report.

"Not yet . . . I see," Grandma repeated. "Nothing happening yet."

I was miserable. I was lonely. Grandma didn't notice. I even missed Fudge banging his pots and pans together. In the middle of the night the phone rang again. It woke me up and I crept out into the hallway to hear what was going on.

Grandma shouted, "Whoopee! It's out! Good news at last."

She hung up and turned to me. "The medicine has finally worked, Peter. All that castor oil and milk of magnesia and prune juice finally worked. The turtle is out!"

"Alive or dead?" I asked.

"PETER WARREN HATCHER, WHAT A QUESTION!" Grandma shouted.

So my brother no longer had a turtle inside of him. And I no longer had a turtle! I didn't like Fudge as much as I thought I did before the phone rang.

The next morning Fudge came home from the hospital. My father carried him into the apartment. My mother's arms were loaded with presents. All for Fudge! My mother put the presents down and kissed him. She said, "Fudgie can have anything he wants. Anything at all. Mommy's so happy her baby's all better!"

It was disgusting. Presents and kisses and attention for Fudge. I couldn't even look at him. He was having fun! He probably wasn't even sorry he ate my turtle.

That night my father came home with the biggest box of all. It wasn't wrapped up or anything but I knew it was another present. I turned away from my father.

"Peter," he said. "This box is a surprise for you!"

"Well, I don't want another turtle," I said. "Don't think you can make me feel better with another turtle . . . because you can't."

"Who said anything about a turtle, son?" Dad asked. "You see, Peter, your mother and I think you've been a good sport about the whole situation. After all, Dribble *was* your pet."

I looked up. Could I be hearing right? Did they really remember about me and Dribble? I put my hand inside the box. I felt something warm and soft and furry. I knew it was a dog, but I pretended to be surprised when he jumped up on my lap and licked me.

Fudge cried, "Ohhh . . . doggie! See . . . doggie!" He ran right over and grabbed my dog's tail.

"Fudge," my father said, taking him away. "This is your

13

brother's dog. Maybe someday you'll have a dog of your own. But this one belongs to Peter. Do you understand?"

Fudge nodded. "Pee-tah's dog."

"That's right," my father said. "Peter's dog!" Then he turned to me. "And just to be sure, son," he said, "we got a dog that's going to grow quite big. *Much* too big for your brother to swallow!"

We all laughed. My dog was neat.

I named him Turtle . . . to remind me.

BETTY MACDONALD
Mrs. Piggle-Wiggle's Magic

Part witch, part fairy godmother, Mrs. Piggle-Wiggle is the most popular person in town. Children love her because she is so much fun, and parents love her because she has a magic cure for all kinds of naughty behavior.

Mr. Burbank absently reached from behind his newspaper for the sugar bowl. His groping fingers hit the toast, the honeycomb, the salt cellar and finally found the sugar bowl. His children Darsie, Alison and Bard nudged each other and laughed. Every morning Daddy felt around on the table for the sugar while he read bad news in the newspaper.

One morning the news was so bad and he was so absent-minded he put currant jelly in his coffee. The children were anxious for a repeat performance and hopefully pushed everything but the sugar in the path of his searching hand. This morning as soon as Mr. Burbank had found the sugar he let the paper down with a bang. "The sugar bowl's empty," he said in an aggrieved, hurt way.

Mrs. Burbank, who was buttering toast said, "Darsie, run out to the kitchen and fill the sugar bowl, dear. The sugar's in the big red can."

Darsie obediently got up, took the sugar bowl and went out to the kitchen. After a long long time he came back to the breakfast table with a plate of cinnamon rolls.

"What are these for?" his father said. "And where is the sugar?"

"Sugar?" said Darsie. "What about sugar?"

"I told you to fill the sugar bowl," said Mrs. Burbank.

"Oh," said Darsie, "I thought you said, 'Get the cinnamon roll.' "

All three children looked at each other and laughed loudly. Finally Mr. and Mrs. Burbank laughed too. Darsie went out and filled the sugar bowl and Mr. Burbank, after three cups of coffee, missed his bus and decided to walk as far as the school with the children.

Just as they were going out the front door, Alison remembered her arithmetic book and dashed upstairs for it. In a minute she leaned over the bannister and called, "Mother, did you see my arithmetic book?"

Mrs. Burbank said, "What does it look like?"

Alison said, "It's blue and not very thick."

Mrs. Burbank said, "I think it's on the table in the hall."

Alison said, "How did it get out there?"

Mrs. Burbank said, "Out where? I said it's on the table in the hall."

Alison said, "Oh, I thought you said it's out in the stable in a stall." All three children roared with laughter.

Alison found her arithmetic book and they all left the house laughing and repeating, "Out in the stable in a stall."

Mr. Burbank said, "Come on, come on, we haven't all day." He walked briskly along the street, his footsteps ringing loudly and purposefully in the thin autumn air. The children giggled and jostled along behind him, their progress so uneven and broken by "thought you said" and shrieks of laughter that Mr. Burbank reached the corner first, in fact almost before they had left the yard. He stopped to wait for them and to survey the city spread out below him in the morning sunshine. He was glad he lived on a hill, he was glad he was alive and he was glad he had a little boy nine, a little girl seven and a little boy six.

When the children had caught up with him he said, "Look, children. See how beautiful the city looks from up here. Watch the fog rise over there."

"Where's the dog?" said Bard.

"What dog?" asked Darsie.

"What color are the dog's eyes?" asked Alison.

"What on earth are you talking about?" said Mr. Burbank. "I said, 'Watch the fog rise over there.'"

"Oh," Bard said, "I thought you said, 'Watch the dog's eyes glare.'" All the children laughed and laughed. Mr. Burbank said, "What nonsense," but it was a beautiful morning so he laughed with his lighthearted children.

When they were halfway down the next block, the children suddenly stopped stock still in front of a pretty white house and yelled in unison, "Marilyn! Mar-ee-lun! Come on, we'll be late!"

Mr. Burbank said, "That's no way to do. If you want Marilyn, go to the door and ask for her."

The children looked surprised but went obediently up to

the door and rang the bell. Marilyn's mother opened the door and said something to the children which seemed to send them into convulsions of mirth. Doubled over with laughter and holding their sides, they came down the walk to their father.

"Now what's so funny?" Mr. Burbank asked.

Darsie said, "Marilyn's mother said Marilyn fell in the toaster and is burnt up dead."

Mr. Burbank said, "What did Marilyn's mother really say and why isn't Marilyn going to school."

Alison said, "She said Marilyn fell in her coaster and hurt her head and Darsie thought she said Marilyn fell in the toaster and is burnt up dead." She went into another paroxysm of laughter.

Mr. Burbank didn't laugh. Instead he bent down and examined Darsie's ears, which were large and pink and soft and quite clean.

"They *should* work," said Mr. Burbank, looking at the other children's ears. They all seemed quite normal. The children wanted to know what he was doing.

Bard said, "What are you doing that for, Daddy?"

Mr. Burbank said, "I'm trying to decide whether I should get you an ear trumpet."

"Beer crumpet? What's that?" Bard said.

The other children repeated after him, "Beer crumpet? Beer crumpet?" They all laughed but Mr. Burbank, who had had enough. He said, "Come on. I'll supervise a race to school. On your marks, get set, go!"

When Mr. Burbank reached his office the very first thing he did was to call Mrs. Burbank. He said, "Mary, have our children ever had scarlet fever?"

She said, "Now you know they haven't, Bernard."

"Well," he said, "have they ever had ear infections?"

"Goodness, no," said Mrs. Burbank. "They've never had anything. They are the healthiest children in the neighborhood. What's the matter?"

Mr. Burbank said, "Plenty. They can't any of them hear well. I told them to look at the fog rise and they thought I was talking about dog's eyes. Marilyn's mother said that Marilyn fell off her coaster and hurt her head and they thought she said Marilyn fell in the toaster and was . . ."

". . . Burnt up dead," Mrs. Burbank finished for him.

"Bernard, did you ever hear of anyone falling in a toaster? Of course not. There is nothing wrong with our children's ears. It is just that they are going through that awful Thought-You-Said phase."

"Well let's get them out of it," said Mr. Burbank. "They sound like dopes. Dog's eyes, indeed."

Mrs. Burbank said, "Don't worry, dear, I'll take care of it."

As soon as she finished talking to Mr. Burbank, Mrs. Burbank called Marilyn's mother to find out about Marilyn, if she was badly hurt and if there was anything she could do. Marilyn's mother said Marilyn was just fine but the doctor thought she should be quiet for a day or two.

When Mrs. Burbank asked Marilyn's mother if she had ever had any trouble with Thought-You-Said, and told about the sugar bowl and the cinnamon rolls, the arithmetic book in the stable in the stall, about Marilyn's fall in the toaster and the dog's eyes, Marilyn's mother said, "Oh, Mrs. Burbank, I'm so glad you called and told me all this. You see Marilyn has been doing the same thing all morning and I was terribly afraid that the blow on her head had affected her mind. When I asked her if she wanted crumpets or toast she said, 'Bumped on the nose, who?' When I asked her if her head pained her she said, 'I thought you said, Is the bed painted yet?' "

Mrs. Burbank said, "I'm going to call up Mrs. Teagle and see if Terry or Theresa are Thought-You-Saids. She is such a good manager that if they have Thought-You-Saiditis she's probably thought of a cure." Marilyn's mother asked Mrs. Burbank to call her back if she got any useful information and they said goodbye.

Then Mrs. Burbank called Mrs. Teagle. She told her all about the Thought-You-Saiditis and asked if she had had any similar experience with Terry or Theresa. Mrs. Teagle said, "Ohwa, nowa, Mrs. Burrrrbank. Youwa see we have allaways studied korrect speeeeeech and wea all speak korrectly. Thee cheeldren alaways pronounce all theirrrr vowels and all theirrr consonants and therefore we neverrrr have any trouble under-standing each otherrrrr. Perhaps the trouble lies with you and Mr. Burbank—perrrhaps you do not speak deestincktly. Perhaps the poor leetle cheeldrun cannot underrrrstahnd you. I am holding lit-tul speeeeeech clahsses everrrry ahfternoon and eef you and Mrrrr. Burrrbank are interrrest-ed I would be glad to hahve you attend. I wouldn't carrrrre to hahve the cheeldrun becawse I am afrrrraid they might corrupt my cheeldrun's perrrrfect speeeeeech."

Mrs. Burbank thanked Mrs. Teagle for her kind offer and

told her that perhaps she was right. That she and Mr. Burbank would try to speak more distinctly and if things didn't improve within the week they might join the speech classes. Mrs. Teagle said, "Glahd to bee of help annnny tihum, Mrs. Burrbank," and hung up.

That night when Mr. Burbank came home she told him about calling Mrs. Teagle, and told him that she thought that from now on they should both try to speak more carefully so that their poor little children could understand them.

That night at dinner Mr. Burbank announced in a very loud voice, "Pleeeeeese pahsssssss the butterrrrrr!" The children all exchanged glances and whispers, then laughed. The butter remained cool and comfortable on its little plate in front of Darsie.

Mr. Burbank looked accusingly at Mrs. Burbank. She said in a high unnatural voice, "Cheeeldrun, leesten to meee. Pleeeeese pahssss youh fahtherrr the butterrrrrr!"

"Oh," said Darsie, "did you say pass the butter. I thought you said, 'Fleas gasp and mutter.' "

Alison said, "I thought you said, 'He's pa's mother.' "

Bard said, "I thought you said, 'Freeze Pat's brother.' "

Mr. Burbank said in a low grim voice, "I said 'Please pass the butter.' " Darsie passed it to him with a beaming smile.

The next morning after breakfast, Mr. Burbank called from upstairs, "Where's my briefcase, anybody seen my briefcase?"

Alison said, "Who's got a thief's face?"

Darsie said, "Beef paste, what do you want that for?"

Bard said, "Leaf race, I thought he said leaf race." They all laughed loudly and did not look for the briefcase.

They could hear their mother and father banging doors and scuffling around upstairs but they were so busy Thought-You-

Saiding they didn't even notice that Bard was standing in front of the briefcase, which was leaning against the radiator in the front hall.

Finally Mr. Burbank came running downstairs, wild-eyed and almost too late for his bus. He called to Mrs. Burbank, "If you find it, dear, bring it right down to the office. I must have it this morning." He slammed the front door and ran like the wind for his bus.

Mrs. Burbank was giving the children their final inspection before school when she saw the briefcase leaning against the wall right behind Bard's fat little legs. She said, "Why children, why didn't you tell Daddy his briefcase was down here. You must have seen it! Now I'll have to make a special trip all the way down to take it to him. Why didn't you tell him?" She looked sternly at her three children.

Alison said, "Briefcase! I didn't know that's what he wanted, I thought he said, 'Thief's face.' "

Darsie said, "I didn't know he wanted his briefcase, I thought he said, 'Beef paste.' "

Bard said, "I thought he said 'leaf race.' "

Mrs. Burbank said, "You know perfectly well that Daddy wouldn't talk about a thief's face, beef paste or leaf races. That's just nonsense and I'm getting good and tired of all this Thought-You-Said business." She sent them off to school with a little push and without a kiss.

But the Thought-You-Saiditis continued all the rest of that week. By Friday morning Mr. and Mrs. Burbank were so irritable they didn't even want to come downstairs and eat breakfast with the Thought-You-Saiders. They tried to solve the problem by not speaking to the children but of course the telephone rang and Mrs. Burbank said to Alison, "Answer the phone" and Alison didn't move and her father said, "ANSWER THE PHONE!" and Alison said, "Oh, answer the phone, I thought you said, 'This ham's got a bone'" and Darsie said, "I thought you said, 'The dancers are home'" and Bard said, "I thought you said, uh, uh, uh, 'The jam's all alone.'" It was the last straw. Mr. Burbank said, "This nonsense has got to stop, now. I'm not going to eat another meal with the Thought-You-Saids."

As soon as the children had left for school and even before she washed the breakfast dishes, Mrs. Burbank decided that she must do something about the Thought-You-Saiders. She poured herself another cup of coffee and sat down at the breakfast table and thought and thought. Ole Boy, the dog, came and sat beside her and she gave him a small piece of ham and stroked his head and wondered and wondered what to do.

She was just going to call Mr. Burbank's mother when the telephone rang again. Mrs. Burbank answered it. It was Mrs. Piggle-Wiggle and she wanted the children to come for tea. Mrs. Burbank said, "Oh, Mrs. Piggle-Wiggle, I am so delighted that you called. I was just sitting here at the breakfast table wondering what in the world to do." And so she told Mrs. Piggle-Wiggle about the Thought-You-Saiders.

Mrs. Piggle-Wiggle said, "There is a regular epidemic of Thought-You-Saiditis all over town. It really is a very harmless disease but can be most annoying to parents, especially when they are trying to hurry. I have suffered with it myself this past

week. Put on your shoes is Thought-You-Said sat on a fuse— Get me a tack is Thought-You-Said butter a cracker, and on and on. Fortunately the cure is very simple. I have a magic powder which you sprinkle in the children's ears tonight. It will make their hearing so keen that they'll be able to hear spiders stamping across the floor, leaves crashing to the ground, flowers snapping open their petals and fireflies striking the matches that light their lanterns. I must warn you that tomorrow when the children are wearing the magic hearing powder, you mustn't pop corn, run the vacuum cleaner or serve dry crunchy breakfast foods. The noise would be too painful to them. I'll send the powder over when the children stop by after school. You might lend a little to Marilyn's mother. Goodbye and good luck." Mrs. Piggle-Wiggle hung up the phone.

After school the children came rushing in to deliver the package from Mrs. Piggle-Wiggle and to change their clothes. Mrs. Piggle-Wiggle's package contained a tiny little box of white powder. Mrs. Burbank felt the powder and smelled it—it felt like talcum powder and it smelled like ginger. She put it under the pile of clean handkerchiefs in her handkerchief box. That evening after the children were in bed, she told Mr. Burbank about it. He thought the magic powder sounded wonderful and decided to try a little in his own ears.

Mrs. Burbank went up and got the bottle and Mr. Burbank put a pinch in his left ear. Immediately he shouted, "TURN OFF THAT TERRIBLE RADIO. IT'S KILLING ME." Mrs. Burbank rushed and turned the radio off. Mr. Burbank said, "It's thundering, we must be going to have a storm." Mrs. Burbank listened. She couldn't hear any thunder. She opened the front door and went out and looked at the sky. It was a clear dark blue and spangled with stars. The night was as still and quiet as a picture. Mr. Burbank shouted, "The storm's getting closer. Almost overhead now!"

Mrs. Burbank came in and closed the door. She said, "Bernard Burbank, it's a cold, clear, perfectly peaceful night. There is no thunder."

Mr. Burbank said, "Listen. Don't you hear it. Deafening—that's what it is. Deafening!" Mrs. Burbank listened very carefully. Then she heard from the kitchen a soft very faint thumping noise. She went out to investigate and found Ole Boy the dog, lying under the kitchen table scratching and bumping his elbow on the floor. She gave Ole Boy a dog biscuit and put him out, then she went back to the living room and asked Mr. Burbank if the storm had passed over.

He said, "Do you have to stamp your feet like that? You certainly must be getting fat, you sound like a coal truck when you walk."

Mrs. Burbank, who was very slight, looked down at her soft red house slippers and said, "Bernard, I think you had better wash that magic powder out of your ear because I'm going to go out right now and get some graham crackers and think of the torture you'll go through if I drop a crumb."

Mr. Burbank said, "Stop shouting!"

Mrs. Burbank said, "I'm whispering, dear," so Mr. Burbank went upstairs to wash out his ear. When he snapped on the light in the bathroom he flinched because it sounded like a pistol shot. When he turned on the faucet it sounded like Niagara Falls and when he accidentally brushed a hairpin off the window sill it sounded like a huge iron chain crashing to the tiled floor.

Mr. Burbank filled the bathroom glass with warm water. He had decided that that would be the best way to wash out the magic powder, and was just about to pour some in his ear when from behind the bathtub he heard the most awful screaming, screeching, whining noise. He straightened up, put down the glass and peered over by the bathtub. He didn't see anything. He bent down over the basin again and picked up the glass. He was just about to pour the warm water in his ear when the horrible, screaming, squealing noise came again, this time right by his head. Mr. Burbank was so scared he dropped the glass, spilled the water and banged his head on the faucet. He looked all around but he couldn't see anything. The noise came again. This time a little fainter and from behind the Venetian blind. He raised the blind and looked carefully. He couldn't see a thing. The terrible noise came again, this time by the mirror; then Mr. Burbank saw what it was. A big mosquito. He grabbed a washcloth and without thinking of his magic hearing, swatted the mosquito. The screams of agony that immediately filled the bathroom were horrible. Mr. Burbank hurriedly turned on the warm water and stuck his ear right under the faucet. Whew, what a relief!

He picked the dead mosquito up by one leg and put it in the wastebasket, then he called to Mrs. Burbank. "Hey, Mary, I'm all right now but I think we'd better go easy with that magic powder in the children's ears. It's awfully strong."

Mrs. Burbank said, "Perhaps you used too much. Here, I'll measure it out. I'll use a toothpick and I'll just put a grain or so in the right ear of each child. Come on now, help me."

They tiptoed into the children's rooms and put a toothpick full of the magic powder in each one's right ear. Even in his sleep Darsie was saying, "Miss Anderson, I didn't hear you say, 'Hand me that ruler'—I thought you said, 'Bananas are cooler.' "

Mr. and Mrs. Burbank looked at their sleeping son and then at each other. "Just wait until tomorrow, Darsie old boy," said Mr. Burbank.

The next morning at seven o'clock, Bard came running into his parents' room and said, "Mother, Daddy, there is a terrible noise in our room. It sounds like sawing." Mr. and Mrs. Burbank got out of bed, put on their robes and went in to investigate. They couldn't hear a thing. Darsie said, "Isn't that an awful noise, Daddy? Do you think it's a buzz bomb?" Mr. and Mrs. Burbank looked and looked but they couldn't see or hear anything.

Mr. Burbank told the children to get dressed and come down to breakfast. Bard began to cry. He said, "We'll come down, Daddy, but you don't have to yell at us."

Mr. Burbank said in a very quiet whisper, "Your hearing must be very good this morning. I didn't yell—in fact I almost whispered." Then he said, "Exactly where is the buzzing noise coming from, Darsie? Listen carefully and tell me."

Darsie said, "Right there by the curtain."

Mr. Burbank pulled back the curtain and found a very small fly buzzing and buzzing in a corner of the window. Remembering his experience with the mosquito, he didn't dare swat the fly, so he opened the window, unlatched the screen and pushed the fly off the window sill. It flew happily away.

Darsie said, "Daddy, I can't stand this awful crunching

noise my shoelaces make when I push them through the holes. It sounds like bones breaking."

Mr. Burbank said, "Here, I have an idea." He tied his handkerchief around Darsie's head like a bandage. "This'll fix it," he said softly.

"Whistle biscuit!" Darsie said. "I thought you said 'Whistle biscuit.' " His father jerked the handkerchief off and said, "Hurry down to breakfast."

At breakfast Alison said, "Oh, Mother, I can't stand the sound of you buttering that toast. It sounds like hoeing on cement."

Bard said, "Hoeing on cement! I thought you said, I thought you said, uh, er ah . . ." He took a spoonful of oatmeal and never finished the sentence. A piece of toast popped out of the toaster. All three children jumped.

Darsie said, "Mother, you should warn us when you're going to make so much noise."

Mrs. Burbank said, "I'm sorry but it didn't seem loud to me. I guess my ears aren't very good."

Alison said, "Come on, boys, let's go to school."

Darsie said, "I thought you said Poison, I mean I thought you said, Poison, I mean . . . Oh, I don't know what I meant."

Alison said, "Ole Boy's breathing so loud I can't hear a thing. And does he have to splash his tongue around in his mouth like that, Mother?"

Mrs. Burbank called Ole Boy and gave him a piece of bacon. He snapped and gulped and all three children jumped and shuddered.

"What a noise," said Alison, glaring balefully at poor Ole Boy. "He's just like some terrible kind of a jungle beast."

Mrs. Burbank said, "Come, children, put on your coats and go to school."

Alison said, "Spit on your coats. I thought you said spit on your coats." Nobody laughed.

Darsie said, "Don't talk so loud, Alison, it hurts my ears."

Bard said, "Didn't you hear what Mother said. She didn't say, 'Spit on your coats.' She said, 'Put on your coats.' "

Alison said, "I know it. I can hear. Let's go."

The front door closed quietly and Mrs. Burbank said to her husband, who was groping for the sugar, "That's the first time in five years they haven't banged the front door. Here's the sugar, dear, and you have four minutes before the next bus."

Just then the front door opened and the three children came crying into the house.

Alison said, "Mother, we just can't stand it. The sidewalk is covered with leaves and when we walk through them the noise is so dreadful we just can't bear it. It sounds like hundreds of giants chopping wood."

Bard said, "It sounds like millions of paper bags."

Darsie said, "It sounds like thousands of houses burning up. Crackle, crackle, crash."

Mrs. Burbank said, "Well, Bernard, I think we'd better wash out their ears and we'll give Mrs. Piggle-Wiggle our heartiest thanks."

Mr. Burbank said, "What's she done wrong?"

"Who?" said Mrs. Burbank.

"Mrs. Piggle-Wiggle," said Mr. Burbank.

"What are you talking about?" said Mrs. Burbank. "I said that we should give Mrs. Piggle-Wiggle our heartiest thanks."

"Oh," said Mr. Burbank. "I thought you said 'Go give Mrs. Piggle-Wiggle your hardest spanks.' "

The children looked disgusted.

DOROTHY CANFIELD FISHER
Understood Betsy

Raised by her highstrung Aunt Frances, Elizabeth Ann has been overprotected all her life. But now she's come to live with her Putney cousins in Vermont. The Putneys seem to have their own strange ideas about everything—even what it's like to take a test in school.

Now, you know what an examination did to Elizabeth Ann. Or haven't I told you yet?

Well, if I haven't, it's because words fail me. If there is anything horrid that an examination *did*n't do to Elizabeth Ann, I have yet to hear of it. It began years ago, before ever she went to school, when she heard Aunt Frances talking about how *she* had dreaded examinations when she was a child, and how they dried up her mouth and made her ears ring and her head ache and her knees get all weak and her mind a perfect blank, so that she didn't know what two and two made. Of course Elizabeth Ann didn't feel *all* those things right off at her first examination, but by the time she had had several and had rushed to tell Aunt Frances about how awful they were and the two of them had sympathized with one another and compared symptoms and then wept about her resulting low marks, why, she not only had all the symptoms Aunt Frances had ever had, but a good many more of her own invention.

Well, she had had them all and had them hard this afternoon, when the Superintendent was there. Her mouth had gone dry and her knees had shaken and her elbows had felt as though they had no more bones in them than so much jelly, and her eyes had smarted, and oh, what answers she had made! That dreadful tight panic had clutched at her throat whenever the Superintendent had looked at her, and she had disgraced herself ten times over. She went hot and cold to think of it, and felt quite sick with hurt vanity. She who did so well every day and was so much looked up to by her classmates, what *must* they be thinking of her! To tell the truth, she had been crying as she walked along through the woods, because she was so sorry for herself. Her eyes were all red still, and her throat sore from the big lump in it.

And now she would live it all over again as she told the Putney cousins. For of course they must be told. She had always told Aunt Frances everything that happened in school. It happened that Aunt Abigail had been taking a nap when she got home from school, and so she had come out to the sap-house, where Cousin Ann and Uncle Henry were making syrup, to have it over with as soon as possible. She went up to the little slab house now, dragging her feet and hanging her head, and opened the door.

Cousin Ann, in a very short old skirt and a man's coat and

high rubber boots, was just poking some more wood into the big fire which blazed furiously under the broad, flat pan where the sap was boiling. The rough, brown hut was filled with white steam and that sweetest of all odors, hot maple syrup. Cousin Ann turned her head, her face very red with the heat of the fire, and nodded at the child.

"Hello, Betsy, you're just in time. I've saved out a cupful of hot syrup for you, all ready to wax."

Betsy hardly heard this, although she had been wild about waxed sugar on snow ever since her very first taste of it. "Cousin Ann," she said unhappily, "the Superintendent visited our school this afternoon."

"Did he?" said Cousin Ann, dipping a thermometer into the boiling syrup.

"Yes, and we had *examinations*!" said Betsy.

"Did you?" said Cousin Ann, holding the thermometer up to the light and looking at it.

"And you know how perfectly awful examinations make you feel," said Betsy, very near to tears again.

"Why, no," said Cousin Ann, sorting over syrup tins. "They never made me feel awful. I thought they were sort of fun."

"*Fun!*" cried Betsy indignantly, staring through the beginnings of her tears.

"Why, yes. Like taking a dare, don't you know. Somebody stumps you to jump off the hitching-post, and you do it to show 'em. I always used to think examinations were like that. Somebody stumps you to spell 'pneumonia,' and you do it to show 'em. Here's your cup of syrup. You'd better go right out and wax it while it's hot."

Elizabeth Ann automatically took the cup in her hand, but she did not look at it. "But supposing you get so scared you can't spell 'pneumonia' or anything else!" she said feelingly. "That's what happened to me. You know how your mouth gets all dry and your knees . . ." She stopped. Cousin Ann had said she did *not* know all about those things. "Well, anyhow, I got so scared I could hardly stand *up*! And I made the most awful mistakes—things I know just as *well*! I spelled 'doubt' without any *b* and 'separate' with an *e*, and I said Iowa was bounded on the north by *Wisconsin*, and I . . ."

"Oh, well," said Cousin Ann, "it doesn't matter if you

really know the right answers, does it? That's the important thing."

This was an idea which had never in all her life entered Betsy's brain and she did not take it in at all now. She only shook her head miserably and went on in a doleful tone. "And I said 13 and 8 are 22! and I wrote March without any capital M, and I . . ."

"Look here, Betsy, do you *want* to tell me all this?" Cousin Ann spoke in the quick, ringing voice she had once in a while, which made everybody, from old Shep up, open his eyes and get his wits about him. Betsy gathered hers and thought hard; and she came to an unexpected conclusion. No, she didn't really want to tell Cousin Ann all about it. Why was she doing it? Because she thought that was the thing to do. "Because if you don't really want to," went on Cousin Ann, "I don't see that it's doing anybody any good. I guess Hemlock Mountain will stand right there just the same even if you did forget to put a *b* in 'doubt.' And your syrup will be too cool to wax right if you don't take it out pretty soon."

She turned back to stoke the fire, and Elizabeth Ann, in a daze, found herself walking out of the door. It fell shut after her, and there she was under the clear, pale-blue sky, with the sun just hovering over the rim of Hemlock Mountain. She looked up at the big mountains, all blue and silver with shadows and snow, and wondered what in the world Cousin Ann had meant. Of course Hemlock Mountain would stand there just the same. But what of it? What did that have to do with her arithmetic, with anything? She had failed in her examination, hadn't she?

RICHARD PECK
Ghosts I Have Been

It is Halloween night, 1913. Blossom Culp is about to give her arch-rival, Alexander Armsworth, and his gang a good scare. But before her mission is accomplished, there's a surprise in store for her, too.

Out in the Horace Mann schoolyard it was hard work not to overhear the gang's plans for Halloween mischief. They whispered about it every recess, boxing each other about the head and ears as boys do. Their Halloween plan was nothing more than to turn over people's outhouses. Progress in Bluff City is spotty. Only the chosen few have indoor plumbing. Much of the town on my side of the tracks is still dotted with privies. I had little trouble plotting the gang's course.

Since ghosts were still on the minds of many people, I

planned a costume to feature myself as one. By dark on Halloween night, I had ready a garment made out of old bed linens. One ragged sheet provided me with a full skirt and trailing train. I devised two batwing sleeves from a pair of pillowslips. I shook a full cup of cake flour over my face and hair and worked it in. To complete my disguise as the shade of a dead girl, I draped a mosquito bar over my head as a veil. And I carried a candle in my hand and a box of safety matches in my shoe top to light up my frightful face when the moment was right.

As I stepped out into the evening, the town was alive with young children trick-or-treating from house to house. Half scared of themselves and each other, they kept to the roads and front walks. I flitted through backyards, not wanting to give the little ones a turn. Though it was a clear night, there were wisps of fog. I moved with small quick steps, and my white skirts billowed behind me for all the world like floating. Listen, I wouldn't have liked to meet *me* in a dark alley.

Glowing a ghastly white, I glided down garden rows and past woven-wire fences, lingering behind woodpiles to observe how my drapings settled. There was a nip in the air, but I was warmed by my plans.

They were to figure out which of the outhouses Alexander's gang would push over first. I reflected on what a lot of trouble this gave innocent people and considered I was doing the property owners a favor. I might cure the gang of vandalism permanently.

The first privy I come to was on the back of Old Man Leverette's place. He's a retired farmer moved to town, but he keeps to his country ways and is not the type to invest in an indoor toilet. His outhouse stood like a sentry box against the rising moon. Here was a temptation the boys could not resist. I waited like a terrible statue for a time, seeming to hear the gang's stealthy footsteps in the distance. For the practice I sighed and moaned a little.

My intention was to step just inside the privy and pull the door shut. Then when the gang approached to tip it over, I planned to step out, with the lighted candle, and moan eerily. If this wouldn't strike them half dead with horror, what would? I grinned under my mosquito bar at my plans. Alas, I grinned too soon.

As there was no breeze that night, I fished the matches out of my shoe top and lit my candle as I stepped up to Old Man Leverette's privy door.

At this point, things went seriously wrong. I had one foot inside when I come face to face with Old Man Leverette himself. He was in his privy, using it. His nightshirt was hitched up about his hips. My candle threw dreadful shadows in the tiny room, and light fell on Old Man Leverette's startled face and on the torn pages of the Montgomery Ward catalogue in his aged hands.

Near enough to the grave himself, he let out a kind of Indian war whoop. He rose up, thought better of it, and flopped back down on the seat. I was as startled as he was, and the wind from his gasping breath set the candle flame bobbing.

"Whoooo, whoooo, whooo in the Sam Hill are *you?*" Old Man Leverette howled.

"I beg your pardon, I'm sure," I said, not wanting to identify myself. I took a step backwards, but his hand snaked out and grabbed my wrist. Pages from the catalogue fluttered away like moths. My presence of mind failed me and I said, "I just happened to be passing."

"So was I!" Old Man Leverette roared.

He could tell by grasping my wrist that I was human. Giving it a painful wrenching, he pushed me out the door,

which closed between us. As I lifted my sheets to take flight, I heard his voice from inside still roaring, "Don't light out, missy! I got business with you!"

As near fear as I'd ever been, I waited until Old Man Leverette stepped out into the yard. Lit by the moon, we seemed a pair of ghosts, what with his white nightshirt and a shock of flowing white hair above his lion's face.

"If you're trick-or-treatin'," he said, still gasping, "you can go around to the front door of the house and take your chances like anybody else!"

My candle had gone out by then, and I'd thrown my veil back from my face. He fixed me with a watery eye, but couldn't place me. "And just who do you happen to be?" he said, and waited for an answer.

"Letty Shambaugh," I replied, naming a stuck-up girl in my grade whose name occurred to me.

"Explain yourself before I cut a switch and stripe your legs!"

It wasn't easy to explain to Old Man Leverette that I had his best interests at heart and only meant to save his outhouse from a tipping over. And how would he like to be tipped over *in* it? I nearly added this, but didn't.

He is one of these people who don't like being convinced. But when I mentioned a gang of boys planning to knock over every outhouse between here and the city limits, he began to nod. I didn't name these boys, but I made it clear that I meant to teach them a lesson. If not in the Leverette privy, then in another.

My words began to work. Old Man Leverette worried the stubble on his chin with a gnarled hand. Presently he said, "There's sense to your plan, Letty. But I don't know but what I can improve on it. You can scare hell out of them in the privy, and I'll send 'em on their way with a plan of my own. Don't move. I'll be back directly." Then he stalked off to the house. His nightshirt strained around his big white legs.

He returned, marching down his punkin patch with a shotgun on his shoulder. "Now then," he said, taking over, "you can get yourself into the privy, and I'll hunker down over there behind my compost heap. I got a notion we won't have long to wait. Do your best, and I'll do the rest.

"And you just as well leave your veil up. You're spooky enough lookin' without it."

There was hardly enough air in the privy to get my candle going again. The atmosphere was close and unpleasant. I was reminded of mummies buried upright in their coffins before I heard the sure sounds of a gang of boys trying to be quiet. I drew my veil down.

The boys crashed through the undergrowth behind the privy. I hoped they didn't mean to tip from the back and flatten the door to the ground before I could float out of it. But they only lingered back there, egging one another on. A good example of cowardice is boys in a bunch. I had an idea this was their first privy of the evening. And with any luck at all, their last.

Giving the sides a shove or two, they circled around and went to work on the front. They began to rock my hiding place, but its posts were well sunk. It started to give, though, just as I pushed back the door and stepped out, nearly into the straining arms of Alexander Armsworth.

The candle flickered and guttered between my white veil and his suddenly white face. His arms fell from the door jamb, and he let out the high whinny of a fire-crazed horse. Bub and Champ were at work on the far side of the door and missed my entrance. But they couldn't miss Alexander. He keeled backwards and fell flat on the ground. "A HAUNT! I AM CURSED!"

he screamed and lay on his back like a turned turtle, with his fists jammed into his eyes.

Bub and Champ were transfixed by this behavior. So was Les Dawson, who was standing farther off, supervising the job. I moved beyond the shadow of the door, pulled my veil tight at my throat, and held the candle directly beneath my chin. "Ohhhh! Woe to all here," I moaned in a far-off, cultivated voice, rather like that of our teacher, Miss Mae Spaulding. Bub and Champ gave me one look and ran directly into each other's arms. Then they stumbled forward, sprawling over Alexander, who was still on his back in the weeds. The three rolled together like puppies. Being farther off, Les held his ground. I raised a ghostly finger and pointed directly at him.

This moved him. Just as he wheeled in the direction of a high wood fence along the side of the property, Old Man Leverette reared up from behind him and let out another of his war whoops. It would have curdled milk and blood alike.

Already traveling, Les took a kind of skip in the air. The three on the ground were scuttling crab fashion toward the fence themselves, but they flattened when they heard the war cry.

Old Man Leverette's whoop had not died away before he aimed his shotgun in the air and fired off one barrel of rock salt. People later reported hearing the explosion as far away as the town square. There was a flash of flame from the muzzle, and for some seconds rock salt spattered like hail over the backyard and privy roof.

Les Dawson had hit the fence at his top speed by then, but crumpled down into a summer-squash vine, evidently thinking he was killed. In the next second Bub, Champ, and Alexander were on the fence, clinging to it a moment, and then over the top. Les, being gangly, made two tries at the fence top before he could heave himself over; he was sobbing aloud. For a long moment his backside was high in the air as he tried to calculate the drop on the far side of the fence. Temptation overcame Old Man Leverette.

He grabbed up his shotgun, jammed the butt into his shoulder, and squeezed off the other barrel of rock salt. His large target was Les Dawson's behind.

Of all the screams and whoops that rent the air that night, Les's was the loudest. He seemed to take flight from the top of the fence, like an aeroplane fueled by rock salt, and he fell in an arc on the far side, howling all the way to the ground.

Old Man Leverette whooped again, very nearly helpless with laughter. His shotgun clattered to earth. He gasped and called out, "Well, Letty, I reckon we showed 'em. You, Letty! You hear me?"

But I'd put out my candle by then and was making tracks toward home. I faded away behind a stand of dry hollyhocks, grinning as I went at the notion of Letty Shambaugh putting in such a night's work.

ANN CAMERON

The Stories Julian Tells

I'm going to make something special for your mother," my father said.

My mother was out shopping. My father was in the kitchen, looking at the pots and the pans and the jars of this and that.

"What are you going to make?" I said.

"A pudding," he said.

My father is a big man with wild black hair. When he laughs, the sun laughs in the windowpanes. When he thinks, you can almost see his thoughts sitting on all the tables and chairs. When he is angry, me and my little brother, Huey, shiver to the bottom of our shoes.

"What kind of pudding will you make?" Huey said.

"A wonderful pudding," my father said. "It will taste like a whole raft of lemons. It will taste like a night on the sea."

Then he took down a knife and sliced five lemons in half. He squeezed the first one. Juice squirted in my eye.

"Stand back!" he said, and squeezed again. The seeds flew out on the floor. "Pick up those seeds, Huey!" he said.

Huey took the broom and swept them up.

My father cracked some eggs and put the yolks in a pan and the whites in a bowl. He rolled up his sleeves and pushed back his hair and beat up the yolks. "Sugar, Julian!" he said, and I poured in the sugar.

He went on beating. Then he put in lemon juice and cream and set the pan on the stove. The pudding bubbled and he stirred it fast. Cream splashed on the stove.

"Wipe that up, Huey!" he said.

Huey did.

It was hot by the stove. My father loosened his collar and pushed at his sleeves. The stuff in the pan was getting thicker and thicker. He held the beater up high in the air. "Just right!" he said, and sniffed in the smell of the pudding.

He whipped the egg whites and mixed them into the pudding. The pudding looked softer and lighter than air.

"Done!" he said. He washed all the pots, splashing water on the floor, and wiped the counter so fast his hair made circles around his head.

"Perfect!" he said. "Now I'm going to take a nap. If something important happens, bother me. If nothing important happens, don't bother me. And—the pudding is for your mother. Leave the pudding alone!"

He went to the living room and was asleep in a minute, sitting straight up in his chair.

Huey and I guarded the pudding.

"Oh, it's a wonderful pudding," Huey said.

"With waves on the top like the ocean," I said.

"I wonder how it tastes," Huey said.

"Leave the pudding alone," I said.

"If I just put my finger in—there—I'll know how it tastes," Huey said.

And he did it.

"You did it!" I said. "How does it taste?"

"It tastes like a whole raft of lemons," he said. "It tastes like a night on the sea."

"You've made a hole in the pudding!" I said. "But since you did it, I'll have a taste." And it tasted like a whole night of lemons. It tasted like floating at sea.

"It's such a big pudding," Huey said. "It can't hurt to have a little more."

"Since you took more, I'll have more," I said.

"That was a bigger lick than I took!" Huey said. "I'm going to have more again."

"Whoops!" I said.

"You put in your whole hand!" Huey said. "Look at the pudding you spilled on the floor!"

"I am going to clean it up," I said. And I took the rag from the sink.

"That's not really clean," Huey said.

"It's the best I can do," I said.

"Look at the pudding!" Huey said.

It looked like craters on the moon. "We have to smooth this over," I said. "So it looks the way it did before! Let's get spoons."

And we evened the top of the pudding with spoons, and while we evened it, we ate some more.

"There isn't much left," I said.

"We were supposed to leave the pudding alone," Huey said.

"We'd better get away from here," I said. We ran into our

bedroom and crawled under the bed. After a long time we heard my father's voice.

"Come into the kitchen, dear," he said. "I have something for you."

"Why, what is it?" my mother said, out in the kitchen.

Under the bed, Huey and I pressed ourselves to the wall.

"Look," said my father, out in the kitchen. "A wonderful pudding."

"Where is the pudding?" my mother said.

"WHERE ARE YOU BOYS?" my father said. His voice went through every crack and corner of the house.

We felt like two leaves in a storm.

"WHERE ARE YOU? I SAID!" My father's voice was booming.

Huey whispered to me, "I'm scared."

We heard my father walking slowly through the rooms. "Huey!" he called. "Julian!"

We could see his feet. He was coming into our room.

He lifted the bedspread. There was his face, and his eyes like black lightning. He grabbed us by the legs and pulled. "STAND UP!" he said.

We stood.

"What do you have to tell me?" he said.

"We went outside," Huey said, "and when we came back, the pudding was gone!"

"Then why were you hiding under the bed?" my father said.

We didn't say anything. We looked at the floor.

"I can tell you one thing," he said. "There is going to be some beating here now! There is going to be some whipping!"

The curtains at the window were shaking. Huey was holding my hand.

"Go into the kitchen!" my father said. "Right now!"

We went into the kitchen.

"Come here, Huey!" my father said.

Huey walked toward him, his hands behind his back.

"See these eggs?" my father said. He cracked them and put the yolks in a pan and set the pan on the counter. He stood a chair by the counter. "Stand up here," he said to Huey.

Huey stood on the chair by the counter.

"Now it's time for your beating!" my father said.

Huey started to cry. His tears fell in with the egg yolks.

"Take this!" my father said. My father handed him the egg-beater. "Now beat those eggs," he said. "I want this to be a good beating!"

"Oh!" Huey said. He stopped crying. And he beat the egg yolks.

"Now you, Julian, stand here!" my father said.

I stood on a chair by the table.

"I hope you're ready for your whipping!"

I didn't answer. I was afraid to say yes or no.

"Here!" he said, and he set the egg whites in front of me. "I want these whipped and whipped well!"

"Yes, sir!" I said, and started whipping.

My father watched us. My mother came into the kitchen and watched us.

After a while Huey said, "This is hard work."

"That's too bad," my father said. "Your beating's not done!" And he added sugar and cream and lemon juice to Huey's pan and put the pan on the stove. And Huey went on beating.

"My arm hurts from whipping," I said.

"That's too bad," my father said. "Your whipping's not done."

So I whipped and whipped, and Huey beat and beat.

"Hold that beater in the air, Huey!" my father said.

Huey held it in the air.

"See!" my father said. "A good pudding stays on the beater. It's thick enough now. Your beating's done." Then he turned to me. "Let's see those egg whites, Julian!" he said. They were puffed up and fluffy. "Congratulations, Julian!" he said. "Your whipping's done."

He mixed the egg whites into the pudding himself. Then he passed the pudding to my mother.

"A wonderful pudding," she said. "Would you like some, boys?"

"No thank you," we said.

She picked up a spoon. "Why, this tastes like a whole raft of lemons," she said. "This tastes like a night on the sea."

BETSY BYARS
The Midnight Fox

To begin with, I did not want to go to the farm. I was
perfectly happy at home. I remember I was sitting at the
desk in my room and I had a brand new $1.98 Cessna 180
model. I was just taking off the cellophane when my mom came
in. I was feeling good because I had the model, and all evening
to work on it, and then my mom told me in an excited way that
I was going to Aunt Millie's farm for two whole months. I felt
terrible.

"I don't want to go to any farm for two months," I said.

"But, Tommy, why not?"

"Because I just don't want to."

"Maybe you don't *now*," my mom said, "but after you think about it for a bit, you will. It's just that I've taken you by surprise. I probably shouldn't have come bursting in like—"

"I will never want to go."

She looked at me with a puzzled shrug. "I thought you would be so pleased."

"Well, I'm not."

"What's wrong?"

"There's nothing wrong. I would just hate to stay on a farm, that's all."

"How do you know? You can't even remember Aunt Millie's farm. You don't know whether you'd like it now or not."

"I know. I knew I wasn't going to like camp, and I didn't. I knew I wasn't going to like figs, and I don't. I knew I wasn't—"

"The trouble with you, Tommy, is that you don't *try* to like new things."

"You shouldn't have to *try* to like things. You should just very easily, without even thinking about it at all, *like* them."

"All right," she said, and her upper lip was beginning to get tight. "When I first saw this farm, I very easily, without thinking about it at all, *loved* it. It is the prettiest farm I ever saw. It's in the hills and there are great big apple trees to climb and there are cows and horses and—"

"Animals hate me."

"Tom, I have never heard anything so silly in my life. Animals do not hate you."

"They do. How about that dog that came running up at about a hundred miles an hour and bit me for no reason? I suppose that dog loved me!"

"The lady explained that. The dog had a little ham bone and you stepped on it and the dog thought you were going to take it. Anyway," she continued quickly, "just wait till you see the baby lambs. There is nothing dearer in the world. They are—"

"I'll probably be the only kid in the world to be stampeded to death by a bunch of baby lambs."

"Tom!"

"I tell you, animals don't like me. Perfectly strange animals come charging at me all the time."

My mom ignored this and went on about the fun I would have in the garden, and especially gathering eggs. There was, according to her, no such fun in the world as going out to the henhouse, sticking your hand under some strange hen, grabbing an egg, and running back to the house with it for breakfast. I could picture that. I would be running to the house with my egg, see, having all this fun, and then there would be a noise like a freight train behind me. A terrible noise growing louder and louder, and I would look around and there would come about two hundred chickens running me down. CHA-ROOOOOM! Me flattened on the ground while the lead hen snatches the egg from my crushed hand and returns in triumph to the coop.

My mom could see I wasn't listening to her, so she stopped talking about the fun and said, "I should think, Tom, that even if you do not particularly want to go to the farm—"

"I don't want to go at all."

"—even if you do not *particularly* want to go to the farm," she continued patiently, "you would realize how much this trip means to your father and me. It is the only chance we will ever have to go to Europe. The only chance."

My mom and dad were going to Europe with about fifty

other very athletic people, and they were going to bicycle through five countries and sleep in fields and barns. You can see that parents who would do that could never understand someone not wanting to go to the farm. I could not understand it myself completely. I just knew that I did not want to go, that I would never want to go, and that if I had to go, I would hate, loathe, and despise every minute of it.

"Don't you want your father and me to have this trip?"

"Yes."

"You're not acting like it."

"I want you to have the trip. I want you to have a hundred trips if you want them, just as long as I don't have to go to any crummy farm."

"You make it sound like a punishment."

"Why can't I stay here?"

"Because there's no one for you to stay with," she said.

"There's Mrs. Albergotti." This shows how desperate I was. Mrs. Albergotti was the kind of sitter who would come in the room where I was sleeping to see if I was still breathing.

"Mrs. Albergotti cannot stay with you for two months."

"Why not?"

"Because she has a family of her own. Now, Tom, will you be reasonable? You are not a baby anymore. You are almost ten years old."

"I am being reasonable."

My mother looked at me for a long time without saying anything. I lifted the lid off my model box. Usually this was a great moment for me. It was usually so great that trumpets should have blown—TA-DAAAAAAA! This time I looked down at the gray plastic pieces and they were just gray plastic pieces.

"Your father will talk to you when he gets home," she said,

and left the room. I could hear her cross the hall into her room and shut the door. My mom cried easily. The week before we had been watching a TV show about an old elephant who couldn't do his circus routine anymore, and suddenly I heard a terrible sob, and I looked over and it was my mom crying about the old elephant. Well, we all laughed, and she laughed too, only it was not so funny to hear my mom crying now, not because of an old elephant, but because of me.

That evening my father came in and talked to me. My dad is a high-school coach who likes to tell about things like the Lehigh-Central basketball game, when he won the game in the last two seconds with a free throw. If anything, I knew that he would be less understanding than my mom. He had not under-stood, for example, why I did not want to be in Little League even after he had watched me strike out seventeen times straight.

"This is a wonderful opportunity," my dad said enthusiastically. "Wonderful! There's a pond there—did you know that? You can go swimming every day if you like."

"I'm not much of a swimmer," I reminded him. This was the understatement of the year. Having a body that would not float would be a great handicap to anybody.

"Well, you can learn! That is why this is such a wonderful opportunity." Then he said earnestly, "If you go to the farm with the right attitude, Tom, that's the main thing. With the right attitude, two months on a farm can make a world of difference in you both mentally and physically."

"I like myself the way I am." I continued working on my model, which was what I had been doing when this conversation started.

"Put down the model, Son."

I put down the model but kept it in my hands so he would know I was very eager for the conversation to be over.

"Son, this trip means a lot to your mother. She has never had a real vacation in her whole life. Remember last summer when we were all packed to go to the Smokies and you got the measles?"

"Yes."

"And she stayed home and nursed you and never complained once about it, did she?"

"Well, no."

"Now she has a chance for a real trip and I want her to have it. I want her to go to Europe and see everything she's wanted to see all her life. And I don't want her to be worried about you the whole time. As long as she thinks you don't want to go to the farm, she is going to worry."

"But I *don't* want to go."

My father sighed. "You don't have to let her know that.

For once in your life you could think of someone besides yourself!"

Sometimes when my dad said something like that to me—well, I wouldn't actually cry or anything; my nose would just start to run. It did this all the time really. One time after school my teacher said, "Tom, I am very disappointed in you. You simply are not working up to capacity this term." Well, I wanted to tell her that I could not work up to capacity sometimes, the same as anybody else, that she need not expect me to be perfect just because my parents were teachers, only I couldn't say anything because my nose started to run.

Now I put my hand up to my nose and said, "All right, I *want* to go to the farm." Then I picked up my model and started pretending to work, because my eyes were kind of wet too.

My father never knew when to leave me alone. Now was the time for him to say, "Fine," and walk out of the room. Instead he just stood there. After a minute he cleared his throat and said, "You won't be sorry, Son. You're doing a fine thing for your mother."

Silence from me. Nose running worse than ever. Couldn't even see what pieces I was forcing together.

"And I bet—I just bet that you're going to have the time of your life on that farm. Millie says they've got some baby pigs. I bet you can have one."

"I have always wanted a baby pig," I said. I thought sure he would know I was being sarcastic, because *no one* has always wanted a baby pig. Maybe some farm girls would see one little pig that didn't look too bad and say, "Hey, let's dress it up," and they would play with it and feed it from a baby bottle, but no one has *always* wanted a baby pig.

But my father seemed pleased and clapped me on the back. "Good going!" This was what he said to his players when one of them excelled. "I'll tell your mother." He went to the door, then paused and said carefully, "I'll tell her you've changed your mind and are eager to go to the farm. Right?"

"Yes, tell her that."

He went out and I wiped my nose and eyes and looked down at my model, which was practically ruined. I have never had less fun for $1.98 in my whole life.

We left for the farm the next morning after breakfast. No one had much to say, so my mom turned on the radio and we listened to a disc jockey play hit songs from the past. About noon we stopped for a picnic lunch by a place that advertised candy, fireworks, toys, real arrowheads, flags, coins, and souvenirs from all fifty states. I used to like to spend hours looking at that kind of stuff, but that day I didn't even feel like going inside. Finally, after we ate, my dad said, "Come on, sport, I'll buy you something," so we went in and I selected a little totem pole that had been made in Japan, and then he made me get this fake plastic ice cube which had a fake fly in it and we went out and put it in Mom's cup for a joke. It was a very dismal morning.

The rest of the way I just sat in the back seat with my eyes closed. I started thinking about a movie I saw once where some farm people sent to the orphanage for a boy, because they wanted someone to help with the hard work on the farm. Instead of the boy, the orphanage sent them a puny girl, and there was tremendous disappointment. I thought now that perhaps Aunt Millie and Uncle Fred were letting me come because they thought I was a great athlete with muscles like potatoes who could toss hay into the loft without spilling a straw. They would be very excited, of course, at the thought of this wonderful summer helper, and as our car drove up, they would be standing

in the yard saying things like "Now we have someone to break the wild horses for us," and "Now we have someone to get the boulders out of the north forty." Then I would step out and they would cry, "But where's the *big* boy?" and I would say, "I'm the only boy there is." They would try to hide their disappointment, but finally Aunt Millie would start crying and run into the house.

I then went on to imagine a wonderful ending, where I turned out to be such a merry boy that I brightened the entire household, bringing fun to a dark house, but this didn't cheer me up, because it seemed to me that any farm people would rather have a sullen muscular worker than a skinny one, no matter how merry.

While I was thinking about this, we turned off onto the dirt road that led to the farm. My dad started blowing the horn to announce our arrival. When we got to the house, where the drive made a big circle and was all neatly edged with whitewashed stones, he called out, "Anybody home?"

Right away Aunt Millie came running out of the house, drying her hands on her apron and shouting, "Fred! Fred! They're here."

I got out of the car—I never felt less muscular in my whole life except in gym class—but she was so busy hugging Mom that she didn't notice me.

"It's been so *long*!" she was saying.

My mom started crying and said, "Oh, Millie, it is so *good* to see you. You are exactly the same, and this farm is exactly the same!" and then she cried some more.

"Now, Fran," my dad said.

"And this is Tom," Aunt Millie said, turning to me. She was not really my aunt but my second cousin, but I called her Aunt Millie, so I said, "Hello, Aunt Millie. It's nice to see you."

"Well, it's nice to see you. I'm so glad to have a boy around this place again. All my boys have grown up and gone, and it's lonesome." She patted my shoulder, and then she turned back to Mom and said, "Hazeline went riding with her boyfriend, but I *told* her to be back in time to see you. I said, 'Hazeline, Fran has not seen you in years and you be home.' "

"I still remember how fat and sweet she was when she was a baby," Mom said.

"I guess you do. Why, you *were* her mama that summer. Me flat on my back and you—she thought you were her mama."

My father had gotten my suitcase out while they were talking, and now we all went into the house and had lemonade and cake with Uncle Fred.

We talked some more about Hazeline, and Uncle Fred told about this prize pig of his, and Dad told some basketball stories, and then—it seemed like we had just been in the house about one second—my dad said, "Fran, we are going to have to get started if we want to get home tonight."

"You're not leaving!" Aunt Millie said. My feelings exactly.

"We have to."

"But we wanted you at least to stay the night."

"We can't. That's what we wanted to do," Mom said, "but the couple we're riding to New York with want to leave first thing in the morning. Tom says he doesn't mind, but I feel awful just dropping him and running."

"Oh, now, Tom is going to get along fine, aren't you, Tom?"

"Sure."

We walked out on the porch without saying anything, but at the steps Mom said, "Now you be a real good boy, Tom, and do what Aunt Millie tells you."

"I will."

"We'll get on just fine," Aunt Millie said, patting my shoulder again.

"I know." Mom hugged Aunt Millie and said, "This is the nicest thing that anyone has ever done for me." Then she hugged me real hard, got into the car, and turned her face away.

My dad said, "Well, so long, sport," and socked me on the arm.

I said, "Have a nice trip." I was pleased that my nose wasn't running or anything, because I felt terrible.

My dad started the car and they drove off. Mom kept her head turned, but Dad waved and honked the horn all the way to the highway.

"Now, you watch," Aunt Millie said. "Hazeline and her boyfriend will come driving up in about ten minutes all full of apologies. I *told* her to be here. That girl! You want to come on back in the house and have some more lemonade?"

"No, I'll just walk around a little bit," I said.

"Sure."

She went back into the house and I sat on the steps. My dad was always talking about control. He said control was the most important thing there was to an athlete, and he was always telling me I should have more of it. I couldn't imagine anyone having any more control than it took to sit quietly on the steps, nose and eyes dry, while being abandoned.

Sometimes my dad would get real disgusted with me because I didn't control myself too well. I used to cry pretty easily if I got hurt or if something was worrying me.

I remembered one time when Petie Burkis came over to my house and told me that he knew a way that you could figure out when you were going to die—the very day! He learned this from a sitter he'd had the night before. It was all according to the wrinkles in your hand—you counted them a certain way. Well, we sat right down and counted the wrinkles in my hand. It took over an hour, and it came out that I was going to die in my seventy-ninth year, on either the eighty-second or eighty-third day. Petie said probably I would fall terribly ill on the eighty-second and last until just after midnight on the eighty-third.

Then we started counting the wrinkles in Petie's hand. He had a peculiar hand, and it came out that he was going to die on the two hundred and seventy-ninth day of his ninth year. Well, Petie was nine years old right then, so he said, "Get a calendar, quick, get a calendar," and he looked like he was already getting sick.

We looked all over the house before we finally found a

wallet-sized insurance calendar, and then we got down on our stomachs and began to count the days. We were saying the numbers together—two hundred and seventy-six, two hundred and seventy-seven, two hundred and seventy-eight—and I can still hear the terrible way it sounded when we both said, "two hundred and seventy-nine." It was like the last sound in the world, because it turned out that Petie was going to die the next Saturday.

I said, "Let's do it again."

We did it again, very slowly and carefully this time, but it still came out the same—two hundred and seventy-nine, next Saturday.

Petie felt awful, I could see that, and I felt even worse, and if there had been any way in the world I could give him nineteen or twenty of my seventy-nine years, I would have done it in a minute. He said, "I better get home," like he meant, "before something happens," and then he left and I was too upset to try and stop him. I went into the house and my mom said, "What's wrong now?"

I said what was wrong was that Petie was going to die on Saturday, and right away she started laughing. I said, "Well, I certainly wouldn't think it was so hilarious if *your* best friend was going to die this Saturday," and I went out of the room.

She caught up with me in the hall and hugged me, and then she sat down on the telephone stool and made me look at her, and said, "Tommy, Petie is *not* going to die this Saturday."

"How do you know?"

"I just *know*, Tom."

"How?"

"Well, look at him. He is in perfect health. He is absolutely the healthiest boy I know."

"Healthy people are hit by cars every day, or fall down wells. You don't have to be sick to die."

"This is some fool thing you and Petie have cooked up. I think you enjoy getting all worked up about nothing."

"We do not."

"Well, I can tell you absolutely, positively that Petie is not going to die on Saturday."

"All right, then, can he come over and spend the day and night with me?" My mom was very particular about people not getting hurt in our yard. Like she would say, "I hope those little kids are not going to get hurt riding their bikes in our driveway," as if it would be perfectly all right if they were hurt just out of our drive, in the street somewhere.

"Yes, you may have him over."

This made me feel a little better, but as soon as my dad got home, he came in and talked to me for over an hour about self-control and not letting myself get worked up over foolish things. He seemed to think I enjoyed getting worked up and upset over my friend's death. I didn't want to worry about things. I wanted to be peaceful and calm like everyone else, only sometimes I couldn't.

Anyway, Petie came over on Saturday and we were careful all day. We didn't even go to bed until it was twelve o'clock. Then, before we got in bed, we went out into the hall, and in the dark we found the telephone and dialed the time to make sure. When the operator said, "The time is twelve–o–two," Petie started jumping up and down and saying, "I'm spared, I'm spared."

My dad said, "Be quiet out there."

We went in and lay down on the bed, and for about an hour all we said were things like, "Whew!" and "What a relief!" and "I really, honestly thought I was going to die, Tom, didn't you?"

I thought about that, and how now that I was controlling myself perfectly, now that there could not be one single complaint of any kind about my absolutely perfect control, there was no one around to see it.

SHIRLEY JACKSON
Life Among the Savages

The day Laurie started kindergarten he renounced corduroy overalls with bibs and began wearing blue jeans with a belt; I watched him go off the first morning with the older girl next door, seeing clearly that an era of my life was ended, my sweet-voiced nursery-school tot replaced by a long-trousered, swaggering character who forgot to stop at the corner and wave goodbye to me.

He came home the same way, the front door slamming

open, his cap on the floor, and the voice suddenly become raucous shouting, "Isn't anybody *here*?"

At lunch he spoke insolently to his father, spilled Jannie's milk, and remarked that his teacher said that we were not to take the name of the Lord in vain.

"How *was* school today?" I asked, elaborately casual.

"All right," he said.

"Did you learn anything?" his father asked.

Laurie regarded his father coldly. "I didn't learn nothing," he said.

"Anything," I said. "Didn't learn anything."

"The teacher spanked a boy, though," Laurie said, addressing his bread and butter. "For being fresh," he added with his mouth full.

"What did he do?" I asked. "Who was it?"

Laurie thought. "It was Charles," he said. "He was fresh. The teacher spanked him and made him stand in a corner. He was awfully fresh."

"What did he do?" I asked again, but Laurie slid off his chair, took a cookie, and left, while his father was still saying, "See here, young man."

The next day Laurie remarked at lunch, as soon as he sat down, "Well, Charles was bad again today." He grinned enormously and said, "Today Charles hit the teacher."

"Good heavens," I said, mindful of the Lord's name, "I suppose he got spanked again?"

"He sure did," Laurie said. "Look up," he said to his father.

"What?" his father said, looking up.

"Look down," Laurie said. "Look at my thumb. Gee, you're dumb." He began to laugh insanely.

"Why did Charles hit the teacher?" I asked quickly.

"Because she tried to make him color with red crayons," Laurie said. "Charles wanted to color with green crayons so he hit the teacher and she spanked him and said nobody play with Charles but everybody did."

The third day—it was Wednesday of the first week—Charles bounced a seesaw onto the head of a little girl and made her bleed and the teacher made him stay inside all during recess. Thursday Charles had to stand in a corner during storytime because he kept pounding his feet on the floor. Friday Charles was deprived of blackboard privileges because he threw chalk.

On Saturday I remarked to my husband, "Do you think kindergarten is too upsetting for Laurie? All this toughness and bad grammar, and this Charles boy sounds like such a bad influence."

"It'll be all right," my husband said reassuringly. "Bound to be people like Charles in the world. Might as well meet them now as later."

On Monday Laurie came home late, full of news. "Charles," he shouted as he came up the hill; I was waiting anxiously on the front steps. "Charles," Laurie yelled all the way up the hill, "Charles was bad again."

"Come right in," I said as soon as he came close enough. "Lunch is waiting."

"You know what Charles did?" he demanded, following me through the door. "Charles yelled so in school they sent a boy in from first grade to tell the teacher she had to make Charles keep quiet, and so Charles had to stay after school. And so all the children stayed to watch him."

"What did he do?" I asked.

"He just sat there," Laurie said, climbing into his chair at the table. "Hi Pop, y'old dust mop."

"Charles had to stay after school today," I told my husband. "Everyone stayed with him."

"What does this Charles look like?" my husband asked Laurie. "What's his other name?"

"He's bigger than me," Laurie said. "And he doesn't have any rubbers and he doesn't ever wear a jacket."

Monday night was the first Parent-Teachers meeting, and only the fact that Jannie had a cold kept me from going; I wanted passionately to meet Charles' mother. On Tuesday Laurie remarked suddenly, "Our teacher had a friend come see her in school today."

"Charles' mother?" my husband and I asked simultaneously.

"Naaah," Laurie said scornfully. "It was a man who came and made us do exercises. Look." He climbed down from his chair and squatted down and touched his toes. "Like this," he said. He got solemnly back into his chair and said, picking up his fork, "Charles didn't even *do* exercises."

"That's fine," I said heartily. "Didn't Charles want to do exercises?"

"Naaah," Laurie said. "Charles was so fresh to the teacher's friend he wasn't *let* do exercises."

"Fresh again?" I said.

"He kicked the teacher's friend," Laurie said. "The teacher's friend told Charles to touch his toes like I just did and Charles kicked him."

"What are they going to do about Charles, do you suppose?" Laurie's father asked him.

Laurie shrugged elaborately. "Throw him out of school, I guess," he said.

Wednesday and Thursday were routine; Charles yelled during story hour and hit a boy in the stomach and made him cry. On Friday Charles stayed after school again and so did all the other children.

With the third week of kindergarten Charles was an institution in our family; Jannie was being a Charles when she cried all afternoon; Laurie did a Charles when he filled his wagon full of mud and pulled it through the kitchen; even my husband, when he caught his elbow in the telephone cord and pulled telephone, ash tray, and a bowl of flowers off the table, said, after the first minute, "Looks like Charles."

During the third and fourth weeks there seemed to be a reformation in Charles; Laurie reported grimly at lunch on Thursday of the third week, "Charles was so good today the teacher gave him an apple."

"What?" I said, and my husband added warily, "You mean Charles?"

"Charles," Laurie said. "He gave the crayons around and he picked up the books afterward and the teacher said he was her helper."

"What happened?" I asked incredulously.

"He was her helper, that's all," Laurie said, and shrugged.

"Can this be true, about Charles?" I asked my husband that night. "Can something like this happen?"

"Wait and see," my husband said cynically. "When you've got a Charles to deal with, this may mean he's only plotting."

He seemed to be wrong. For over a week Charles was the teacher's helper; each day he handed things out and he picked things up; no one had to stay after school.

"The P.T.A. meeting's next week again," I told my husband one evening. "I'm going to find Charles' mother there."

"Ask her what happened to Charles," my husband said. "I'd like to know."

"I'd like to know myself," I said.

On Friday of that week things were back to normal. "You know what Charles did today?" Laurie demanded at the lunch table, in a voice slightly awed. "He told a little girl to say a word and she said it and the teacher washed her mouth out with soap and Charles laughed."

"What word?" his father asked unwisely, and Laurie said, "I'll have to whisper it to you, it's so bad." He got down off his

chair and went around to his father. His father bent his head down and Laurie whispered joyfully. His father's eyes widened.

"Did Charles tell the little girl to say *that*?" he asked respectfully.

"She said it *twice*," Laurie said. "Charles told her to say it *twice*."

"What happened to Charles?" my husband asked.

"Nothing," Laurie said. "He was passing out the crayons."

Monday morning Charles abandoned the little girl and said the evil word himself three or four times, getting his mouth washed out with soap each time. He also threw chalk.

My husband came to the door with me that evening as I set out for the P.T.A. meeting. "Invite her over for a cup of tea after the meeting," he said. "I want to get a look at her."

"If only she's there," I said prayerfully.

"She'll be there," my husband said. "I don't see how they could hold a P.T.A. meeting without Charles' mother."

At the meeting I sat restlessly, scanning each comfortable matronly face, trying to determine which one hid the secret of Charles. None of them looked to me haggard enough. No one stood up in the meeting and apologized for the way her son had been acting. No one mentioned Charles.

After the meeting I identified and sought out Laurie's kindergarten teacher. She had a plate with a cup of tea and a piece of chocolate cake; I had a plate with a cup of tea and a piece of marshmallow cake. We maneuvered up to one another cautiously and smiled.

"I've been so anxious to meet you," I said. "I'm Laurie's mother."

"We're all so interested in Laurie," she said.

"Well, he certainly likes kindergarten," I said. "He talks about it all the time."

"We had a little trouble adjusting, the first week or so," she said primly, "but now he's a fine little helper. With lapses, of course."

"Laurie usually adjusts very quickly," I said. "I suppose this time it's Charles' influence."

"Charles?"

"Yes," I said, laughing, "you must have your hands full in that kindergarten, with Charles."

"Charles?" she said. "We don't have any Charles in the kindergarten."

SAKI

The Lumber-Room

The children were to be driven, as a special treat, to the sands at Jagborough. Nicholas was not to be of the party; he was in disgrace. Only that morning he had refused to eat his wholesome bread-and-milk on the seemingly frivolous ground that there was a frog in it. Older and wiser and better people had told him that there could not possibly be a frog in his bread-and-milk and that he was not to talk nonsense; he continued, nevertheless, to talk what seemed the veriest nonsense, and described with much detail the coloration and markings of the alleged frog. The dramatic part of the incident was that there really was a frog in Nicholas' basin of bread-and-milk; he had put it there himself, so he felt entitled to know something about it. The sin of taking a frog from the garden and putting it into a bowl of wholesome bread-and-milk was enlarged on at great length, but the fact that stood out clearest in the whole affair, as it presented itself to the mind of Nicholas, was that the older, wiser, and better people had been proved to be profoundly in error in matters about which they had expressed the utmost assurance.

"You said there couldn't possibly be a frog in my bread-and-milk; there *was* a frog in my bread-and-milk," he repeated, with the insistence of a skilled tactician who does not intend to shift from favorable ground.

So his boy-cousin and girl-cousin and his quite uninteresting younger brother were to be taken to Jagborough sands that afternoon and he was to stay at home. His cousins' aunt, who insisted, by an unwarranted stretch of imagination, in styling herself his aunt also, had hastily invented the Jagborough expedition in order to impress on Nicholas the delights that he had justly forfeited by his disgraceful conduct at the breakfast-table. It was her habit, whenever one of the children fell from grace, to improvise something of a festival nature from which the offender would be rigorously debarred; if all the children sinned collectively they were suddenly informed of a circus in a neighboring town, a circus of unrivaled merit and uncounted elephants, to which, but for their depravity, they would have been taken that very day.

A few decent tears were looked for on the part of Nicholas when the moment for the departure of the expedition arrived. As a matter of fact, however, all the crying was done by his girl-cousin, who scraped her knee rather painfully against the step of the carriage as she was scrambling in.

"How she did howl," said Nicholas cheerfully, as the party drove off without any of the elation of high spirits that should have characterized it.

"She'll soon get over that," said the aunt; "it will be a glorious afternoon for racing about over those beautiful sands. How they will enjoy themselves!"

"Bobby won't enjoy himself much, and he won't race much either," said Nicholas with a grim chuckle; "his boots are hurting him. They're too tight."

"Why didn't he tell me they were hurting?" asked the aunt with some asperity.

"He told you twice, but you weren't listening. You often don't listen when we tell you important things."

"You are not to go into the gooseberry garden," said the aunt, changing the subject.

"Why not?" demanded Nicholas.

"Because you are in disgrace," said the aunt loftily.

Nicholas did not admit the flawlessness of the reasoning; he felt perfectly capable of being in disgrace and in a gooseberry garden at the same moment. His face took on an expression of considerable obstinacy. It was clear to his aunt that he was determined to get into the gooseberry garden, "only," as she remarked to herself, "because I have told him he is not to."

Now the gooseberry garden had two doors by which it might be entered, and once a small person like Nicholas could slip in there he could effectually disappear from view amid the masking growth of artichokes, raspberry canes, and fruit bushes. The aunt had many other things to do that afternoon, but she spent an hour or two in trivial gardening operations among flower beds and shrubberies, whence she could keep a watchful eye on the two doors that led to the forbidden paradise. She was a woman of few ideas, with immense powers of concentration.

Nicholas made one or two sorties into the front garden, wriggling his way with obvious stealth of purpose towards one or other of the doors, but never able for a moment to evade the aunt's watchful eye. As a matter of fact, he had no intention of trying to get into the gooseberry garden, but it was extremely convenient for him that his aunt should believe that he had; it was a belief that would keep her on self-imposed sentry-duty for the greater part of the afternoon. Having thoroughly confirmed and fortified her suspicions, Nicholas slipped back into the house and rapidly put into execution a plan of action that had long germinated in his brain. By standing on a chair in the library one could reach a shelf on which reposed a fat, important-looking key. The key was as important as it looked; it was the instrument which kept the mysteries of the lumber-room secure from unauthorized intrusion, which opened a way only for aunts and such-like privileged persons. Nicholas had not had much experience of the art of fitting keys into keyholes and turning locks, but for some days past he had practiced with the key of the schoolroom door; he did not believe in trusting too much to luck and accident. The key turned stiffly in the lock, but it turned. The door opened, and Nicholas was in an un-known land, compared with which the gooseberry garden was a stale delight, a mere material pleasure.

Often and often Nicholas had pictured to himself what the lumber-room might be like, that region that was so carefully sealed from youthful eyes and concerning which no questions were ever answered. It came up to his expectations. In the first place it was large and dimly lit, one high window opening on to the forbidden garden being its only source of illumination. In the second place it was a storehouse of unimagined treasures. The aunt-by-assertion was one of those people who think that things spoil by use and consign them to dust and damp by way of preserving them. Such parts of the house as Nicholas knew best were rather bare and cheerless, but here there were wonderful things for the eye to feast on. First and foremost there was a piece of framed tapestry that was evidently meant to be a fire-screen. To Nicholas it was a living, breathing story; he sat down on a roll of Indian hangings, glowing in wonderful colors beneath a layer of dust, and took in all the details of the tapestry picture. A man, dressed in the hunting costume of some remote period, had just transfixed a stag with an arrow; it could not have been a difficult shot because the stag was only one or two paces away from him; in the thickly growing vegetation that the picture suggested it would not have been difficult to creep up to a feeding stag, and the two spotted dogs that were springing forward to join in the chase had evidently been trained to keep to heel till the arrow was discharged. That part of the picture was simple, if interesting, but did the huntsman see, what Nicholas saw, that four galloping wolves were coming in his direction through the wood? There might be more than four of them hidden behind the trees, and in any case would the man and his

dogs be able to cope with the four wolves if they made an attack? The man had only two arrows left in his quiver, and he might miss with one or both of them; all one knew about his skill in shooting was that he could hit a large stag at a ridiculously short range. Nicholas sat for many golden minutes revolving the possibilities of the scene; he was inclined to think that there were more than four wolves and that the man and his dogs were in a tight corner.

But there were other objects of delight and interest claiming his instant attention: there were quaint twisted candlesticks in the shape of snakes, and a teapot fashioned like a china duck, out of whose open beak the tea was supposed to come. How dull and shapeless the nursery teapot seemed in comparison! And there was a carved sandal-wood box packed tight with aromatic cotton-wool, and between the layers of cotton-wool were little brass figures, hump-necked bulls, and peacocks and goblins, delightful to see and to handle. Less promising in appearance was a large square book with plain black covers; Nicholas peeped into it, and, behold, it was full of colored pictures of birds. And such birds! In the garden, and in the lanes when he went for a walk, Nicholas came across a few birds, of which the largest were an occasional magpie or woodpigeon; here were herons and bustards, kites, toucans, tiger-bitterns, brush turkeys, ibises, golden pheasants, a whole portrait gallery of undreamed-of creatures. And as he was admiring the coloring of the mandarin duck and assigning a life-history to it, the voice of his aunt in shrill vociferation of his name came from the gooseberry garden without. She had grown suspicious at his long disappearance, and had leapt to the conclusion that he had climbed over the wall behind the sheltering screen of the lilac bushes; she was now engaged in an energetic and rather hopeless search for him among the artichokes and raspberry canes.

"Nicholas, Nicholas!" she screamed. "You are to come out of this at once. It's no use trying to hide there; I can see you all the time."

It was probably the first time for twenty years that anyone had smiled in that lumber-room.

Presently the angry repetitions of Nicholas' name gave way to a shriek, and a cry for somebody to come quickly. Nicholas shut the book, restored it carefully to its place in a corner, and shook some dust from a neighboring pile of newspapers over it. Then he crept from the room, locked the door, and replaced the key exactly where he had found it. His aunt was still calling his name when he sauntered into the front garden.

"Who's calling?" he asked.

"Me," came the answer from the other side of the wall; "didn't you hear me? I've been looking for you in the gooseberry garden, and I've slipped into the rain-water tank. Luckily there's no water in it, but the sides are slippery and I can't get out. Fetch the little ladder from under the cherry tree—"

"I was told I wasn't to go into the gooseberry garden," said Nicholas promptly.

"I told you not to, and now I tell you that you may," came the voice from the rain-water tank, rather impatiently.

"Your voice doesn't sound like aunt's," objected Nicholas; "you may be the Evil One tempting me to be disobedient. Aunt often tells me that the Evil One tempts me and that I always yield. This time I'm not going to yield."

"Don't talk nonsense," said the prisoner in the tank; "go and fetch the ladder."

"Will there be strawberry jam for tea?" asked Nicholas innocently.

"Certainly there will be," said the aunt, privately resolving that Nicholas should have none of it.

"Now I know that you are the Evil One and not aunt,"
shouted Nicholas gleefully; "when we asked aunt for strawberry
jam yesterday she said there wasn't any. I know there are four
jars of it in the store cupboard, because I looked, and of course
you know it's there, but *she* doesn't, because she said there
wasn't any. Oh, Devil, you *have* sold yourself!"

There was an unusual sense of luxury in being able to talk
to an aunt as though one was talking to the Evil One, but
Nicholas knew, with childish discernment, that such luxuries
were not to be over-indulged in. He walked noisily away, and it
was a kitchenmaid, in search of parsley, who eventually rescued
the aunt from the rain-water tank.

Tea that evening was partaken in a fearsome silence. The
tide had been at its highest when the children had arrived at
Jagborough Cove, so there had been no sands to play on—a

circumstance that the aunt had overlooked in the haste of organizing her punitive expedition. The tightness of Bobby's boots had had disastrous effect on his temper the whole of the afternoon, and altogether the children could not have been said to have enjoyed themselves. The aunt maintained the frozen muteness of one who has suffered undignified and unmerited detention in a rain-water tank for thirty-five minutes. As for Nicholas, he, too, was silent, in the absorption of one who has much to think about; it was just possible, he considered, that the huntsman would escape with his hounds while the wolves feasted on the stricken stag.

RUDYARD KIPLING
The Elephant's Child

In the High and Far-Off Times the Elephant, O Best Beloved, had no trunk. He had only a blackish, bulgy nose, as big as a boot, that he could wriggle about from side to side; but he couldn't pick up things with it. But there was one Elephant—a new Elephant—an Elephant's Child—who was full of 'satiable curtiosity, and that means he asked ever so many questions. *And* he lived in Africa, and he filled all Africa with his 'satiable curtiosities. He asked his tall aunt, the Ostrich, why her tail-feathers grew just so, and his tall aunt the Ostrich spanked him with her hard, hard claw. He asked his tall uncle, the Giraffe, what made his skin spotty, and his tall uncle, the Giraffe, spanked him with his hard, hard hoof. And still he was full of 'satiable curtiosity! He asked his broad aunt, the Hippopotamus, why her eyes were red, and his broad aunt, the Hippopotamus, spanked him with her broad, broad hoof; and he asked his hairy uncle, the Baboon, why melons tasted just so, and his hairy uncle, the Baboon, spanked him with his hairy, hairy paw. And *still* he was full of 'satiable curtiosity! He asked questions about everything that he saw, or heard, or felt, or smelt, or touched, and all his uncles and his aunts spanked him. And still he was full of 'satiable curtiosity!

One fine morning in the middle of the Precession of the Equinoxes this 'satiable Elephant's Child asked a new fine question that he had never asked before. He asked, "What does the Crocodile have for dinner?" Then everybody said "Hush!" in a loud and dretful tone, and they spanked him immediately and directly, without stopping, for a long time.

By and by, when that was finished, he came upon Kolokolo Bird sitting in the middle of a wait-a-bit thorn-bush, and he said, "My father has spanked me, and my mother has spanked me; all my aunts and uncles have spanked me for my 'satiable curtiosity; and *still* I want to know what the Crocodile has for dinner!"

Then Kolokolo Bird said with a mournful cry, "Go to the banks of the great gray-green, greasy Limpopo River, all set about with fever-trees, and find out."

That very next morning, when there was nothing left of the Equinoxes, because the Precession had preceded according to precedent, this 'satiable Elephant's Child took a hundred pounds of bananas (the little short red kind), and a hundred pounds of sugar cane (the long purple kind), and seventeen melons (the greeny-crackly kind), and said to all his dear families, "Good-bye. I am going to the great gray-green, greasy Limpopo River, all set about with fever-trees, to find out what the Crocodile has for dinner." And they all spanked him once more for luck, though he asked them most politely to stop.

Then he went away, a little warm, but not at all astonished, eating melons, and throwing the rind about, because he could not pick it up.

He went from Graham's Town to Kimberley, and from Kimberley to Khama's Country, and from Khama's Country he went east by north, eating melons all the time, till at last he came to the banks of the great gray-green, greasy Limpopo River, all set about with fever-trees, precisely as Kolokolo Bird had said.

Now you must know and understand, O Best Beloved, that till that very week, and day, and hour, and minute, this 'satiable Elephant's Child had never seen a Crocodile, and did not know what one was like. It was all his 'satiable curtiosity.

The first thing that he found was a Bi-Colored-Python-Rock-Snake curled round a rock.

" 'Scuse me," said the Elephant's Child most politely, "but have you seen such a thing as a Crocodile in these promiscuous parts?"

"*Have* I seen a Crocodile?" said the Bi-Colored-Python-Rock-Snake in a voice of dretful scorn. "What will you ask me next?"

" 'Scuse me," said the Elephant's Child, "but could you kindly tell me what he has for dinner?"

Then the Bi-Colored-Python-Rock-Snake uncoiled himself very quickly from the rock, and spanked the Elephant's Child with his scalesome, flailsome tail.

"That is odd," said the Elephant's Child, "because my

father and my mother, and my uncle and my aunt, not to mention my other aunt, the Hippopotamus, and my other uncle, the Baboon, have all spanked me for my 'satiable curtiosity—and I suppose this is the same thing.'

So he said good-bye very politely to the Bi-Colored-Python-Rock-Snake, and helped to coil him up on the rock again, and went on, a little warm, but not at all astonished, eating melons, and throwing the rind about, because he could not pick it up, till he trod on what he thought was a log of wood at the very edge of the great gray-green, greasy Limpopo River, all set about with fever-trees.

But it was really the Crocodile, O Best Beloved, and the Crocodile winked one eye—like this!

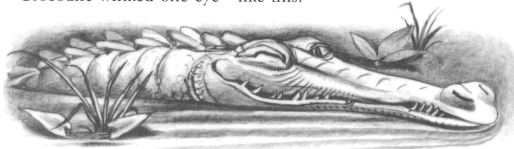

" 'Scuse me," said the Elephant's Child most politely, "but do you happen to have seen a Crocodile in these promiscuous parts?"

Then the Crocodile winked the other eye, and lifted half his tail out of the mud; and the Elephant's Child stepped back most politely, because he did not wish to be spanked again.

"Come hither, Little One," said the Crocodile. "Why do you ask such things?"

" 'Scuse me," said the Elephant's Child most politely, "but my father has spanked me, my mother has spanked me, not to mention my tall aunt, the Ostrich, and my tall uncle, the Giraffe, who can kick ever so hard, as well as my broad aunt, the Hippopotamus, and my hairy uncle, the Baboon, *and* including the Bi-Colored-Python-Rock-Snake, with the scalesome, flailsome tail, just up the bank, who spanks harder than any of them; and *so*, if it's quite all the same to you, I don't want to be spanked anymore."

"Come hither, Little One," said the Crocodile, "for I am the Crocodile," and he wept crocodile tears to show it was quite true.

Then the Elephant's Child grew all breathless, and panted, and kneeled down on the bank, and said, "You are the very person I have been looking for all these long days. Will you please tell me what you have for dinner?"

"Come hither, Little One," said the Crocodile, "and I'll whisper."

Then the Elephant's Child put his head down close to the Crocodile's musky, tusky mouth, and the Crocodile caught him by his little nose, which up to that very week, day, hour, and minute, had been no bigger than a boot, though much more useful.

"I think," said the Crocodile—and he said it between his teeth, like this—"I think today I will begin with Elephant's Child!"

At this, O Best Beloved, the Elephant's Child was much annoyed, and he said, speaking through his nose, like this, "Led go! You are hurtig be!"

Then the Bi-Colored-Python-Rock-Snake scuffled down from the bank and said, "My young friend, if you do not now, immediately and instantly, pull as hard as ever you can, it is my opinion that your acquaintance in the large-pattern leather ulster" (and by this he meant the Crocodile) "will jerk you into yonder limpid stream before you can say Jack Robinson."

This is the way Bi-Colored-Python-Rock-Snake always talked.

Then the Elephant's Child sat back on his little haunches, and pulled, and pulled, and pulled, and his nose began to stretch. And the Crocodile floundered into the water, making it all creamy with great sweeps of his tail, and *he* pulled, and pulled, and pulled.

And the Elephant's Child's nose kept on stretching; and the Elephant's Child spread all his little four legs and pulled, and pulled, and pulled, and his nose kept on stretching; and the Crocodile threshed his tail like an oar, and *he* pulled, and pulled, and pulled, and at each pull the Elephant's Child's nose grew longer and longer—and it hurt him hijjus!

Then the Elephant's Child felt his legs slipping, and he said through his nose, which was now nearly five feet long, "This is too butch for be!"

Then the Bi-Colored-Python-Rock-Snake came down from the bank, and knotted himself in a double-clove-hitch round the Elephant's Child's hind legs, and said, "Rash and inexperienced traveler, we will now seriously devote ourselves to a little high tension, because if we do not, it is my impression that yonder self-propelling man-of-war with the armor-plated upper deck" (and by this, O Best Beloved, he meant the Crocodile), "will permanently vitiate your future career."

That is the way all Bi-Colored-Python-Rock-Snakes always talk.

So he pulled, and the Elephant's Child pulled, and the Crocodile pulled; but the Elephant's Child and the Bi-Colored-Python-Rock-Snake pulled hardest; and at last the Crocodile let go of the Elephant's Child's nose with a plop that you could hear all up and down the Limpopo.

Then the Elephant's Child sat down most hard and sudden; but first he was careful to say "Thank you" to the Bi-

Colored-Python-Rock-Snake; and next he was kind to his poor pulled nose, and wrapped it all up in cool banana leaves, and hung it in the great gray-green, greasy Limpopo to cool.

"What are you doing that for?" said the Bi-Colored-Python-Rock-Snake.

" 'Scuse me," said the Elephant's Child, "but my nose is badly out of shape, and I am waiting for it to shrink."

"Then you will have to wait a long time," said the Bi-Colored-Python-Rock-Snake. "Some people do not know what is good for them."

The Elephant's Child sat there for three days waiting for his nose to shrink. But it never grew any shorter, and, besides, it made him squint. For, O Best Beloved, you will see and understand that the Crocodile had pulled it out into a really truly trunk same as all Elephants have today.

At the end of the third day a fly came and stung him on the shoulder, and before he knew what he was doing he lifted up his trunk and hit that fly dead with the end of it.

" 'Vantage number one!" said the Bi-Colored-Python-Rock-Snake. "You couldn't have done that with a mere-smear nose. Try and eat a little now."

Before he thought what he was doing the Elephant's Child put out his trunk and plucked a large bundle of grass, dusted it clean against his forelegs, and stuffed it into his mouth.

" 'Vantage number two!" said the Bi-Colored-Python-Rock-Snake. "You couldn't have done that with a mere-smear nose. Don't you think the sun is very hot here?"

"It is," said the Elephant's Child, and before he thought what he was doing he schlooped up a schloop of mud from the banks of the great gray-green, greasy Limpopo, and slapped it on his head, where it made a cool schloopy-sloshy mud-cap all trickly behind his ears.

" 'Vantage number three!" said the Bi-Colored-Python-Rock-Snake. "You couldn't have done that with a mere-smear nose. Now how do you feel about being spanked again?"

" 'Scuse me," said the Elephant's Child, "but I should not like it at all."

"How would you like to spank somebody?" said the Bi-Colored-Python-Rock-Snake.

"I should like it very much indeed," said the Elephant's Child.

"Well," said the Bi-Colored-Python-Rock-Snake, "you will find that new nose of yours very useful to spank people with."

"Thank you," said the Elephant's Child. "I'll remember that; and now I think I'll go home to all my dear families and try."

So the Elephant's Child went home across Africa frisking and whisking his trunk. When he wanted fruit to eat he pulled fruit down from a tree, instead of waiting for it to fall as he used to do. When he wanted grass he plucked grass up from the ground, instead of going on his knees as he used to do. When the flies bit him he broke off the branch of a tree and used it as a fly whisk; and he made himself a new, cool, slushy-squshy mud-cap whenever the sun was hot. When he felt lonely walking through Africa he sang to himself down his trunk, and the noise was louder than several brass bands. He went especially out of his way to find a broad Hippopotamus (she was no relation of his), and he spanked her very hard, to make sure that the Bi-Colored-Python-Rock-Snake had spoken the truth about his new trunk. The rest of the time he picked up the melon rinds that he had dropped on his way to the Limpopo—for he was a Tidy Pachyderm.

One dark evening he came back to all his dear families, and he coiled up his trunk and said, "How do you do?" They were very glad to see him, and immediately said, "Come here and be spanked for your 'satiable curtiosity."

"Pooh," said the Elephant's Child. "I don't think you peoples know anything about spanking; but *I* do, and I'll show you."

Then he uncurled his trunk and knocked two of his dear brothers head over heels.

"O Bananas!" said they. "Where did you learn that trick, and what have you done to your nose?"

"I got a new one from the Crocodile on the banks of the great gray-green, greasy Limpopo River," said the Elephant's Child. "I asked him what he had for dinner, and he gave me this to keep."

"It looks very ugly," said his hairy uncle, the Baboon.

"It does," said the Elephant's Child. "But it's very useful," and he picked up his hairy uncle, the Baboon, by one hairy leg, and hove him into a hornets' nest.

Then that bad Elephant's Child spanked all his dear families for a long time, till they were very warm and greatly astonished. He pulled out his tall Ostrich aunt's tail-feathers; and he caught his tall uncle, the Giraffe, by the hind leg, and dragged him through a thorn-bush; and he shouted at his broad aunt, the Hippopotamus, and blew bubbles into her ear when she was sleeping in the water after meals; but he never let anyone touch Kolokolo Bird.

At last things grew so exciting that his dear families went off one by one in a hurry to the banks of the great gray-green, greasy Limpopo River, all set about with fever-trees, to borrow new noses from the Crocodile. When they came back nobody spanked anybody anymore; and ever since that day, O Best Beloved, all the Elephants you will ever see, besides all those that you won't, have trunks precisely like the trunk of the 'satiable Elephant's Child.

JAMES THURBER
The Moth and the Star

A young and impressionable moth once set his heart on a certain star. He told his mother about this and she counseled him to set his heart on a bridge lamp instead. "Stars aren't the thing to hang around," she said. "Lamps are the thing to hang around." "You get somewhere that way," said the moth's father. "You don't get anywhere chasing stars." But the moth would not heed the words of either parent. Every evening at dusk when the star came out he would start flying toward it and every morning at dawn he would crawl back home worn out with his vain endeavor. One day his father said to him, "You haven't burned a wing in months, boy, and it looks to me as if you were never going to. All your brothers have been badly burned flying around street lamps and all your sisters have been terribly singed flying around house lamps. Come on, now, get out of here and get yourself scorched! A big strapping moth like you without a mark on him!"

The moth left his father's house, but he would not fly around street lamps and he would not fly around house lamps. He went right on trying to reach the star, which was four and one-third light years, or twenty-five trillion miles, away. The moth thought it was just caught in the top branches of the elm. He never did reach the star, but he went right on trying, night after night, and when he was a very, very old moth he began to think that he really had reached the star and he went around saying so. This gave him a deep and lasting pleasure, and he lived to a great old age. His parents and his brothers and his sisters had all been burned to death when they were quite young.

MORAL: *Who flies afar from the sphere of our sorrow is here today and here tomorrow.*

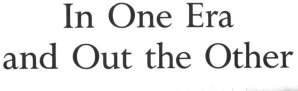

In One Era
and Out the Other

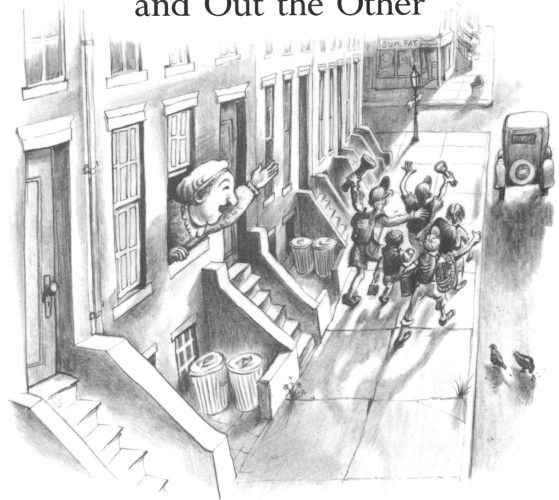

At least once each summer we kids went off on a hike, but never without strong opposition from Mama. When it came to the open road Mama had a closed mind. Anything beyond our immediate neighborhood was wilderness. Once she set foot out of the house she lost her bearings. When she did venture out she traveled by landmarks.

For a visit to Aunt Bessie she got on the trolley at our corner and got off at a corner where there was a furniture store with a brown bed in the window. The road to Aunt Naomi passed two churches, one movie house, one large school, one small school, and a tailor shop.

Sometimes, just to make sure, she would ask the conductor questions like "This is the second school?" or "Where do the tracks go round and round and come out under an elevator?"

She would often lose patience, get off the trolley, and go in search of two churches, which she somehow always found. After a while she gave up the trolley completely, and would walk from our house, following the tracks past two churches, one movie house, one large school, one small school, and a tailor shop to Aunt Naomi's house. When the tailor moved away she wound up in the trolley yard.

Her method of dissuading us from venturing out into the unknown was to make the entire project appear ridiculous.

"You're going on a what?"

"We're going on a hike."

"What's a hike?" Mama would ask.

When we started to explain it, the whole idea did in fact become ludicrous.

"We go walking, Ma."

"Walking? For that you have to leave home? What's the matter with walking right here? You walk; I'll watch."

"You don't understand, Ma. We take lunch along."

"I'll give you lunch here, and you can march right around the table"—and she would start singing a march, clapping her hands rhythmically.

"Ma, we climb mountains in the woods."

She couldn't understand why it was so much more enjoyable to fall off a mountain than off a fire escape.

"And how about the wild animals in the woods?"

"Wild animals? What kind of wild animals?"

"A bear, for instance. A bear could eat you up."

"Ma, bears don't eat little children."

"Okay, so he won't eat you, but he could take a bite and spit out! I'm telling you now, if a wild animal eats you up, don't come running to me. And who's going with you?"

"Well, there's Georgie . . ."

"Georgie! Not him! He's a real wild animal!" She then went on to list all the conditions for the trip. "And remember one thing, don't tear your pants; and remember one thing, don't eat wild berries and bring me home the cramps; and remember one thing, don't tell me tomorrow morning that you're too tired to go to school; and remember one thing, wear rubbers, a sweater, warm underwear, and an umbrella, and a hat; and remember one thing, if you should get lost in the jungle, call up so I'll know you're all right. And don't dare come home without color in your cheeks. I wish I was young and free like you. Take soap."

Since the consent was specifically granted for the next day only, that night none of us slept. There was always a chance that it might rain. Brother Albert stayed at the crystal set all night like a ship's radio operator with his earphones on, listening to weather bulletins and repeating them aloud for the rest of us. "It's clearing in Nebraska. Hot air masses coming up from the Gulf. They say it's good for planting alfalfa. Storm warning off the coast of Newfoundland. It's drizzling in Montreal."

At 6:00 A.M. we were ready for Operation Hike, rain or shine, but we had to wait for Papa to get up. We didn't need his permission, but we did need his blanket.

Into the valley of Central Park marched the six hundred bowed down with knapsacks, flashlights, a Cracker Jack box compass-mirror (so you could tell not only where you were lost but who was lost), a thermos bottle (semi-automatic—you had to fill it, but it emptied by itself), and an axe. Onward! Forward!

Upward! "Ours not to reason why." Philip was always the leader. He was the one to get lost first. Jerry was the lookout. He would yell, "Look out!" and fall off a cliff. None of us knew how long we were supposed to march. We went on because we wouldn't know what to do if we stopped. One brave coward finally spoke up. "I can't go on anymore. The heat is killing me. Let's start the fire here."

No hike was complete without Georgie and his Uncle Bernie's World War I bugle. This kid had lungs like a vacuum cleaner. With him outside the walls of Jericho, they could have sent the rest of the army home. He used to stand on a hill and let go a blast that had the Staten Island ferries running into each other.

Lunch, naturally, was packed in a shoe box—sandwiches, fruit, cheese, and napkins—all squashed together neatly. The lid would open by itself every twenty minutes for air.

It happened every time, the Miracle of the Sandwiches. One kid always got a brilliant idea. "Hey, I got a brilliant idea. I'm tired of my mother's sandwiches. Let's everybody exchange sandwiches." All the kids exchanged sandwiches, and miraculously we all ended up with salami.

Albert was the true nature lover. "You know, you can learn a lot about human nature from the ants," he always said as he lifted up rock after rock to study his favorite insects. And he was right. While he was studying the ants someone swiped his apple.

We came home with color in our cheeks—green. To make sure we could go again, we didn't forget Mama. We brought her a bouquet. She took one whiff and broke out in red blotches. Papa yelled but didn't lay a hand on us. He was afraid it was catching.

BEVERLY CLEARY
Beezus and Ramona

When Beezus came home from school on the afternoon of her tenth birthday, she felt that so far the day had been perfect—packages by her plate at breakfast, a new dress to wear to school, the whole class singing "Happy Birthday" just for her. But the best part was still to come. Aunt Beatrice was coming for dinner.

Beezus could hardly wait to tell her aunt about acting the part of Sacajawea leading Lewis and Clark across the plains to Oregon at a P.T.A. meeting. And of course Aunt Beatrice would bring more presents—very special presents, because she was Aunt Beatrice's namesake. And at dinner there would be a beautiful birthday cake with ten candles. Mother had probably worked all afternoon baking and decorating the cake and now had it hidden away in a cupboard.

When Mother kissed Beezus she had said, "I'm sorry, Beezus, but I'll have to ask you to keep Ramona out of the kitchen for a while."

"Why?" asked Beezus, thinking her mother was planning a surprise.

"So I can bake your birthday cake," Mother explained.

"Isn't it baked yet?" exclaimed Beezus. "Oh, Mother."

"This has been one of those days when I couldn't seem to get anything done," said Mother. "It was my morning for the nursery-school car pool. After I picked up all the children and drove them to nursery school and came home and did the breakfast dishes and made the beds, it was time to pick up the children and take them all home again. And after lunch I started the cake and had just creamed the sugar and butter in the electric mixer when I was called to the telephone. When I came back, what do you think had happened?"

"What?" asked Beezus, pretty sure Ramona had something to do with it.

"Ramona had dropped all the eggs in the house into the batter and had started the mixer," said Mother.

"Shells and all?" asked Beezus, horrified.

"Shells and all," repeated Mother wearily. "And so I had to get out the car again and drive to market and buy more eggs."

"Ramona, what did you have to go and do a thing like that for?" Beezus demanded of her little sister, who was playing with her doll Bendix.

"To see what would happen," answered Ramona.

She doesn't look a bit sorry, thought Beezus crossly. Spoiling my birthday cake like that!

"Don't worry, dear. There's still plenty of time to bake another," said Mother. "If you'll just keep Ramona out of the kitchen, I can get it into the oven in no time at all."

That made Beezus feel better. At least she would have a birthday cake, even if it did mean looking after Ramona for a while.

"Read to me," Ramona demanded. "Read about Big Steve."

"I'll read to you, but I won't read that book," said Beezus, going to the bookcase. She really wanted to read one of her birthday books, called 202 *Things to Do on a Rainy Afternoon*, but she knew Ramona would insist on a story. "How about 'Hänsel and Gretel'?" she asked. Next to stories with lots of noise, Ramona liked stories about witches, goblins, or ogres.

"Yes, I like 'Hänsel and Gretel'," agreed Ramona, as she climbed on the davenport and sat Bendix beside her. "O.K., I'm ready. Now you can begin."

Beezus curled up at the other end of the davenport with *Grimm's Fairy Tales*. "Once upon a time . . ." she began, and Ramona listened contentedly. When she did not have to make noises like machinery Beezus enjoyed reading to Ramona, and this afternoon reading aloud was particularly pleasant, with Mother in the kitchen baking a birthday cake. As Beezus read she listened to the whir of the mixer and the sound of eggs being cracked against a bowl.

Beezus read about Hänsel's leaving a trail of crumbs behind him as he and Gretel went into the woods. She read the part Ramona liked best, about the witch's trying to fatten Hänsel. Ramona listened wide-eyed until Beezus came to the end of the story, where Gretel pushed the witch into the oven and escaped through the woods with her brother.

"That's a good story," said Ramona, as she jumped down from the davenport.

Surprised that Ramona didn't demand another story, Beezus picked up *202 Things to Do on a Rainy Afternoon* and began to read. She was learning how to make a necklace out of beans and pumpkin seeds painted with fingernail polish when a lovely sweet vanilla fragrance began to fill the house, and Beezus knew her birthday cake was safely in the oven at last.

Ramona's unusual silence made Beezus glance up from her book. "Ramona!" she cried, when she saw what her little sister was doing. "Stop that right away!"

Ramona was busy pulling graham-cracker crumbs out of the pocket of her overalls and sprinkling them across the rug. "I'm Hänsel leaving a trail of crumbs through the woods," she said, digging more crumbs out of her pocket. "My father is a poor woodcutter."

"Oh, Ramona," said Beezus, but she had to giggle at the picture of Father as a poor woodcutter.

Ramona sprinkled more crumbs on the rug, and Beezus knew she had to do something about it. "Why don't you pretend you're Gretel?" she suggested, because Gretel would not leave crumbs on the rug.

"O.K.," agreed Ramona.

That was easy, thought Beezus, and went on reading about making a complete set of doll furniture out of old milk cartons. How good her birthday cake smelled! She hoped Mother would remember she had asked for pink frosting. She heard the oven door open and close. Mother must be peeking into the oven to see how my cake is coming along, she thought.

Beezus read on, absorbed in the directions for making a vase out of an old tomato-juice can. Something smells funny, she thought as she turned a page. Then she stopped and sniffed. The air was no longer filled with the lovely warm fragrance of a baking cake. It was filled with a horrid rubbery smell. That's funny, thought Beezus. I wonder what it can be. She sniffed again. Maybe somebody was burning trash outside and the smell was coming in through the window.

Mother came into the living room from the bedroom. "Beezus, do you smell something rubbery?" she asked anxiously.

"Yes, and it smells awful," said Beezus. Ramona held her nose.

Mother sniffed again. "It smells as if something is scorching, too."

Beezus went into the kitchen, where she found the smell so strong that it made her cough. "It's worse in here, Mother," she called, as she looked to see if anything was burning on the stove. Then Beezus remembered the oven. "Mother," she said in a worried voice, "you don't suppose something has happened to my birthday cake again?"

"Of course not," said Mother, coming into the kitchen and opening the window. "What could happen to it?"

Just to be sure, Beezus cautiously opened the oven door. "Mother!" she cried, horrified at what she saw. "Look!" Ramona's rubber doll, Bendix, leaned over the edge of the cake pan, her head and arms buried in the batter. Her dress was scorched to a golden tan. "Oh, Mother!" repeated Beezus. Her birthday cake, her beautiful, fragrant birthday cake, was ruined.

"Is the witch done yet?" Ramona asked.

"Ramona—" began Mother and stopped. She couldn't

think of anything to say. Silently she turned off the oven and, with a pot holder, pulled out the doll and the remains of the cake.

"Ramona Geraldine Quimby!" said Beezus angrily. "You're just awful, that's what you are! Just plain awful. Spoiling your own sister's birthday cake!"

"You told me to pretend I was Gretel," protested Ramona. "And Gretel pushed the witch into the oven."

Beezus looked at the cake and burst into tears. Ramona promptly began to cry too. This made Beezus even angrier. "You stop crying," she ordered Ramona furiously. "It was my birthday cake and I'm the one that's supposed to be crying."

"Girls!" said Mother in a tired voice. "Ramona, you have been very naughty. You know better than to put anything into the oven. Now go to your room and stay there until I say you can come out."

Sniffling, Ramona started toward the bedroom.

"And don't you dare put your toys on my bed," said Beezus. "Mother, can you fix the cake?"

"I'm afraid not." Mother poked at the cake with her finger. "It's fallen, and anyway it would probably taste like burnt rubber."

Beezus tried to brush the tears out of her eyes. "Ramona always spoils everything. Now I won't have any birthday cake, and Aunt Beatrice is coming and it won't be like a birthday at all."

"I know Ramona is a problem but we'll just have to be patient, because she's little," said Mother, as she scraped the cake into the garbage can. "And you will still have a cake. I'll phone your Aunt Beatrice and have her bring one from the bakery."

"Oh, Mother, will you?" asked Beezus.

"That's what I'll do," said Mother. "Now run along and wash your face and you'll feel better."

But as Beezus held her face cloth under the faucet she was not at all sure she would feel better. For Ramona to spoil one birthday cake was bad enough, but *two* . . . Probably nobody else in the whole world had a little sister who had spoiled two birthday cakes on the same day.

Beezus scrubbed away the tear stains, feeling more and more sorry for herself for having such a little sister. If Ramona were only bigger, things might be different; but since she was so much younger, she would always be . . . well, a pest. Then the terrible thought came to Beezus again—the thought she had had the time Ramona bit into all the apples and the time she shoved the dog into the bathroom. She tried not to think the thought, but she couldn't help it. There were times when she did not love Ramona. This was one of them. Everyone knew sisters were supposed to love each other. Look how much Mother and Aunt Beatrice loved each other. Beezus felt very gloomy indeed as she dried her face. She was a terrible girl who did not love her little sister. Like a wicked sister in a fairy tale. And on her birthday, too, a day that was supposed to be happy.

When Beezus went into the living room, Mother switched off the vacuum cleaner, which had been sucking up the crumbs Ramona had sprinkled on the rug. "Aunt Beatrice said she would be delighted to bring a cake. She knows a bakery that makes very special birthday cakes," she said, smiling at Beezus. "You mustn't let Ramona spoil your birthday."

Beezus felt a little better. She curled up on the davenport again with *202 Things to Do on a Rainy Afternoon* and read about making Christmas tree ornaments out of cellophane straws, until she heard her aunt's car turn into the driveway. Then she flung her book aside and ran out to greet her.

"Happy birthday, darling!" cried Aunt Beatrice, as she set the brake and opened the door of her yellow convertible.

Joyfully Beezus ran over to the car and kissed her aunt. "Did you bring the cake?" she asked.

"I certainly did," answered Aunt Beatrice. "The best birthday cake I could find. And that isn't all I brought. Here, help me carry these packages while I carry the cake. We mustn't let anything happen to *this* cake!"

And the way Aunt Beatrice laughed made Beezus laugh too. Her aunt gave her three packages, two large and one small, to carry.

"The little package is for Ramona," explained Aunt Beatrice. "So she won't feel left out."

Mother came out of the house and hugged her sister. "Hello, Bea," she said. "I'm so glad you could come. What would I ever do without you?"

"It's good to see you, Dorothy," answered Aunt Beatrice. "And what's an aunt for if she can't come to the rescue with a birthday cake once in a while?"

As Beezus watched her mother and her aunt, arm in arm, go into the house, she thought how different they were—Mother so tall and comfortable-looking and Aunt Beatrice so small and gay—and yet how happy they looked together. Smiling, Beezus carried the gifts into the house. Aunt Beatrice always brought such beautiful packages, wrapped in fancy paper and tied with big, fluffy bows.

Aunt Beatrice handed the cake box to Mother. "Be sure you put it in a safe place," she said, and laughed again.

"May I open the packages now?" Beezus asked eagerly, although she felt it was almost too bad to untie such beautiful bows.

"Of course you may," answered Aunt Beatrice. "Where's Ramona?"

A subdued Ramona came out of the bedroom to receive her present. She tore off the wrapping, but Beezus painstakingly untied the ribbon on one of her presents and removed the paper carefully so she wouldn't tear it. Her new book, *202 Things to Do on a Rainy Afternoon*, suggested pasting pretty paper on a gallon ice-cream carton to make a wastebasket.

"Oh, Aunt Beatrice," exclaimed Beezus, as she opened her first package. It was a real grown-up sewing box. It had two sizes of scissors, a fat red pincushion that looked like a tomato, an emery bag that looked like a ripe strawberry, and a tape measure that pulled out of a shiny box. When Beezus pushed the button on the box, the tape measure snapped back inside. The box also had needles, pins, and a thimble. Beezus never wore a thimble, but she thought it would be nice to have one in case she ever wanted to use one. "Oh, Aunt Beatrice," she said, "it's the most wonderful sewing box in the whole world. I'll make you two pot holders for Christmas!" Then, as Aunt Beatrice laughed, Beezus clapped her hand over her mouth. The pot holder was supposed to be a surprise.

Ramona had unwrapped a little steam shovel made of red and yellow plastic, which she was now pushing happily around the rug.

Breathlessly Beezus lifted the lid of the second box. "Oh, Aunt Beatrice!" she exclaimed, as she lifted out a dress that was a lovely shade of blue.

"It's just the right shade of blue to match your eyes," explained Aunt Beatrice.

"Is it really?" asked Beezus, delighted that her pretty young aunt liked blue eyes. She was about to tell her about being Sacajawea for the P.T.A. when Father came home from work, and before long dinner was on the table. Mother lit the candles and turned off the dining-room light. How pretty everything looks, thought Beezus. I wish we had candles on the table every night.

After Father had served the chicken and mashed potatoes and peas and Mother had passed the hot rolls, Beezus decided the time had come to tell Aunt Beatrice about being Sacajawea. "Do you know what I did last week?" she began.

"I want some jelly," said Ramona.

"You mean, 'Please pass the jelly,' " corrected Mother, while Beezus waited patiently.

"No, what did you do last week?" asked Aunt Beatrice.

"Well, last week I—" Beezus began again.

"I like purple jelly better than red jelly," said Ramona.

"Ramona, stop interrupting your sister," said Father.

"Well, I *do* like purple jelly better than red jelly," insisted Ramona.

"Never mind," said Mother. "Go on, Beezus."

"Last week—" said Beezus, looking at her aunt, who smiled as if she understood.

"Excuse me, Beezus," Mother cut in. "Ramona, we do not put jelly on our mashed potatoes."

"I like jelly on my mashed potatoes." Ramona stirred potato and jelly around with her fork.

"Ramona, you heard what your mother said." Father looked stern.

"If I can put butter on my mashed potatoes, why can't I put jelly? I put butter and jelly on toast," said Ramona.

Father couldn't help laughing. "That's a hard question to answer."

"But Mother—" Beezus began.

"I *like* jelly on my mashed potatoes," interrupted Ramona, looking sulky.

"You can't have jelly on your mashed potatoes, because you aren't supposed to," said Beezus crossly, forgetting Sacajawea for the moment.

"That's as good an answer as any," agreed Father. "There are some things we don't do, because we aren't supposed to."

Ramona looked even more sulky.

"Where is my Merry Sunshine?" Mother asked.

Ramona scowled. "I am *too* a Merry Sunshine!" she shouted angrily.

"Ramona," said Mother quietly, "you may go to your room until you can behave yourself."

And serves you right, too, thought Beezus.

"I am *too* a Merry Sunshine," insisted Ramona, but she got down from the table and ran out of the room.

Everyone was silent for a moment. "Beezus, what was it you were trying to tell me?" Aunt Beatrice asked.

And finally Beezus got to tell about leading Lewis and Clark to Oregon, with a doll tied to Mother's breadboard for a papoose, and how her teacher told her what a clever girl she was to think of using a breadboard for a papoose board. Somehow she did not feel the same about telling the story after all Ramona's interruptions. Being Sacajawea for the P.T.A. did not seem very important now. No matter what she did, Ramona always managed to spoil it. Unhappily, Beezus went on eating her chicken and peas. It was another one of those terrible times when she did not love her little sister.

"You mustn't let Ramona get you down," whispered Mother.

Beezus did not answer. What a terrible girl she was not to love her little sister! How shocked and surprised Mother would be if she knew.

"Beezus, you look as if something is bothering you," remarked Aunt Beatrice.

Beezus looked down at her plate. How could she ever tell such an awful thing?

"Why don't you tell us what is wrong?" Aunt Beatrice suggested. "Perhaps we could help."

She sounded so interested and so understanding that Beezus discovered she really wanted to tell what was on her mind. "Sometimes I just don't love Ramona!" she blurted out, to get it over with. There! She had said it right out loud. And on her birthday, too. Now everyone would know what a terrible girl she was.

"My goodness, is that all that bothers you?" Mother sounded surprised.

Beezus nodded miserably.

"Why, there's no reason why you *should* love Ramona all the time," Mother went on. "After all, there are probably lots of times when she doesn't love you."

Now it was Beezus' turn to be surprised—surprised and relieved at the same time. She wondered why she hadn't thought of it that way before.

Aunt Beatrice smiled. "Dorothy," she said to Mother, "do you remember the time I—" She began to laugh so hard she couldn't finish the sentence.

"You took my doll with the beautiful yellow curls and dyed her hair with black shoe dye," finished Mother, and the two grown-up sisters went into gales of laughter. "I didn't love you a bit that time," admitted Mother. "I was mad at you for days."

"And you were always so bossy, because you were older," said Aunt Beatrice. "I'm sure I didn't love you at all when you were supposed to take me to school and made me walk about six feet behind you, because you didn't want people to know you had to look after me."

"Mother!" exclaimed Beezus in shocked delight.

"Did I do that?" laughed Mother. "I had forgotten all about it."

"What else did Mother do?" Beezus asked eagerly.

"She was terribly fussy," said Aunt Beatrice. "We had to share a room and she used to get mad because I was untidy. Once she threw all my paper dolls into the wastebasket, because I had left them on her side of the dresser. That was another time we didn't love each other."

Fascinated, Beezus hoped this interesting conversation would continue. Imagine Mother and Aunt Beatrice quarreling!

"Oh, but the worst thing of all!" said Mother. "Remember—"

"I'll never forget!" exclaimed Aunt Beatrice, as if she knew what Mother was talking about. "Wasn't I awful?"

"Perfectly terrible," agreed Mother, wiping her eyes because she was laughing so hard.

"What happened?" begged Beezus, who could not wait to find out what dreadful thing Aunt Beatrice had done when she was a girl. "Mother, tell what happened."

"It all began when the girls began to take autograph albums to school," began Mother and then went off into another fit of laughter. "Oh, Beatrice, you tell it."

"Of course I wanted an autograph album too," continued Aunt Beatrice. Beezus nodded, because she, too, had an autograph album. "Well, your mother, who was always very sensible, saved her allowance and bought a beautiful album with a red cover stamped in gold. How I envied her!"

"As soon as your Aunt Beatrice got her allowance she always ran right over to the school store and spent it," added Mother.

"Yes, and on the most awful junk," agreed Aunt Beatrice. "Licorice whips, and pencils that were square instead of round, and I don't know what all."

"Yes, but what about the autograph album?" Beezus asked.

"Well, when I—oh, I'm almost ashamed to tell it," said Aunt Beatrice.

"Oh, go on," urged Mother. "It's priceless."

"Well, when I saw your mother with that brand-new autograph album that she bought, because she was so sensible, I was annoyed, because I wanted one too and I hadn't saved my allowance. And then she asked me if I'd like to sign my name in it."

"It was my night to set the table," added Mother. "I never should have left her alone with it."

"But what happened?" Beezus could hardly wait to find out.

"I sat down at the desk and picked up a pen, planning to write on the last page, 'By hook or by crook I'll be the last in your book,' " said Aunt Beatrice.

"Oh, did people write that in those days, too?" Beezus was surprised, because she had thought this was something very new to write in an autograph album.

"But I didn't write it," continued Aunt Beatrice. "I just sat there wishing I had an autograph album, and then I took the pen and wrote my name on every single page in the book!"

"Aunt Beatrice! You didn't! Not in Mother's brand-new

autograph album!" Beezus was horrified and delighted at the same time. What a terrible thing to do!

"She certainly did," said Mother, "and not just plain Beatrice Haswell, either. She wrote Beatrice Ann Haswell, Miss Bea Haswell, B. A. Haswell, Esquire, and everything she could think of. When she couldn't think of any more ways to write her name she started all over again."

"Oh, Aunt Beatrice, how perfectly awful," exclaimed Beezus, with a touch of admiration in her voice.

"Yes, wasn't it?" agreed Aunt Beatrice. "I don't know what got into me."

"And what did Mother do?" inquired Beezus, eager for the whole story.

"We had a dreadful quarrel and I got spanked," said Aunt Beatrice. "Your mother didn't love me one little bit for a long, long time. And I wouldn't admit it, but I felt terrible because I had spoiled her autograph album. Fortunately Christmas came along about that time and we were both given albums and that put an end to the whole thing."

Why, thought Beezus, Aunt Beatrice used to be every bit as awful as Ramona. And yet look how nice she is now. Beezus could scarcely believe it. And now Mother and Aunt Beatrice, who had quarreled when they were girls, loved each other and thought the things they had done were funny! They actually laughed about it. Well, maybe when she was grown-up she would think it was funny that Ramona had put eggshells in one birthday cake and baked her rubber doll with another. Maybe she wouldn't think Ramona was so exasperating, after all. Maybe that was just the way things were with sisters. A lovely feeling of relief came over Beezus. What if she *didn't* love Ramona all the time? It didn't matter at all. She was just like any other sister.

"Mother," whispered Beezus, happier than she had felt in a long time, "I hope Ramona comes back before we have my birthday cake."

"Don't worry," Mother said, smiling. "I'm sure she wouldn't miss it for anything."

And sure enough, in a few minutes Ramona appeared from the bedroom and took her place at the table. "I can behave myself," she said.

"It's about time," observed Father.

Beezus watched Ramona eating her cold mashed potatoes and jelly and thought how much easier things would be now that she could look at her sister when she was exasperating and think, Ha-ha, Ramona, this is one of those times when I don't have to love you.

"Girls with birthdays don't have to help clear the table," said Mother, beginning to carry out the dishes.

Beezus waited expectantly for the most important moment of the day. She heard her mother take the cake out of its box and strike a match to light the candles. "Oh," she breathed happily, when Mother appeared in the doorway with the cake in her hands. It was the most beautiful cake she had ever seen—pink with a wreath of white roses made of icing, and ten pink candles that threw a soft glowing light on Mother's face.

" 'Happy birthday to you,' " sang Mother and Father and Aunt Beatrice and Ramona. " 'Happy birthday, dear Beezus, happy birthday to you.' "

"Make a wish," said Father.

Beezus paused a minute. Then she closed her eyes and thought, I wish all my birthdays would turn out to be as wonderful as this one finally did. She opened her eyes and blew as hard as she could.

"Your wish is granted!" cried Aunt Beatrice, smiling across the ten smoking candles.

" 'Happy birthday, dear Beezus, happy birthday to you!' " sang Ramona at the top of her voice.

"All right, Ramona," said Mother with a touch of exasperation in her voice. "Once is enough."

But at that moment Beezus did not think her little sister was exasperating at all.

ROALD DAHL
The Witches

*It's the annual witches' convention. What's on the
agenda? You'll see!*

Children are rrree-volting!" screamed The Grand High
Witch. "Vee vill vipe them all avay! Vee vill scrrrub them
off the face of the earth! Vee vill flush them down the drain!"

"Yes, yes!" chanted the audience. "Wipe them away! Scrub
them off the earth! Flush them down the drain!"

"Children are foul and filthy!" thundered The Grand High
Witch.

"They are! They are!" chorused the English witches. "They
are foul and filthy!"

"Children are dirty and stinky!" screamed The Grand High Witch.

"Dirty and stinky!" cried the audience, getting more and more worked up.

"Children are smelling of *dogs' drrroppings*!" screeched The Grand High Witch.

"Pooooooo!" cried the audience. "Pooooooo! Pooooooo! Pooooooo!"

"They are vurse than dogs' drrroppings!" screeched The Grand High Witch. "Dogs' drrroppings is smelling like violets and prrrimroses compared vith children!"

"Violets and primroses!" chanted the audience. They were clapping and cheering almost every word spoken from the platform. The speaker seemed to have them completely under her spell.

"To talk about children is making me sick!" screamed The Grand High Witch. "I am feeling sick even *thinking* about them! Fetch me a basin!"

The Grand High Witch paused and glared at the mass of eager faces in the audience. They waited, wanting more.

"So now!" barked The Grand High Witch. "So now I am having a plan! I am having a giganticus plan for getting rrrid of every single child in the whole of Inkland!"

The witches gasped. They gaped. They turned and gave each other ghoulish grins of excitement.

"Yes!" thundered The Grand High Witch. "Vee shall svish them and svollop them and vee shall make to disappear every single smelly little brrrat in Inkland in vun strrroke!"

"Whoopee!" cried the witches, clapping their hands. "You are brilliant, O Your Grandness! You are fantabulous!"

"Shut up and listen!" snapped The Grand High Witch. "Listen very carefully and let us not be having any muck-ups!"

The audience leaned forward, eager to learn how this magic was going to be performed.

"Each and every vun of you," thundered The Grand High Witch, "is to go back to your home towns immediately and rrree-sign from your jobs. Rrree-sign! Give notice! Rrree-tire!"

"We will!" they cried. "We will resign from our jobs!"

"And after you have rrree-signed from your jobs," The Grand High Witch went on, "each and every vun of you vill be going out and you vill be buying . . ." She paused.

"What will we be buying?" they cried. "Tell us, O Brilliant One, what is it we shall be buying?"

"Sveet-shops!" shouted The Grand High Witch.

"Sweet-shops!" they cried. "We are going to buy sweet-shops! What a frumptious wheeze!"

"Each of you vill be buying for herself a sveet-shop. You vill be buying the very best and most rrree-spectable sveet-shops in Inkland."

"We will! We will!" they answered. Their dreadful voices were like a chorus of dentists' drills all grinding away together.

"I am vonting no tuppenny-ha'penny crrrummy little tobacco-selling-newspaper-sveet-shops!" shouted The Grand High Witch. "I am vonting you to get only the very best shops filled up high vith piles and piles of luscious sveets and tasty chocs!"

"The best!" they cried. "We shall buy the best sweet-shops in town!"

"You vill be having no trouble in getting vot you vont," shouted The Grand High Witch, "because you vill be offering four times as much as a shop is vurth and nobody is rrree-fusing an offer like that! Money is not a prrroblem to us vitches as you know very vell. I have brrrought vith me six trrrunks stuffed full of Inklish bank notes, all new and crrrisp. And all of them," she added with a fiendish leer, "all of them homemade."

The witches in the audience grinned, appreciating this joke.

At that point, one foolish witch got so excited at the possibilities presented by owning a sweet-shop that she leapt to her feet and shouted, "The children will come flocking to my shop and I will feed them poisoned sweets and poisoned chocs and wipe them all out like weasels!"

The room became suddenly silent. I saw the tiny body of The Grand High Witch stiffen and then go rigid with rage. "Who spoke?" she shrieked. "It vos *you*! You over there!"

The culprit sat down fast and covered her face with her clawed hands.

"You blithering bumpkin!" screeched The Grand High Witch. "You brrrainless bogvumper! Are you not rrree-alizing that if you are going rrround poisoning little children you vill be caught in five minutes flat? Never in my life am I hearing such a boshvolloping suggestion coming from a vitch!"

The entire audience cowered and shook. I'm quite sure they all thought, as I did, that the terrible white-hot sparks were about to start flying again.

Curiously enough, they didn't.

"If such a tomfiddling idea is all you can be coming up vith," thundered The Grand High Witch, "then it is no vunder Inkland is still svorming vith rrrotten little children!"

There was another silence. The Grand High Witch glared at the witches in the audience. "Do you not know," she shouted at them, "that vee vitches are vurrrking only vith magic?"

"We know, Your Grandness!" they all answered. "Of course we know!"

The Grand High Witch grated her bony gloved hands against each other and cried out, "So each of you is owning a magnificent sveet-shop! The next move is that each of you vill be announcing in the vindow of your shop that on a certain day you vill be having a Great Gala Opening vith frree sveets and chocs to every child!"

"That will bring them in, the greedy little brutes!" cried the audience. "They'll be fighting to get through the doors!"

"Next," continued The Grand High Witch, "you vill prepare yourselves for this Great Gala Opening by filling every choc and every sveet in your shop vith my very latest and grrreatest magic formula! This is known as FORMULA 86 DELAYED ACTION MOUSE-MAKER!"

"Delayed Action Mouse-Maker!" they chanted. "She's done it again! Her Grandness has concocted yet another of her wondrous magic child-killers! How do we make it, O Brilliant One?"

"Exercise patience," answered The Grand High Witch. "First, I am explaining to you how my Formula 86 Delayed Action Mouse-Maker is vurrrking. Listen carefully."

"We are listening!" cried the audience, who were now jumping up and down in their chairs with excitement.

"Delayed Action Mouse-Maker is a green liqvid," explained The Grand High Witch, "and vun droplet in each choc or sveet vill be qvite enough. So here is vot happens:

"Child eats choc vich has in it Delayed Action Mouse-Maker liqvid . . .

"Child goes home feeling fine . . .

"Child goes to bed, still feeling fine . . .

"Child vakes up in the morning still okay . . .

"Child goes to school still feeling fine . . .

"Formula, you understand, is *delayed action*, and is not vurrrking yet."

"We understand, O Brainy One!" cried the audience. "But when does it start working?"

"It is starting to vurrrk at exactly nine o'clock, vhen the child is arriving at school!" shouted The Grand High Witch triumphantly. "Child arrives at school. Delayed Action Mouse-Maker immediately starts to vurrrk. Child starts to shrrrink. Child is starting to grow fur. Child is starting to grow tail. All is happening in prrreecisely twenty-six seconds. After twenty-six seconds, child is not a child any longer. It is a mouse!"

"A mouse!" cried the witches. "What a frumptious thought!"

"Classrooms vill all be svorrrming vith mice!" shouted The Grand High Witch. "Chaos and pandemonium vill be rrreigning in every school in Inkland! Teachers vill be hopping up and down! Vimmen teachers vill be standing on desks and holding up skirts and yelling, 'Help, help, help!' "

"They will! They will!" cried the audience.

"And vot," shouted The Grand High Witch, "is happening next in every school?"

"Tell us!" they cried. "Tell us, O Brainy One!"

The Grand High Witch stretched her stringy neck forward and grinned at the audience, showing two rows of pointed teeth, slightly blue. She raised her voice louder than ever and shouted, *"Mouse-trrraps is coming out!"*

"Mouse-traps!" cried the witches.

"And cheese!" shouted The Grand High Witch. "Teachers is all rrrushing and rrrunning out and getting mouse-trrraps and baiting them vith cheese and putting them down all over school! Mice is nibbling cheese! Mouse-trrraps is going off! All over school, mouse-trrraps is going *snappety-snap* and mouse-heads is rrrolling across the floors like marbles! All over Inkland, in everrry school in Inkland, noise of snapping mouse-trrraps vill be heard!"

At this point, the disgusting old Grand High Witch began to do a sort of witch's dance up and down the platform, stamping her feet and clapping her hands. The entire audience joined in the clapping and the foot-stamping. They were making such a tremendous racket that I thought surely Mr. Stringer would hear it and come banging at the door. But he didn't.

Then, above all the noise, I heard the voice of The Grand High Witch screaming out some sort of an awful gloating song:

"Down vith children! Do them in!
Boil their bones and fry their skin!
Bish them, sqvish them, bash them, mash
    them!
Brrreak them, shake them, slash them, smash
    them!
Offer chocs vith magic powder!
Say 'Eat up!' then say it louder.
Crrram them full of sticky eats,
Send them home still guzzling sveets.
And in the morning little fools
Go marching off to separate schools.
A girl feels sick and goes all pale.
She yells, 'Hey look! I've grrrown a tail!'
A boy who's standing next to her
Screams, 'Help! I think I'm grrrowing fur!'
Another shouts, 'Vee look like frrreaks!
There's viskers growing on our cheeks!'
A boy who vos extremely tall
Cries out, 'Vot's wrong? I'm grrrowing small!'

Four tiny legs begin to sprrrout
From everybody rrround about.
And all at vunce, all in a trrrice,
There are no children! Only MICE!
In every school is mice galore
All rrrunning rrround the school-rrroom floor!
And all the poor demented teachers
Is yelling, 'Hey, who are these crrreatures?'
They stand upon the desks and shout,
'Get out, you filthy mice! Get out!
Vill someone fetch some mouse-trrraps, please!
And don't forrrget to bring the cheese!'
Now mouse-trrraps come and every trrrap
Goes *snippy-snip* and *snappy-snap*.
The mouse-trrraps have a powerful spring,
The springs go *crack* and *snap* and *ping*!

Is lovely noise for us to hear!
Is music to a vitch's ear!
Dead mice is every place arrround,
Piled two feet deep upon the grrround,
Vith teachers searching left and rrright,
But not a single child in sight!
The teachers cry, 'Vot's going on?
Oh vhere have all the children gone?
Is half-past nine and as a rrrule
They're never late as this for school!'
Poor teachers don't know vot to do.
Some sit and rrread, and just a few
Amuse themselves throughout the day
By sweeping all the mice avay.
AND ALL US VITCHES SHOUT HOORAY!"

NORTON JUSTER
The Phantom Tollbooth

The mysterious gift of a magic tollbooth takes young Milo to a strange, topsy-turvy world. Accompanied by Tock, a huge watchdog who actually ticks, Milo soon sees that even the simple act of asking directions can turn into a comical word game.

Milo and Tock walked up to the door, whose brass nameplate read simply THE GIANT, and knocked.

"Good afternoon," said the perfectly ordinary-sized man who answered the door.

"Are you the giant?" asked Tock doubtfully.

"To be sure," he replied proudly. "I'm the smallest giant in the world. What can I do for you?"

"Are we lost?" said Milo.

"That's a difficult question," said the giant. "Why don't you go around back and ask the midget?" And he closed the door.

They walked to the rear of the house, which looked exactly like the front, and knocked at the door, whose nameplate read THE MIDGET.

"How are you?" inquired the man, who looked exactly like the giant.

"Are you the midget?" asked Tock again, with a hint of uncertainty in his voice.

"Unquestionably," he answered. "I'm the tallest midget in the world. May I help you?"

"Do you think we're lost?" repeated Milo.

"That's a very complicated problem," he said. "Why don't you go around to the side and ask the fat man?" And he, too, quickly disappeared.

The side of the house looked very like the front and back, and the door flew open the very instant they knocked.

"How nice of you to come by," exclaimed the man, who could have been the midget's twin brother.

"You must be the fat man," said Tock, learning not to count too much on appearance.

"The thinnest one in the world," he replied brightly; "but if you have any questions, I suggest you try the thin man, on the other side of the house."

Just as they suspected, the other side of the house looked the same as the front, the back, and the side, and the door was again answered by a man who looked precisely like the other three.

"What a pleasant surprise!" he cried happily. "I haven't had a visitor in as long as I can remember."

"How long is that?" asked Milo.

"I'm sure I don't know," he replied. "Now pardon me; I have to answer the door."

"But you just did," said Tock.

"Oh yes, I'd forgotten."

"Are you the fattest thin man in the world?" asked Tock.

"Do you know one that's fatter?" he asked impatiently.

"I think you're all the same man," said Milo emphatically.

"S-S-S-S-S-H-H-H-H-H-H-H," he cautioned, putting his finger up to his lips and drawing Milo closer. "Do you want to ruin everything? You see, to tall men I'm a midget, and to short men I'm a giant; to the skinny ones I'm a fat man, and to the fat ones I'm a thin man. That way I can hold four jobs at once. As you can see, though, I'm neither tall nor short nor fat nor thin. In fact, I'm quite ordinary, but there are so many ordinary men that no one asks their opinion about anything. Now what is your question?"

132

"Are we lost?" asked Milo once again.

"H-h-m-m-m," said the man, scratching his head. "I haven't had such a difficult question in as long as I can remember. Would you mind repeating it? It's slipped my mind."

Milo asked the question for the fifth time.

"My, my," the man mumbled. "I know one thing for certain; it's much harder to tell whether you *are* lost than whether you *were* lost, for, on many occasions, where you're going is exactly where you are. On the other hand, you often find that where you've been is not at all where you should have gone, and, since it's much more difficult to find your way back from someplace you've never left, I suggest you go there immediately and then decide. If you have any more questions, please ask the giant." And he slammed his door and pulled down the shade.

NATALIE BABBITT
The Harps of Heaven

There were two brothers in the World once named Basil and Jack—Basil was the fat one—a pair of mean, low, quarrelsome fellows who hated each other right from the start and would never have stayed together if it weren't for the fact that no one else could stand them for a minute. They had begun to fight when they were babies and fought all their lives, so that one or the other was always black and blue; but still they had gone into business together and had managed to become quite famous, at least with the law, for they were positively the best thieves in the World.

There wasn't anything that Basil and Jack couldn't steal if they wanted to, and most of the time they wanted to. Then they would sell what they stole and spend all the money on whiskey and iodine, the first to get them ready for a fight and the second to patch them up afterward. But one night they went too far, for each in secret had bought a pistol, and in the middle of the fight they shot each other dead. However, this drastic event made very little difference between them, for when they arrived at the gates of Hell, which happened almost at once—there being no question in anyone's mind as to where they belonged—they began another fight on the spot over who should go in first.

When the Devil heard all the commotion, he was pleased as punch. "It's Basil and Jack!" he said to himself. "And not a moment too soon!"

Now, what the Devil meant by that was this: there was a peevish piano teacher in Hell—sent down for nagging—whose principal quarrel with the place was the music. There was bound to be better music in Heaven, she said, since they had so many lovely harps there, while in Hell, she said, there wasn't even one harp, lovely or otherwise.

The Devil had been stung by these remarks, for he was proud of Hell. But it was all too true that he had no harps, and he had decided that the only way to get a good one was to steal it from Heaven. And the only way to do *that* was to send up Basil and Jack. "If anyone can steal a harp from Heaven, it's Basil and Jack," he said to himself, "and now at last they're here!"

So, as soon as the brothers were settled in, the Devil had

them brought to his throne room. "Basil and Jack!" he said joyfully. "Basil and Jack at last."

"That's us," said Jack.

And Basil said, "None other!"

"Splendid!" said the Devil. "I've got a job for you." And he went on to tell them the problem.

Well, the brothers were just as glad to get busy again, so they heard the Devil out, and the whole thing appealed to them hugely.

"That's the stuff," said Basil.

And Jack said, "Right!"

"You'll need a good plan, though," said the Devil. "A really good plan."

"Nothing to that," said the brothers. "There's no job anywhere too tricky for *us*."

"So I've heard," said the Devil, "and I hope it's true. I've set my heart, such as it is, on having a harp in Hell. I can't go up myself—they'd know me in a minute. But you two can do it if anyone can."

So Basil and Jack thought up a plan, and the plan was to disguise themselves as angels. "We'll just go up all sweet-like," they said, "and pretend to have lost our way. Then we'll slip in, grab the merchandise, slip out, and be back in time for supper."

"Splendid!" said the Devil, and he gave them the costumes they needed and sent them on their way.

It took a good while to get there, for they had to pass round the World on the way, and the wings the Devil gave them took time to get used to. But at least they didn't fight, for neither wanted to spoil his costume, and after a while they arrived at the gates of Heaven, out of breath but full of confidence.

Now, confidence is all right, but it isn't everything, for at this point things began to go wrong in ways that the brothers had never in the World expected. Here they were at the gates, but a Person was sitting there with a harp at his side, and this Person looked at them, looked at their costumes, smiled, and said at last in a gentle tone, "Why, it's Jack and Basil, isn't it? Let's see now. *You* must be Basil, because Basil is the fat one, and *you* must be Jack. What brings you up this way?"

"Oh," said Basil.

And Jack said, "Well . . ."

"Never mind," said the Person at the gates. "I already know why you've come. And I must say you look very nice in your costumes."

No one in all their lives had ever called the brothers nice, and Jack had it in mind to say, "Nuts!" But he didn't quite dare, somehow, and Basil just stood there with his mouth open.

"You're here for a harp," said the Person at the gates. "Well, that's all right. There are plenty of harps in Heaven, and this one here beside me is for you. There isn't any need to steal one."

"Oh!" said Jack.

And Basil said, "Well."

And they were both severely disappointed.

But the Person at the gates only smiled and picked up the harp—a small triangular harp made of gold, with cupids carved on its frame and strings like sunbeams—and handed it to them. "Goodbye then," said the Person at the gates.

So Jack took the harp and off the brothers went, back round the World to Hell.

It took a good deal longer to go down than it had to come up—a fact about which one may draw one's own conclusions—and the brothers, who were already cross about missing the chance to steal, soon grew bored with flying and began to argue.

"Here," said Basil. "Let *me* take the harp for a while. There's no reason *you* should get to have it all the time."

"I'll be hanged if I will," said Jack. "You'd only drop it."

"Selfish!" said Basil.

And Jack said, "Clumsy!"

"Donkey!" said Basil.

"Pig!" said Jack.

"You're another."

"Am not."

"Are too."

And right there in the air between Heaven and Hell, Basil and Jack began to fight.

It was a glorious fight, with a great tearing of costumes, and a great snatching out of feathers from wings, and a great noise full of yells, thumps, swats, and wallops; and right in the middle was the poor little harp, yanked this way and that like tug of war.

They fought all the way back to Hell and arrived at last in terrible condition.

"Where's the harp?" said the Devil, who had heard them coming. "Hand it over." He took it away from them, cradled it in one arm, and ran his thumb across the strings.

But instead of sounding sweeter than zephyrs, the harp gave off a discord that made all three of them wince.

"*Now* see what you've done with your silly fighting," said the Devil. "My harp's all out of tune!"

"Oh," said Basil.

And Jack said, "Well."

"And I don't know how to tune it!" said the Devil.

"Neither do I," said Jack.

And Basil said, "Me either."

And that, of course, was that, for the pity of it was that there wasn't a soul—no one in all of Hell—who knew how to tune a harp from Heaven, not even the piano teacher.

"Well," said the Devil to Basil and Jack, "you'll just have to go back and get another."

"If you say so," said Basil and Jack.

"I do," said the Devil.

So back they went just as they were, in their ragged costumes, and the flying was harder than ever with so many feathers missing from their wings. But still they got there at last without too much complaining, and found the Person still sitting at the gates.

"Why, Jack and Basil! Here you are again!" said the Person.

"That's it," said Jack.

And Basil said, "Right."

But they were more than a little embarrassed.

"You've come for another harp, I expect," said the Person at the gates, observing the tears in their costumes.

"Right," said Basil.

And Jack said, "That's it."

"Nothing easier," said the Person. And he took another harp exactly like the first one from under his robe, and held it out to them.

This time Basil took the harp and off they started once again for Hell. But after they had been flying for a while, Jack couldn't stand it any longer. He gave Basil a poke and said, "I never saw anything so silly as you holding on to that harp."

"Says who?" said Basil.

"Says me," said Jack.

"Says pigs," said Basil.

And they were off again, fighting like a frenzy.

This time, however, in the middle of the fight, just when things were getting really satisfying, Basil dropped the harp. Down it fell, straight toward the World, and landed—clunk!—on a mountaintop.

"I told you so," said Jack.

Well, they flew down and found it and took it round the World to Hell just the same, and when they gave it to the Devil, he was very upset.

"Look at this harp!" he said. "It's all bashed out of shape! No one could play a harp in this condition."

"Someone can patch it up," said Basil.

"Ding it out with a hammer or something," said Jack.

But there wasn't a goldsmith in all of Hell who knew how to work on a harp from Heaven, and the piano teacher stood to one side and looked scornful.

"Back you go," said the Devil to the brothers. "One more time. And this time you'd better do it right."

"If you say so," said Basil and Jack.

"I do," said the Devil.

So back they had to go once more, and this time the Person at the gates sighed and shook his head when he saw them. "Jack

140

and Basil!" he said. "Can it really be you again?"

"That's it," said Jack.

And Basil said, "Right."

But they were more embarrassed than ever.

"Well," said the Person at the gates, "there's one harp left. I hope you make it through with this one." And he handed them the third harp, went on into Heaven, and shut the gates behind him.

So Basil and Jack took the harp between them, with both holding on to it, and started back down again toward Hell. And this time they got all the way round the World before anything happened. In fact, they were almost to Hell when Basil's wings, which were in far worse shape than Jack's, came loose from his costume and there he was with no way to keep from falling except to cling to his half of the harp.

"Leave off!" cried Jack, flapping his own wings hard. "You'll drag us both down!"

"I can't leave off!" said Basil. "If I do, I'll fall."

"So fall!" said Jack. "Better you than both of us." And he tried to pry Basil's fingers loose from the harp.

They made quite a picture, there in the air above Hell, grappling and struggling, and in the midst of trying to get a safer grip, Basil snatched at the harp strings and pulled them right out like straws from a broom.

And that was the way they arrived back in Hell, Jack with the harp and Basil with the strings, and the Devil was so angry that his horns smoked. "I'll go myself!" he bellowed. "And take my chances!"

"No use," said Basil.

"There's no harps left," said Jack.

"This was the last one," said both of them together.

And the pity of it was that there was no one in all of Hell

who knew how to put the strings back into a harp from Heaven.

So the Devil had to give it up, angry or not. And to punish Jack and Basil, he made them take piano lessons from the peevish teacher—thereby punishing her as well, since the lessons went on for hundreds of years and the brothers never could learn anything but scales, no matter how much they practiced. And of course she made them practice all the time.

But the Devil kept the harps in his throne room just the same. "At least," he said to himself, "no one can say I don't *have* any." And he pretended to everyone that he could fix the harps any time he wanted to, but just didn't want to for now.

BARBARA ROBINSON

The Best Christmas Pageant Ever

The Herdman kids are the town terrors. They've never so much as set foot in church, but the prospect of free doughnuts lures them to tryouts for the annual nativity pageant. When they wind up with leading roles, everyone's Christmas spirit is put to the test.

The first pageant rehearsal was usually about as much fun as a three-hour ride on the school bus, and just as noisy and crowded. This rehearsal, though, was different. Everybody shut up and settled down right away, for fear of missing something awful that the Herdmans might do.

They got there ten minutes late, sliding into the room like a bunch of outlaws about to shoot up a saloon. When Leroy passed Charlie he knuckled him behind the ear, and one little primary girl yelled as Gladys went by. But Mother had said she was going to ignore everything except blood, and since the primary kid wasn't bleeding, and neither was Charlie, nothing happened.

Mother said, "And here's the Herdman family. We're glad to see you all," which was probably the biggest lie ever said right out loud in the church.

Imogene smiled—the Herdman smile, we called it, sly and sneaky—and there they sat, the closest thing to criminals that we knew about, and they were going to represent the best and most beautiful. No wonder everybody was so worked up.

Mother started to separate everyone into angels and shepherds and guests at the inn, but right away she ran into trouble.

"Who were the shepherds?" Leroy Herdman wanted to know. "Where did they come from?"

Ollie Herdman didn't even know what a shepherd was . . . or, anyway, that's what he said.

"What was the inn?" Claude asked. "What's an inn?"

"It's like a motel," somebody told him, "where people go to spend the night."

"What people?" Claude said. "Jesus?"

"Oh, honestly!" Alice Wendleken grumbled. "Jesus wasn't even born yet! Mary and Joseph went there."

"Why?" Ralph asked.

"What happened first?" Imogene hollered at my mother. "Begin at the beginning!"

That really scared me because the beginning would be the Book of Genesis, where it says "In the beginning . . ." and if we were going to have to start with the Book of Genesis we'd never get through.

The thing was, the Herdmans didn't know anything about the Christmas story. They knew that Christmas was Jesus' birthday, but everything else was news to them—the shepherds, the

Wise Men, the star, the stable, the crowded inn.

It was hard to believe. At least, it was hard for me to believe—Alice Wendleken said she didn't have any trouble believing it. "How would they find out about the Christmas story?" she said. "They don't even know what a Bible is. Look what Gladys did to that Bible last week."

While Imogene was snitching money from the collection plate in my class, Gladys and Ollie drew mustaches and tails on all the disciples in the primary-grade Illustrated Bible.

"They never went to church in their whole life till your little brother told them we got refreshments," Alice said, "and all you ever hear about Christmas in school is how to make ornaments out of aluminum foil. So how would they know about the Christmas story?"

She was right. Of course they might have read about it, but they never read anything except *Amazing Comics*. And they might have heard about it on TV, except that Ralph paid sixty-five cents for their TV at a garage sale, and you couldn't see anything on it unless somebody held on to the antenna. Even then, you couldn't see much.

The only other way for them to hear about the Christmas story was from their parents, and I guess Mr. Herdman never got around to it before he climbed on the railroad train. And it was pretty clear that Mrs. Herdman had given up ever trying to tell them anything.

So they just didn't know. And Mother said she had better begin by reading the Christmas story from the Bible. This was a pain in the neck to most of us because we knew the whole thing backward and forward and never had to be told anything except who we were supposed to be, and where we were supposed to stand.

". . . Joseph and Mary, his espoused wife, being great with child . . ."

"Pregnant!" yelled Ralph Herdman.

Well. That stirred things up. All the big kids began to giggle and all the little kids wanted to know what was so funny, and Mother had to hammer on the floor with a blackboard pointer. "That's enough, Ralph," she said, and went on with the story.

"I don't think it's very nice to say Mary was pregnant," Alice whispered to me.

"But she was," I pointed out. In a way, though, I agreed with her. It sounded too ordinary. Anybody could be pregnant. "Great with child" sounded better for Mary.

"I'm not supposed to talk about people being pregnant." Alice folded her hands in her lap and pinched her lips together. "I'd better tell my mother."

"Tell her what?"

"That your mother is talking about things like that in church. My mother might not want me to be here."

I was pretty sure she would do it. She wanted to be Mary, and she was mad at Mother. I knew, too, that she would make it sound worse than it was and Mrs. Wendleken would get madder than she already was. Mrs. Wendleken didn't even want cats to have kittens or birds to lay eggs, and she wouldn't let Alice play with anybody who had two rabbits.

But there wasn't much I could do about it, except pinch Alice, which I did. She yelped, and Mother separated us and made me sit beside Imogene Herdman and sent Alice to sit in the middle of the baby angels.

I wasn't crazy to sit next to Imogene—after all, I'd spent my whole life staying away from Imogene—but she didn't even notice me . . . not much, anyway.

"Shut up," was all she said. "I want to hear her."

I couldn't believe it. Among other things, the Herdmans were famous for never sitting still and never paying attention to anyone—teachers, parents (their own or anybody else's), the truant officer, the police—yet here they were, eyes glued on my mother and taking in every word.

"What's that?" they would yell whenever they didn't understand the language, and when Mother read about there being no room at the inn, Imogene's jaw dropped and she sat up in her seat.

"My God!" she said. "Not even for Jesus?"

I saw Alice purse her lips together so I knew that was something else Mrs. Wendleken would hear about—swearing in the church.

"Well, now, after all," Mother explained, "nobody knew the baby was going to turn out to be Jesus."

"You said Mary knew," Ralph said. "Why didn't she tell them?"

"*I* would have told them!" Imogene put in. "Boy, would I have told them! What was the matter with Joseph that he didn't tell them? Her pregnant and everything," she grumbled.

"What was that they laid the baby in?" Leroy said. "That manger . . . is that like a bed? Why would they have a bed in the barn?"

"That's just the point," Mother said. "They *didn't* have a bed in the barn, so Mary and Joseph had to use whatever there was. What would you do if you had a new baby and no bed to put the baby in?"

"We put Gladys in a bureau drawer," Imogene volunteered.

"Well, there you are," Mother said, blinking a little. "You didn't have a bed for Gladys so you had to use something else."

"Oh, we had a bed," Ralph said, "only Ollie was still in it and he wouldn't get out. He didn't like Gladys." He elbowed Ollie. "Remember how you didn't like Gladys?"

I thought that was pretty smart of Ollie, not to like Gladys right off the bat.

"*Anyway,*" Mother said, "Mary and Joseph used the manger. A manger is a large wooden feeding trough for animals."

"What were the wadded-up clothes?" Claude wanted to know.

"The what?" Mother said.

"You read about it—'she wrapped him in wadded-up clothes.' "

"*Swaddling* clothes." Mother sighed. "Long ago, people used to wrap their babies very tightly in big pieces of material, so they couldn't move around. It made the babies feel cozy and comfortable."

I thought it probably just made the babies mad. Till then, I didn't know what swaddling clothes were either, and they sounded terrible, so I wasn't too surprised when Imogene got all excited about that.

"You mean they tied him up and put him in a feedbox?" she said. "Where was the Child Welfare?"

The Child Welfare was always checking up on the Herdmans. I'll bet if the Child Welfare had ever found Gladys all tied up in a bureau drawer they would have done something about it.

"And, lo, the Angel of the Lord came upon them," Mother went on, "and the glory of the Lord shone round about them, and—"

"Shazam!" Gladys yelled, flinging her arms out and smacking the kid next to her.

"What?" Mother said. Mother never read *Amazing Comics*.

"Out of the black night with horrible vengeance, the Mighty Marvo—"

"I don't know what you're talking about, Gladys," Mother said. "This is the Angel of the Lord who comes to the shepherds in the fields, and—"

"Out of nowhere, right?" Gladys said. "In the black night, right?"

"Well . . ." Mother looked unhappy. "In a way."

So Gladys sat back down, looking very satisfied, as if this was at least one part of the Christmas story that made sense to her.

"Now when Jesus was born in Bethlehem of Judaea," Mother went on reading, "behold there came Wise Men from the East to Jerusalem, saying—"

"That's you, Leroy," Ralph said, "and Claude and Ollie. So pay attention."

"What does it mean, Wise Men?" Ollie wanted to know. "Were they like schoolteachers?"

"No, dumbbell," Claude said. "It means like President of the United States."

Mother looked surprised, and a little pleased—like she did when Charlie finally learned the times-tables up to five. "Why, that's very close, Claude," she said. "Actually, they were kings."

"Well, it's about time," Imogene muttered. "Maybe they'll tell the innkeeper where to get off, and get the baby out of the barn."

"They saw the young child with Mary, his mother, and fell down and worshipped him, and presented unto him gifts: gold, and frankincense, and myrrh."

"What's that stuff?" Leroy wanted to know.

"Precious oils," Mother said, "and fragrant resins."

"Oil!" Imogene hollered. "What kind of a cheap king hands out oil for a present? You get better presents from the firemen!"

Sometimes the Herdmans got Christmas presents at the

Firemen's Party, but the Santa Claus always had to feel all around the packages to be sure they weren't getting bows and arrows or dart guns or anything like that. Imogene usually got sewing cards or jigsaw puzzles and she never liked them, but I guess she figured they were better than oil.

Then we came to King Herod, and the Herdmans never heard of him either, so Mother had to explain that it was Herod who sent the Wise Men to find the baby Jesus.

"Was it him that sent the crummy presents?" Ollie wanted to know, and Mother said it was worse than that—he planned to have the baby Jesus put to death.

"My God!" Imogene said. "He just got born and already they're out to kill him!"

The Herdmans wanted to know all about Herod—what he looked like, and how rich he was, and whether he fought wars with people.

"He must have been the main king," Claude said, "if he could make the other three do what he wanted them to."

"If I was a king," Leroy said, "I wouldn't let some other king push me around."

"You couldn't help it if he was the main king."

"I'd go be king somewhere else."

They were really interested in Herod, and I figured they liked him. He was so mean he could have been their ancestor—Herod Herdman. But I was wrong.

"Who's going to be Herod in this play?" Leroy said.

"We don't show Herod in our pageant," Mother said. And they all got mad. They wanted somebody to be Herod so they could beat up on him.

I couldn't understand the Herdmans. You would have thought the Christmas story came right out of the F.B.I. files, they got so involved in it—wanted a bloody end to Herod, worried about Mary having her baby in a barn, and called the Wise Men a bunch of dirty spies.

And they left the first rehearsal arguing about whether Joseph should have set fire to the inn, or just chased the inn-keeper into the next county.

EDWARD EAGER
Half Magic

One summer four children find a magic charm. They soon discover that the coin grants only half a wish—to get exactly what they want they have to ask for twice as much. As you will see, half magic leads to double trouble when the children travel back in time to the days of King Arthur.

Next morning there were no secret meetings before breakfast.

Jane stayed in her room and Mark stayed in his room, and in the room they shared Katharine and Martha hardly conversed at all.

Each of the children was too busy making private plans and deciding on favorite wishes.

Breakfast was eaten in silence, but not without the exchange of some excited looks. The children's mother was aware that something was in the air, and wondered what new trial lay in store for her.

When their mother had gone to work and the dishes and other loathly tasks were done, the four children gathered in Katharine and Martha's room. Katharine had already checked to see that the charm still lay in its cubbyhole, unharmed by wish of mouse or termite.

Jane had drawn up some rules.

"The wishes are to go by turns," she said. "Nobody's to make any main wish that doesn't include all the rest of us. If there have to be any smaller wishes later on in the same adventure, the person who wished the main wish gets to make them, except in case of emergency. Like if he loses the charm and one of the other ones finds it. I get to go first."

Katharine had something to say about that.

"I don't see why," she said. "You always get dibs on first 'cause you're the oldest, and grownups always pick Martha 'cause she's the baby, and Mark has a wonderful double life with all this and being a boy, too! Middle ones never get any privileges at all! Besides, who hasn't had a wish of her own yet? Think back!"

It was true. Jane had had the half-fire, and Martha had made Carrie half-talk, and Mark had taken them to half of a desert island.

Jane had to agree that Katharine deserved a chance. But she couldn't keep from giving advice.

"We don't want any old visits with Henry Wadsworth Longfellow," she said. "Make it something that's fun for everybody."

"I'm going to," said Katharine. "But I can't decide between wishing we could all fly like birds and wishing we had all the money in the world."

"Those aren't any good," said Jane. "People always wish those in stories, and it never works out at *all*! They either fly too near the sun and get burned, or end up crushed under all the money!"

"We could make it *paper* money," suggested Katharine.

A discussion followed as to how many million dollars in large bills it would take to crush a person to death. By the time the four children got back to the subject of the magic charm seventeen valuable minutes had been wasted.

But now Mark had an idea.

"We've found out the charm can take us through space," he said. "What about time?"

"You mean travel around in the past?" Jane's eyes were glowing. "See Captain Kidd and Nero?"

"I've always wanted to live back in the olden romantic days," said Katharine, getting excited, too. "In days of old when knights were bold!"

The others were joining in by now. For once the four children were all in complete agreement.

"Put in about tournaments," said Mark.

"And quests," said Jane.

"Put in a good deed, too," said Martha. "Just to be on the safe side."

"Don't forget to say two times everything," said all three. They clustered eagerly around Katharine as she took hold of the charm.

"I wish," said Katharine, "that we may go back twice as far as to the days of King Arthur, and see two tournaments and go on two quests and do two good deeds."

The next thing the four children knew, they were standing in the midst of a crowded highway. Four queens were just passing, riding under a silken canopy. The next moment seven merry milkmaids skipped past, going a-Maying. In the distance a gallant knight was chasing a grimly giant with puissant valor, and in the other direction a grimly giant was chasing a gallant knight for all he was worth. Some pilgrims stopped and asked the four children the way to Canterbury. The four children didn't know.

But by now they were tired of the crowded traffic conditions on the King's Highway, and crossed into a field, where the grass seemed greener and fresher than any they had ever seen in their own time. A tall figure lay on the ground nearby, under an apple tree. It was a knight in full armor, and he was sound asleep.

The four children knew he was asleep, because Martha lifted the visor of his helmet and peeked inside. A gentle snore issued forth.

The knight's sword lay on the ground beside him, and Mark reached to pick it up.

Immediately the sleeping knight awoke, and sat up.

"Who steals my purse steals trash," he said, "but who steals my sword steals honor itself, and him will I harry by wood and by water till I cleave him from his brain-pan to his thigh-bone!"

"I beg your pardon, sir," said Mark.

"We didn't mean anything," said Jane.

"We're sorry," said Katharine.

The knight rubbed his eyes with his mailed fist. Instead of the miscreant thief he had expected to see, he saw Mark and Jane and Katharine and Martha.

"Who be you?" he said. "Hath some grimly foe murdered me in my sleep? Am I in Heaven? Be ye cherubim or seraphim?"

"We be neither," said Katharine. "And this isn't Heaven. We are four children."

"Pish," said the knight. "Ye be like no children these eyes have ever beheld. Your garb is outlandish."

"People who live in tin armor shouldn't make remarks," said Katharine.

At this moment there was an interruption. A lady came riding up on a milk-white palfrey. She seemed considerably excited.

"Hist, gallant knight!" she cried.

The knight rose to his feet, and bowed politely. The lady began batting her eyes, and looking at him in a way that made the children feel ashamed for her.

"Thank Heaven I found you," she went on. "You alone of all the world can help me, if your name be Sir Launcelot, as I am let to know it is!"

The children stared at the knight, open-mouthed with awe.

"Are you really Sir Launcelot?" Mark asked him.

"That is my name," said the knight.

The four children stared at him harder.

Now that he wasn't looking so sleepy they could see that it was true. No other in all the world could wear so manly a bearing, so noble a face. They were in the presence of Sir Launcelot du Lake, the greatest knight in all the Age of Chivalry!

"How is Elaine?" Katharine wanted to know right away, "and little Galahad?"

"I know not the folk you mention," said Sir Launcelot.

"Oh, yes, you do, sooner or later," said Katharine. "You probably just haven't come to them yet."

"Be ye a prophetess?" cried Sir Launcelot, becoming interested. "Can ye read the future? Tell me more!"

But the lady on the milk-white palfrey was growing impatient.

"Away, poppets!" she said, getting between the four children and Sir Launcelot. "Gallant knight, I crave your assistance. In a dolorous tower nearby a dread ogre is distressing some gentlewomen. I am Preceptress of the Distressed Gentlewoman Society. We need your help."

"Naturally," said Sir Launcelot. He whistled, and his trusty horse appeared from behind the apple tree, where it had been cropping apples. Sir Launcelot started to mount the horse.

The four children looked at each other. They did not like what they had seen of the lady at all, and they liked the way she had spoken to them even less.

Katharine stepped forward.

"I wouldn't go if I were you," she said. "It's probably a trap."

The lady gave her an evil look.

"Even so," said Sir Launcelot, "needs must when duty calls." He adjusted his reins.

Katharine drew herself up to her full four feet four.

"As you noticed before, I be a mighty prophetess!" she cried. "And I say unto you, go not where this lady bids. She will bring you nothing but disaster!"

"I shall go where I please," said Sir Launcelot.

"So there!" said the lady.

"You'll be sorry!" said Katharine.

"Enough of parley," said Sir Launcelot. "Never yet did Launcelot turn from a worthy quest. I know who ye be now. Ye be four false wizards come to me in the guise of children to tempt me from my course. 'Tis vain. Out of the way. Flee, churls. Avaunt and quit my sight, thy bones are marrowless. Giddy-up."

Sir Launcelot chirruped to his horse, and the lady chirruped to hers, and away they went, galloping down the King's

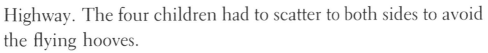

Highway. The four children had to scatter to both sides to avoid the flying hooves.

Of course it was but the work of a moment and a simple problem in fractions for Katharine to wish they all had horses and could follow.

Immediately they had, and they did.

Sir Launcelot turned, and saw the four children close at his heels, mounted now on four dashing chargers.

"Away, fiends!" he said.

"Shan't!" said Katharine.

They went on.

The four children had never ridden horseback before, but they found that it came to them quite easily, though Martha's horse was a bit big for her, and she had trouble posting.

And it was particularly interesting when, every time the lady started casting loving looks at Sir Launcelot, the children would ride up close behind and make jeering noises, and Sir Launcelot would turn in his saddle and shout, "Begone, demons!" at them. This happened every few minutes. Sir Launcelot seemed to get a little angrier each time.

When they had ridden a goodly pace they came to a dark wood, stretching along both sides of the highway. Just at the edge of the wood, the lady cried out that her horse had cast a shoe. Sir Launcelot reined in to go to her aid. The four children stopped at a safe distance.

Then, just as Sir Launcelot was dismounting, three knights rode out of the wood. One was dressed all in red, one in green, and one in black. Before the children could cry out, the knights rushed at Sir Launcelot from behind.

It was three against one and most unfair. But even so, Sir Launcelot's strength would have been as the strength of at least nine if he hadn't been taken by surprise. As it was, he had no time even to touch his hand to his sword before the three knights had seized and disarmed him, bound him hand and foot, flung him across the saddle of his own horse, and galloped off into the wood with him, a hapless prisoner.

The lady turned on the four children.

"Ha ha!" she cried. "Now they will take him to my castle, where he will lie in a deep dungeon and be beaten every day with thorns! And so we shall serve all knights of the Round Table who happen this way! Death to King Arthur!"

"Why, you false thing, you!" said Jane.

"I told him so!" said Katharine.

"Let's go home!" said Martha.

"No, we have to rescue him!" said Mark.

"Ho ho!" said the lady. "Just you try it! Your magic is a mere nothing compared with mine, elfspawn! Know that I am the great enchantress, Morgan le Fay!"

"You *would* be!" said Katharine, who didn't like being called "elfspawn," as who would? "I remember you in the books, always making trouble. I wish you'd go jump in the lake!"

Katharine wasn't thinking of the charm when she wished this, or she might have worded it differently. But that didn't stop the charm.

"Good old charm!" said Mark, as he watched what happened.

Morgan le Fay didn't go jump in the lake; she merely fell in a pool. Luckily there was a pool handy. She slid backwards off her horse and landed in it in a sitting position. And luckier still, the pool had a muddy bottom, and Morgan le Fay stuck there long enough for Katharine to make another, calmer wish, which was that she would *stay* stuck, and unable to use any of her magic, for twice as long as would be necessary.

This done, the four children turned their horses into the

wood, and set about following the wicked knights. Morgan le Fay hurled a few curses after them from among the water weeds, but these soon died away in the distance.

There was no path to follow through the wood. The branches of trees hung low and thick, and the earth beneath them was damp and dark and dank, and no birds sang.

"This," said Katharine, "is what I would call a tulgey wood."

"Don't!" cried Martha. "Suppose something came whiffling through it!"

The four children pressed on. Suddenly they came to a clearing, and there amidst a tangle of lambkill and henbane and deadly nightshade they saw the witch's castle rising just ahead of them. Poison ivy mantled its walls. There were snakes in the moat and bats in the belfry. The four children did not like the look of it at all.

"What do we do now?" said Jane.

"Wish him free, of course," said Mark.

"Just stand out here and wish? That's too easy!" said Katharine.

"I'm not going inside that castle!" said Martha.

"Nay," said Katharine, who did not seem to be so docile today as she used to be. "Ye forget that I be a mighty prophetess. Trust ye unto my clever strategy!"

"Bushwah," said Mark. "Less talk and more action."

Katharine put her hand on the charm. "I wish that two doors of this castle may stand open for us," she said.

So then the children had to look for the one door that did. They found it at last, a little back door with a small drawbridge of its own, over the moat. The drawbridge was down and the door was ajar. The children went over the drawbridge.

"Beware!" croaked the magic talking frogs in the moat.

They went in through the doorway. A long dark passage lay beyond.

"Beware!" squeaked the magic talking mice in the walls.

The children went along the passage. It wound and twisted a good deal. The magic cobwebs hanging from the ceiling brushed at their faces and caught at their clothing, trying to hold them back, but they broke away and pushed on.

At last the passage ended at a heavy doorway. From beyond it came the sound of loud voices raised in something that was probably intended to be music. The children eased the door open a crack and peeked through, into a large hall.

The red knight and the green knight and the black knight were enjoying a hearty meal, and washing down each mouthful with a draught of nut-brown ale. They were singing at the table, which was rude of them, and the words of their song were ruder still:

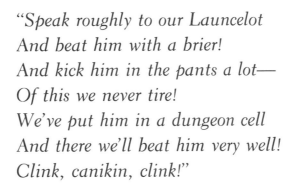

"Speak roughly to our Launcelot
And beat him with a brier!
And kick him in the pants a lot—
Of this we never tire!
We've put him in a dungeon cell
And there we'll beat him very well!
Clink, canikin, clink!"

The four children looked at each other indignantly; then they peeked through again.

Some varlets had appeared in the hall. They cleared away the dishes, left the dessert platter on the table, and departed.

The dessert was a number of round plum puddings, all aflame with blazing blue brandy. The black knight stood up to serve them.

At that moment Katharine remembered a story she had once read. She decided to have some fun with the three knights.

"I wish two of those puddings were stuck to the end of your nose!" she cried, putting her hand on the charm and staring straight at the black knight, through the crack of the doorway. And immediately one of them was.

But this pudding, unlike the one in the story, was still burning blue with brandy-fire; so that not only was it humiliating to the black knight, but hurt a good deal as well. And furthermore, his long black whiskers, of which he was inordinately proud, began to singe badly. He gave a wild howl, and his face turned nearly as black as his garments, with rage.

"Ods blood, who hath played this scurvy trick upon me?" he cried, beating at his nose and whiskers with his hands, and then yelling with pain as the flames scorched his fingers.

"Tee hee hee," tittered the green knight. "You look very funny!"

The black knight whirled on him.

"Be it *you*, then, who hath played this scurvy trick?" he cried.

"No, it be not I," said the green knight, "but you look very funny, just the same!"

"Oh, I do, do I?" shouted the black knight, in a passion. And he whipped his sword out of its scabbard, and swapped off the green knight's head.

The red knight jumped to his feet.

"I say, Albemarle, that was going a bit too far!" he cried.

"Oh, I don't know," said the black knight. "He was exceedingly provoking! Come and help me get this great pudding thing off my nose!"

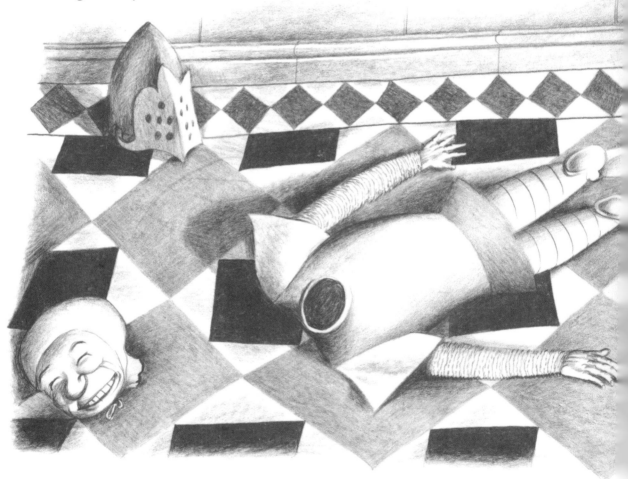

167

"Well," said the red knight, looking at him rather dubiously, "I don't know if I can, but I'll *try!*"

And he whipped *his* sword out of *its* scabbard, and swapped off the pudding from the black knight's nose. Unfortunately (for him) he swapped off a good bit of the nose, too.

The black knight gave a wild bellow and hurled himself at the red knight, sword in hand. The red knight parried his thrust. A moment later they were joined in deadly combat, leaping about the hall, smashing furniture, and hacking off parts of each other with the greatest abandon.

Behind the door, the four children shut their eyes, held their ears, and cowered trembling in each other's arms.

The combat did not last long. Two sword blades flashed in the air, and a second later two heads fell on the floor, followed, more slowly, by two bodies.

There was a silence. Katharine hadn't meant her wish to end in such a gory and final way. But she reminded herself to be bloody, bold, and resolute, and crept through the door into the hall, followed by the three others. All four averted their eyes from what they would have seen if they had looked at the floor.

"I do think you might have managed it neater," said Jane. "How can we get through to the dungeon with all these different pieces of knight lying around underfoot?"

"The point is that I managed it at all," said Katharine, more cheerfully than she felt. "And we don't have to walk; we can wish ourselves there."

She put her hand on the charm and wished that they were twice as far as the dungeon door and that she had two keys to the dungeon in her hand.

After that, of course, it was but a matter of turning the key, and out walked Sir Launcelot, followed by several dozen other knights who had also been prisoners of the enchantress and her friends, and who looked somewhat the worse for their daily beatings.

The other captive knights fell on their knees, kissing the children's hands and hailing them as their deliverers. Sir Launcelot also thanked the children quite politely, but somehow he didn't seem so happy to be free as the children had expected he would.

A moment later, when the other captive knights had left to resume their interrupted quests, the children found out why.

"You saved me by magical means?" Sir Launcelot asked.

"That's right," said Katharine, proudly. "I did it with my little charm."

"That mislikes me much," said Sir Launcelot. "I would it were otherwise."

"Well, really!" said Katharine. "I suppose you'd rather have stayed in there being beaten?"

"Sooner that," said Sir Launcelot, "than bring shame to my honor by taking unfair magical advantage of a foe, however deadly!"

"Well, if you're all that particular," said Katharine, annoyed, "I can easily put them back together again." And she led him into the great hall, and showed him the different pieces of the three knights.

"Please do so," said Sir Launcelot.

"Shall I lock you up in the dungeon again?" asked Katharine, sarcastically. "Doesn't it hurt your conscience that I set you free?"

"That much advantage," said Sir Launcelot, "I think I can take. Some fair jailer's daughter would probably have let me out sooner or later, anyway."

"Oh, is that so?" said Katharine. "I'm sorry I troubled, I'm sure! Is there anything else?"

"Well, yes," said Sir Launcelot. "You might just fetch me my sword and armor, which these cowardly knaves have taken from me."

Thoroughly cross with him by now, Katharine wished the sword and armor back on him; then, working out the fractions carefully, she spoke the wish that was to bring the red knight, the green knight, and the black knight back to life.

It was very interesting watching the different pieces of the different-colored knights reassembling themselves on the hall floor, and the four children were sorry when it was over.

But by then something even more interesting was going on. Because by then Sir Launcelot was fighting the three knights singlehanded, and that was a sight worth coming back many centuries to see.

Sir Launcelot did not seem to appreciate the four children's interest, however.

"Go away. Thank you very much. Good-by," he called, pinning the green knight against the wall with a table, and holding the red and black ones at bay with his sword.

"Can't we help?" Mark wanted to know.

"No. Go away," said Sir Launcelot, cracking the red knight

on the pate, thwacking the black knight in the chest with his backhand swing, and leaping over the table to take a whack at the green one.

"Can't we even *watch?*" Jane wailed.

"No. It makes me nervous. I want to be alone," said Sir Launcelot, ducking under the table to send the red knight sprawling, then turning to face the black and green ones again.

Katharine sighed, and made a wish.

Next moment the four children were on their horses once more, riding along the King's Highway.

"We might at least have waited in the yard," complained Martha. "Now we'll never know how it ended!"

"He'll come out on top; trust *him!*" said Katharine.

SID FLEISCHMAN
McBroom's Almanac

Josh McBroom, proud owner of a fabulous one-acre farm, is an incurable teller of tall tales. Here's a typical McBroom whopper.

It's not generally known, but I invented air conditioning. I read in the paper the idea has already spread to the big cities.

But, shucks, everyone is welcome to it. Folks around here call it McBroom's Natural Winter Extract & Relief for the Summer Dismals. You can make your own, same as us.

February is about the last month you can lay in a supply of prime Winter Extract.

Wait for an infernal cold day. When the mercury in the

thermometer drops to the bottom—you're getting close. But the weather's still a mite too warm.

When the mercury busts the glass bulb and rolls over to the fireplace to get warm—that's Extract weather.

"Will*jill*hester*chester*peter*polly*tim*tom*mary*larry*andlittle*clarinda!*" I shouted to our young'uns. "Bulb's shattered. Fetch the ripsaws, the crosscut saws, and let's get to work!"

Cold? Mercy, it was so cold outside *the wind had frozen solid*.

Didn't we get busy! We began sawing up chunks of frozen wind.

Now, you got to do the thing right. Wind's got a grain, just like wood. So be positive to use the crosscut saw against the grain, and the ripsaw along with it.

It fell dark before we finished harvesting and hauling that Winter Extract to our icehouse. And there stood our neighbor Heck Jones. That skinflint is so mean and miserly he brands the horseflies over at his place for fear someone will rustle 'em.

"Are you hidin' my left sock, McBroom?" he asked.

"Of course not," I said.

"Someone stole it off the clothesline. My best black sock, too! It only had three holes in it. If I catch the thief, I'll have him in a court of law!"

He loped away, grumbling and snarling.

We finished packing sawdust around the chunks of wind to keep them frozen. "Good work, my lambs," I said. "We're all set for the Summer Dismals."

Well, Heck Jones walked around in one sock the rest of winter, and summer, too.

As soon as the days turned sizzle-hot, we'd set a chunk of Winter Extract in the parlor. In a second or three it would begin to thaw—just a cool breeze at first. But when that February wind really got whistling, it would lift the curtains!

One hot night I fetched in a nice chunk of frozen wind without bothering to scrape off the sawdust. A few minutes later I saw a black thing shoot across the room. Something had got frozen in our Winter Extract.

"Heck Jones's sock!" I declared. "I can smell his feet!"

He was sure to think we'd stolen it. He'd have us in a court of law! I made a grab for it, but the February wind was kicking up such a blow it shot the sock past the curtains and far out the window.

I could see Heck Jones asleep in his hammock, one sock on, the other foot bare. The left sock hoisted its tail like a kite in the air and started down.

I declare, if I didn't see it with my own eyes, I'd think I was scrambly-witted. That holey black sock had the instinct of a homing pigeon. It returned right to Heck Jones's left foot and pulled itself on. I think it navigated by scent.

What Heck Jones thought when he awoke and looked at both feet—I can't reckon.

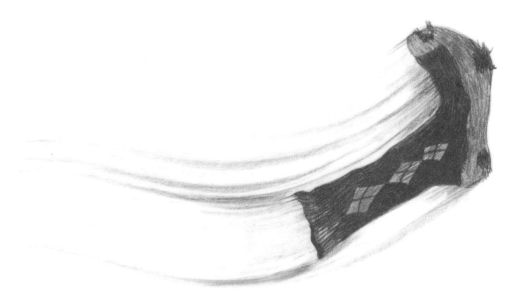

BOB and RAY
Prodigy Street

(*Bouncy type of theme music. Establish and fade for*)

WALLY   Hi there, boys and girls. Let's all gather round for another session of fun and learning on . . . *Prodigy Street.* I know how anxious all you little people are to become smarter than your mommies and daddies. So let's not waste another minute to find out what Mr. Wise Old Owl has to teach us today. I see you have your blackboard all set up there ready to begin, Mr. Owl.

OWL   Yes, I sure do, Wally the Word Man. And today, boys and girls, we're going to learn a lot more about numbers as we study the numeral 1. First, I'm going to put a figure 1 on my Wise Old Owl blackboard. And to help you remember, we'll write out the word "one" right next to it— O-N-E. Now, we'll put—

WALLY   Excuse me, Mr. Wise Old Owl. But I think the boys and girls should notice that the word "one" begins with that "W" sound I was telling them about yesterday on *Prodigy Street*. But it isn't spelled with a "W." How about that?!

OWL   Well, that's certainly interesting, Wally the Word Man. But today's lesson is about numbers. So I want all of you boys and girls to hold up one finger and then count it.

WALLY   But first, kids, you should take a moment to notice that "one" is spelled as if it should be pronounced "own." But always remember—it isn't.

OWL   Pardon me, Wally the Word Man. But I don't think we should confuse the boys and girls with too many ideas at once here. And I'd just asked them to count a finger when I'm afraid you got them off onto something else.

WALLY   I'm terribly sorry, Mr. Wise Old Owl. It's just that we were learning about the letter "W" yesterday. And I thought it would be good to bring up this point while it was fresh in mind. But that was all. So please continue.

OWL   Thank you. . . . Now, kids, hold up one more finger and count again. How many are there this time? That's right— two. So one plus one makes two. Now I'll put the figure 2 on the blackboard—and right next to it, the word "two"— T-W-O.

WALLY   Well, look there, boys and girls! Our old friend, the letter "W," is peeking out at us from the middle of the word "two."

OWL   Look, Wally—I really wish you'd knock it off with this letter "W" business. I'm trying to teach the kids simple addition.

WALLY   Well, actually, that's not a very important thing to know. But the word "two" is unique in our language. See, kids? It's spelled as if it should be pronounced "twah." But always remember—it isn't.

OWL   Wally, nobody needs to know how it's spelled to do arithmetic. For all I know, Einstein couldn't spell it.

WALLY   Well, I don't think our producer is going to be too happy to hear you implying to the boys and girls that Einstein was illiterate.

OWL   I didn't say that. I just mean it's completely beside the point. You don't have to be able to spell numbers to do arithmetic. It's irrelevant. . . . Now hold up another finger, kids, and—

WALLY   Well, I certainly don't consider any phase of the correct use of our language to be irrelevant. And I think you may be right out on your ear when the foundation that finances this show hears what you said.

OWL   Why do you have to twist around everything I say? You English grammar smart alecks are always doing that. And I've got millions of kids out there holding up three fingers waiting for me to tell them what to do next.

WALLY   Well, I suppose you're just going to have them count

their fingers again. So count your fingers, kids . . . Big deal!

OWL   Now, just hold on. Are you trying to make me look foolish in front of all these children?

WALLY   I sure don't have to try very hard to do that, fella.

OWL   Okay, Buster. If you're looking for a knuckle sandwich, you got one. Take that!

(*Sound: Scuffling, furniture and glass breaking, Wally and Owl grunting and groaning. Then*)

WALLY   (*Breathless*) Time's up for today's lesson, kids. But join us again tomorrow on *Prodigy Street* for more—

OWL   (*Breathless*) You can stop holding your fingers up in the air now, boys and girls.

(*Bring in theme music during*)

WALLY   Yeah, stop that. But remember to tune in tomorrow for more fun and learning—same time, same station—on *Prodigy Street*. See you then, Mr. Wise Old Owl.

OWL   Yeah. I suppose so.

(*Theme music up briefly and then out*)

ROBERT McCLOSKEY
Homer Price

One Friday night in November Homer overheard his mother talking on the telephone to Aunt Agnes over in Centerburg. "I'll stop by with the car in about half an hour and we can go to the meeting together," she said, because tonight was the night the Ladies' Club was meeting to discuss plans for a box social and to knit and sew for the Red Cross.

"I think I'll come along and keep Uncle Ulysses company while you and Aunt Agnes are at the meeting," said Homer.

So after Homer had combed his hair and his mother had

looked to see if she had her knitting instructions and the right size needles, they started for town.

Homer's Uncle Ulysses and Aunt Agnes have a very up-and-coming lunch room over in Centerburg, just across from the court house on the town square. Uncle Ulysses is a man with advanced ideas and a weakness for labor-saving devices. He equipped the lunch room with automatic toasters, automatic coffee maker, automatic dish washer, and an automatic dough-nut maker. All just the latest thing in labor-saving devices. Aunt Agnes would throw up her hands and sigh every time Uncle Ulysses bought a new labor-saving device. Sometimes she be-came unkindly disposed toward him for days and days. She was of the opinion that Uncle Ulysses just frittered away his spare time over at the barber shop with the sheriff and the boys, so, what was the good of a labor-saving device that gave you more time to fritter?

When Homer and his mother got to Centerburg they stopped at the lunch room, and after Aunt Agnes had come out and said, "My, how that boy does grow!" which was what she always said, she went off with Homer's mother in the car. Homer went into the lunch room and said, "Howdy, Uncle Ulysses!"

"Oh, hello, Homer. You're just in time," said Uncle Ulysses. "I've been going over this automatic doughnut ma-chine, oiling the machinery and cleaning the works . . . won-derful things, these labor-saving devices."

"Yep," agreed Homer, and he picked up a cloth and started polishing the metal trimmings while Uncle Ulysses tinkered with the inside workings.

"Opfwo-oof!!" sighed Uncle Ulysses and, "Look here, Homer, you've got a mechanical mind. See if you can find where these two pieces fit in. I'm going across to the barber shop for a spell, 'cause there's somethin' I've got to talk to the sheriff about. There won't be much business here until the double feature is over and I'll be back before then."

Then as Uncle Ulysses went out the door he said, "Uh, Homer, after you get the pieces in place, would you mind mixing up a batch of doughnut batter and putting it in the machine? You could turn the switch and make a few doughnuts to have on hand for the crowd after the movie . . . if you don't mind."

"O.K.," said Homer, "I'll take care of everything."

A few minutes later a customer came in and said, "Good evening, Bud."

Homer looked up from putting the last piece in the dough nut machine and said, "Good evening, Sir, what can I do for you?"

"Well, young feller, I'd like a cup o' coffee and some doughnuts," said the customer.

"I'm sorry, Mister, but we won't have any doughnuts for about half an hour, until I can mix some dough and start this machine. I could give you some very fine sugar rolls instead."

"Well, Bud, I'm in no real hurry so I'll just have a cup o' coffee and wait around a bit for the doughnuts. Fresh doughnuts are always worth waiting for is what I always say."

"O.K.," said Homer, and he drew a cup of coffee from Uncle Ulysses' super-automatic coffee maker.

"Nice place you've got here," said the customer.

"Oh, yes," replied Homer, "this is a very up-and-coming lunch room with all the latest improvements."

"Yes," said the stranger, "must be a good business. I'm in business too. A traveling man in outdoor advertising. I'm a sandwich man, Mr. Gabby's my name."

"My name is Homer. I'm glad to meet you, Mr. Gabby. It must be a fine profession, traveling and advertising sandwiches."

"Oh, no," said Mr. Gabby, "I don't advertise sandwiches, I just wear any kind of an ad, one sign on front and one sign on behind, this way . . . Like a sandwich. Ya know what I mean?"

"Oh, I see. That must be fun, and you travel too?" asked Homer as he got out the flour and the baking powder.

"Yeah, I ride the rods between jobs, on freight trains, ya know what I mean?"

"Yes, but isn't that dangerous?" asked Homer.

"Of course there's a certain amount of risk, but you take any method of travel these days, it's all dangerous. Ya know what I mean? Now take airplanes for instance . . ."

Just then a large shiny black car stopped in front of the lunch room and a chauffeur helped a lady out of the rear door. They both came inside and the lady smiled at Homer and said, "We've stopped for a light snack. Some doughnuts and coffee would be simply marvelous."

Then Homer said, "I'm sorry, Ma'm, but the doughnuts won't be ready until I make this batter and start Uncle Ulysses' doughnut machine."

"Well now aren't *you* a clever young man to know how to make *doughnuts*!"

"Well," blushed Homer, "I've really never done it before but I've got a receipt to follow."

"Now, young man, you simply must allow me to help. You know, I haven't made doughnuts for years, but I know the best receipt for doughnuts. It's marvelous, and we really must use it."

"But, Ma'm . . ." said Homer.

"Now just *wait* till you taste these doughnuts," said the lady. "Do you have an apron?" she asked as she took off her fur coat and her rings and her jewelry and rolled up her sleeves. "Charles," she said to the chauffeur, "hand me that baking

powder, that's right, and, young man, we'll need some nutmeg."

So Homer and the chauffeur stood by and handed things and cracked the eggs while the lady mixed and stirred. Mr. Gabby sat on his stool, sipped his coffee, and looked on with great interest.

"There!" said the lady when all of the ingredients were mixed. "Just *wait* till you taste these doughnuts!"

"It looks like an awful lot of batter," said Homer as he stood on a chair and poured it into the doughnut machine with the help of the chauffeur. "It's about *ten* times as much as Uncle Ulysses ever makes."

"But wait till you taste them!" said the lady with an eager look and a smile.

Homer got down from the chair and pushed a button on the machine marked START. Rings of batter started dropping into the hot fat. After a ring of batter was cooked on one side an automatic gadget turned it over and the other side would cook. Then another automatic gadget gave the doughnut a little push and it rolled neatly down a little chute, all ready to eat.

"That's a simply *fascinating* machine," said the lady as she waited for the first doughnut to roll out.

"Here, young man, *you* must have the first one. Now isn't that just *too* delicious!? Isn't it simply marvelous?"

"Yes, Ma'm, it's very good," replied Homer as the lady handed doughnuts to Charles and to Mr. Gabby and asked if they didn't think they were simply divine doughnuts.

"It's an old family receipt!" said the lady with pride.

Homer poured some coffee for the lady and her chauffeur and for Mr. Gabby, and a glass of milk for himself. Then they all sat down at the lunch counter to enjoy another few doughnuts apiece.

"I'm so glad you enjoy my doughnuts," said the lady. "But now, Charles, we really must be going. If you will just take this apron, Homer, and put two dozen doughnuts in a bag to take along, we'll be on our way. And, Charles, don't forget to pay the young man." She rolled down her sleeves and put on her jewelry, then Charles managed to get her into her big fur coat.

"Good night, young man, I haven't had so much fun in years. I *really* haven't!" said the lady as she went out the door and into the big shiny car.

"Those are sure good doughnuts," said Mr. Gabby as the car moved off.

"You bet!" said Homer. Then he and Mr. Gabby stood and watched the automatic doughnut machine make doughnuts.

After a few dozen more doughnuts had rolled down the little chute, Homer said, "I guess that's about enough doughnuts to sell to the after-theater customers. I'd better turn the machine off for a while."

Homer pushed the button marked STOP and there was a little click, but nothing happened. The rings of batter kept right on dropping into the hot fat, and an automatic gadget kept right on turning them over, and another automatic gadget kept right on giving them a little push, and the doughnuts kept right on rolling down the little chute, all ready to eat.

"That's funny," said Homer, "I'm sure that's the right button!" He pushed it again but the automatic doughnut maker kept right on making doughnuts.

"Well I guess I must have put one of those pieces in backwards," said Homer.

"Then it might stop if you pushed the button marked 'start,'" said Mr. Gabby.

Homer did, and the doughnuts still kept rolling down the little chute, just as regular as a clock can tick.

"I guess we could sell a few more doughnuts," said Homer, "but I'd better telephone Uncle Ulysses over at the barber shop." Homer gave the number and while he waited for someone to answer he counted thirty-seven doughnuts roll down the little chute.

Finally someone answered, "Hello! This is the sarber bhop, I mean the barber shop."

"Oh, hello, sheriff. This is Homer. Could I speak to Uncle Ulysses?"

"Well, he's playing pinochle right now," said the sheriff. "Anythin' I can tell 'im?"

"Yes," said Homer. "I pushed the button marked 'stop' on the doughnut machine but the rings of batter keep right on dropping into the hot fat, and an automatic gadget keeps right on turning them over, and another automatic gadget keeps giving them a little push, and the doughnuts keep right on rolling down the little chute! It won't stop!"

"O.K. Wold the hire, I mean, hold the wire and I'll tell 'im." Then Homer looked over his shoulder and counted another twenty-one doughnuts roll down the little chute, all ready to eat. Then the sheriff said, "He'll be right over. . . . Just gotta finish this hand."

"That's good," said Homer. "G'by, sheriff."

The window was full of doughnuts by now so Homer and Mr. Gabby had to hustle around and start stacking them on plates and trays and lining them up on the counter.

"Sure are a lot of doughnuts!" said Homer.

"You bet!" said Mr. Gabby. "I lost count at twelve hundred and two and that was quite a while back."

People had begun to gather outside the lunch room window, and someone was saying, "There are almost as many doughnuts as there are people in Centerburg, and I wonder how in tarnation Ulysses thinks he can sell all of 'em!"

Every once in a while somebody would come inside and buy some, but while somebody bought two to eat and a dozen to take home, the machine made three dozen more.

By the time Uncle Ulysses and the sheriff arrived and pushed through the crowd, the lunch room was a calamity of doughnuts! Doughnuts in the window, doughnuts piled high on the shelves, doughnuts stacked on plates, doughnuts lined up twelve deep all along the counter, and doughnuts still rolling down the little chute, just as regular as a clock can tick.

"Hello, sheriff, hello, Uncle Ulysses, we're having a little trouble here," said Homer.

"Well, I'll be dunked!!" said Uncle Ulysses.

"Dernd ef you won't be when Aggy gits home," said the sheriff.

"Mighty fine doughnuts though. What'll you do with 'em all, Ulysses?"

Uncle Ulysses groaned and said, "What will Aggy say? We'll never sell 'em all."

Then Mr. Gabby, who hadn't said anything for a long time, stopped piling doughnuts and said, "What you need is an advertising man. Ya know what I mean? You got the doughnuts, ya gotta create a market . . . Understand? . . . It's balancing the demand with the supply . . . That sort of thing."

"Yep!" said Homer. "Mr. Gabby's right. We have to enlarge our market. He's an advertising sandwich man, so if we hire him, he can walk up and down in front of the theater and get the customers."

"You're hired, Mr. Gabby!" said Uncle Ulysses.

Then everybody pitched in to paint the signs and to get Mr. Gabby sandwiched between. They painted SALE ON DOUGHNUTS in big letters on the window too.

Meanwhile the rings of batter kept right on dropping into the hot fat, and an automatic gadget kept right on turning them over, and another automatic gadget kept right on giving them a little push, and the doughnuts kept right on rolling down the little chute, just as regular as a clock can tick.

"I certainly hope this advertising works," said Uncle Ulysses, wagging his head. "Aggy'll certainly throw a fit if it don't."

The sheriff went outside to keep order, because there was quite a crowd by now—all looking at the doughnuts and guessing how many thousand there were, and watching new ones roll down the little chute, just as regular as a clock can tick. Homer and Uncle Ulysses kept stacking doughnuts. Once in a while somebody bought a few, but not very often.

Then Mr. Gabby came back and said, "Say, you know there's not much use o' me advertisin' at the theater. The show's all over, and besides almost everybody in town is out front watching that machine make doughnuts!"

"Zeus!" said Uncle Ulysses. "We must get rid of these doughnuts before Aggy gets here!"

"Looks like you will have ta hire a truck ta waul 'em ahay, I mean haul 'em away!!" said the sheriff, who had just come in. Just then there was a noise and a shoving out front and the lady from the shiny black car and her chauffeur came pushing through the crowd and into the lunch room.

"Oh, gracious!" she gasped, ignoring the doughnuts, "I've lost my diamond bracelet, and I know I left it here on the counter," she said, pointing to a place where the doughnuts were piled in stacks of two dozen.

"Yes, Ma'm, I guess you forgot it when you helped make the batter," said Homer.

Then they moved all the doughnuts around and looked for

the diamond bracelet, but they couldn't find it anywhere. Meanwhile the doughnuts kept rolling down the little chute, just as regular as a clock can tick.

After they had looked all around the sheriff cast a suspicious eye on Mr. Gabby, but Homer said, "He's all right, sheriff, he didn't take it. He's a friend of mine."

Then the lady said, "I'll offer a reward of one hundred dollars for that bracelet! It really *must* be found . . . it *really* must!"

"Now don't you worry, lady," said the sheriff. "I'll get your bracelet back!"

"Zeus! This is terrible!" said Uncle Ulysses. "First all of these doughnuts and then on top of that, a lost diamond bracelet . . ."

Mr. Gabby tried to comfort him, and he said, "There's always a bright side. That machine'll probably run outta batter in an hour or two."

If Mr. Gabby hadn't been quick on his feet Uncle Ulysses would have knocked him down, sure as fate.

Then while the lady wrung her hands and said, "We must find it, we *must!*" and Uncle Ulysses was moaning about what Aunt Agnes would say, and the sheriff was eyeing Mr. Gabby, Homer sat down and thought hard.

Before twenty more doughnuts could roll down the little chute he shouted, "SAY! I know where the bracelet is! It was lying here on the counter and got mixed up in the batter by mistake! The bracelet is cooked inside one of these doughnuts!"

"Why . . . I really believe you're right," said the lady through her tears. "Isn't that *amazing*? Simply *amazing!*"

"I'll be durn'd!" said the sheriff.

"OhH-h!" moaned Uncle Ulysses. "Now we have to break up all of these doughnuts to find it. Think of the *pieces*! Think of the *crumbs*! Think of what *Aggy* will say!"

"Nope," said Homer. "We won't have to break them up. I've got a plan."

So Homer and the advertising man took some cardboard and some paint and printed another sign. They put this sign in the window, and the sandwich man wore two more signs that said the same thing and walked around in the crowd out front.

THEN . . . The doughnuts began to sell! *Everybody* wanted to buy doughnuts, *dozens* of doughnuts!

And that's not all. Everybody bought coffee to dunk the doughnuts in too. Those that didn't buy coffee bought milk or soda. It kept Homer and the lady and the chauffeur and Uncle Ulysses and the sheriff busy waiting on the people who wanted to buy doughnuts.

When all but the last couple of hundred doughnuts had

been sold, Rupert Black shouted, "I GAWT IT!!" and sure enough . . . there was the diamond bracelet inside of his doughnut!

Then Rupert went home with a hundred dollars, the citizens of Centerburg went home full of doughnuts, the lady and her chauffeur drove off with the diamond bracelet, and Homer went home with his mother when she stopped by with Aunt Aggy.

As Homer went out of the door he heard Mr. Gabby say, "Neatest trick of merchandising I ever seen," and Aunt Aggy was looking sceptical while Uncle Ulysses was saying, "The rings of batter kept right on dropping into the hot fat, and the automatic gadget kept right on turning them over, and the other automatic gadget kept right on giving them a little push, and the doughnuts kept right on rolling down the little chute just as regular as a clock can tick—they just kept right on a comin', an' a comin', an' a comin', an' a comin'."

E. NESBIT

The Story of the Treasure Seekers

When their widowed father's business starts to fail, the six Bastable children decide to see what they can do to restore the family fortune. They try everything, including digging for treasure in the backyard garden—an unlikely scheme that pays off in an unexpected way.

The best part of books is when things are happening. That is the best part of real things too. This is why I shall not tell you in this story about all the days when nothing happened. You will not catch me saying, "thus the sad days passed slowly by"—or "the years rolled on their weary course"—or "time went on"—because it is silly; of course time goes on—whether you say so or not. So I shall just tell you the nice, interesting parts—and in between you will understand that we had our meals and got up and went to bed, and dull things like that. It would be sickening to write all that down, though of course it happens. I said so to Albert-next-door's uncle, who writes books, and he said, "Quite right, that's what we call selection, a necessity of true art." And he is very clever indeed. So you see.

I have often thought that if the people who write books for children knew a little more it would be better. I shall not tell you anything about us except what I should like to know about if I was reading the story and you were writing it. Albert's uncle says I ought to have put this in the preface, but I never read prefaces, and it is not much good writing things just for people to skip. I wonder other authors have never thought of this.

Well, when we had agreed to dig for treasure we all went down into the cellar and lighted the gas. Oswald would have liked to dig there, but it is stone flags. We looked among the old boxes and broken chairs and fenders and empty bottles and things, and at last we found the spades we had to dig in the sand with when we went to the seaside three years ago. They are not silly, babyish, wooden spades, that split if you look at them, but good iron, with a blue mark across the top of the iron part, and yellow wooden handles. We wasted a little time getting them dusted, because the girls wouldn't dig with spades that had cobwebs on them. Girls would never do for African explorers or anything like that, they are too beastly particular.

It was no use doing the thing by halves. We marked out a sort of square in the moldy part of the garden, about three yards across, and began to dig. But we found nothing except worms and stones—and the ground was very hard.

So we thought we'd try another part of the garden, and we found a place in the big round flower bed, where the ground was much softer. We thought we'd make a smaller hole to begin with, and it was much better. We dug and dug and dug, and it was jolly hard work! We got very hot digging, but we found nothing.

Presently Albert-next-door looked over the wall. We do not like him very much, but we let him play with us sometimes, because his father is dead, and you must not be unkind to orphans, even if their mothers are alive. Albert is always very tidy. He wears frilly collars and velvet knickerbockers. I can't think how he can bear to.

So we said, "Hallo!"

And he said, "What are you up to?"

"We're digging for treasure," said Alice. "An ancient parchment revealed to us the place of concealment. Come over and help us. When we have dug deep enough we shall find a great pot of red clay, full of gold and precious jewels."

Albert-next-door only sniggered and said, "What silly nonsense!" He cannot play properly at all. It is very strange, because he has a very nice uncle. You see, Albert-next-door doesn't care for reading, and he has not read nearly so many books as we have, so he is very foolish and ignorant, but it cannot be helped, and you just have to put up with it when you want him to do anything. Besides, it is wrong to be angry with people for not being so clever as you are yourself. It is not always their fault.

So Oswald said, "Come and dig! Then you shall share the treasure when we've found it."

But he said, "I shan't—I don't like digging—and I'm just going in to my tea."

"Come along and dig, there's a good boy," Alice said. "You can use my spade. It's much the best—"

So he came along and dug, and when once he was over the wall we kept him at it, and we worked as well, of course, and the hole got deep. Pincher worked too—he is our dog and he is very good at digging. He digs for rats in the dustbin sometimes, and gets very dirty. But we love our dog, even when his face wants washing.

"I expect we shall have to make a tunnel," Oswald said, "to reach the rich treasure." So he jumped into the hole and began to dig at one side. After that we took it in turns to dig at the tunnel, and Pincher was most useful in scraping the earth out of the tunnel—he does it with his back feet when you say "Rats!"

and he digs with his front ones, and burrows with his nose as well.

At last the tunnel was nearly a yard long, and big enough to creep along to find the treasure, if only it had been a bit longer. Now it was Albert's turn to go in and dig, but he funked it.

"Take your turn like a man," said Oswald—nobody can say that Oswald doesn't take his turn like a man. But Albert wouldn't. So we had to make him, because it was only fair.

"It's quite easy," Alice said. "You just crawl in and dig with your hands. Then when you come out we can scrape out what you've done, with the spades. Come—be a man. You won't notice it being dark in the tunnel if you shut your eyes tight. We've all been in except Dora—and she doesn't like worms."

"I don't like worms neither." Albert-next-door said this, but we remembered how he had picked a fat red and black worm up in his fingers and thrown it at Dora only the day before.

So we put him in.

But he would not go in head first, the proper way, and dig with his hands as we had done, and though Oswald was angry at the time, for he hates snivelers, yet afterwards he owned that perhaps it was just as well. You should never be afraid to own that perhaps you were mistaken—but it is cowardly to do it unless you are quite sure you are in the wrong.

"Let me go in feet first," said Albert-next-door. "I'll dig with my boots—I will truly, honor bright."

So we let him get in feet first—and he did it very slowly and at last he was in, and only his head sticking out into the hole; and all the rest of him in the tunnel.

"Now dig with your boots," said Oswald, "and, Alice, do catch hold of Pincher, he'll be digging again in another minute,

and perhaps it would be uncomfortable for Albert if Pincher threw the mold into his eyes."

You should always try to think of these little things. Thinking of other people's comfort makes them like you. Alice held Pincher, and we all shouted, "Kick! Dig with your feet, for all you're worth!"

So Albert-next-door began to dig with his feet, and we stood on the ground over him, waiting—and all in a minute the ground gave way, and we tumbled together in a heap; and when we got up there was a little shallow hollow where we had been standing, and Albert-next-door was underneath, stuck quite fast, because the roof of the tunnel had tumbled in on him. He is a horribly unlucky boy to have anything to do with.

It was dreadful the way he cried and screamed, though he had to own it didn't hurt, only it was rather heavy and he couldn't move his legs. We would have dug him out all right enough, in time, but he screamed so we were afraid the police would come, so Dicky climbed over the wall, to tell the cook there to tell Albert-next-door's uncle he had been buried by mistake, and to come and help dig him out.

Dicky was a long time gone. We wondered what had become of him, and all the while the screaming went on and on, for we had taken the loose earth off Albert's face so that he could scream quite easily and comfortably.

Presently Dicky came back and Albert-next-door's uncle came with him. He has very long legs, and his hair is light and his face is brown. He has been to sea, but now he writes books. I like him.

He told his nephew to stow it, so Albert did, and then he asked him if he was hurt—and Albert had to say he wasn't, for though he is a coward, and very unlucky, he is not a liar like some boys are.

"This promises to be a protracted if agreeable task," said Albert-next-door's uncle, rubbing his hands and looking at the hole with Albert's head in it. "I will get another spade." So he fetched the big spade out of the next-door garden toolshed, and began to dig his nephew out.

"Mind you keep very still," he said, "or I might chunk a bit out of you with the spade." Then after a while he said—

"I confess that I am not absolutely insensible to the dramatic interest of the situation. My curiosity is excited. I own that I should like to know how my nephew happened to be buried. But don't tell me if you'd rather not. I suppose no force was used?"

"Only moral force," said Alice. They used to talk a lot about moral force at the High School where she went, and in case you don't know what it means I'll tell you that it is making people do what they don't want to, just by slanging them, or laughing at them, or promising them things if they're good.

"Only moral force, eh?" said Albert-next-door's uncle. "Well?"

"Well," Dora said, "I'm very sorry it happened to Albert—I'd rather it had been one of us. It would have been my turn to go into the tunnel, only I don't like worms, so they let me off. You see we were digging for treasure."

"Yes," said Alice, "and I think we were just coming to the underground passage that leads to the secret hoard, when the tunnel fell in on Albert. He *is* so unlucky," and she sighed.

Then Albert-next-door began to scream again, and his uncle wiped his face—his own face, not Albert's—with his silk handkerchief, and then he put it in his trousers pocket. It seems a strange place to put a handkerchief, but he had his coat and waistcoat off and I suppose he wanted the handkerchief handy. Digging is warm work.

He told Albert-next-door to drop it, or he wouldn't proceed further in the matter, so Albert stopped screaming, and presently his uncle finished digging him out. Albert did look so funny, with his hair all dusty and his velvet suit covered with mold and his face muddy with earth and crying.

We all said how sorry we were, but he wouldn't say a word back to us. He was most awfully sick to think he'd been the one buried, when it might just as well have been one of us. I felt myself that it was hard lines.

"So you were digging for treasure," said Albert-next-door's uncle, wiping his face again with his handkerchief. "Well, I fear that your chances of success are small. I have made a careful study of the whole subject. What I don't know about buried treasure is not worth knowing. And I never knew more than one coin buried in any one garden—and that is generally—Hullo—what's that?"

He pointed to something shining in the hole he had just dragged Albert out of. Oswald picked it up. It was a half-crown. We looked at each other, speechless with surprise and delight, like in books.

"Well, that's lucky, at all events," said Albert-next-door's uncle. "Let's see, that's fivepence each for you."

"It's fourpence—something; I can't do fractions," said Dicky. "There are seven of us, you see."

"Oh, you count Albert as one of yourselves on this occasion, eh?"

"Of course," said Alice, "and I say, he was buried after all. Why shouldn't we let him have the odd somethings, and we'll have fourpence each."

We all agreed to do this, and told Albert-next-door we would bring his share as soon as we could get the half-crown changed. He cheered up a little at that, and his uncle wiped his face again—he did look hot—and began to put on his coat and waistcoat.

When he had done it he stooped and picked up something. He held it up, and you will hardly believe it, but it is quite true—it was another half-crown!

"To think that there should be two!" he said. "In all my experience of buried treasure I never heard of such a thing!"

I wish Albert-next-door's uncle would come treasure-seeking with us regularly; he must have very sharp eyes: for Dora says she was looking just the minute before at the very place where the second half-crown was picked up from, and *she* never saw it.

ISAAC BASHEVIS SINGER

The Fools of Chelm and the Stupid Carp

In Chelm, a city of fools, every housewife bought fish for the Sabbath. The rich bought large fish, the poor small ones. They were bought on Thursday, cut up, chopped, and made into gefilte fish on Friday, and eaten on the Sabbath.

One Thursday morning the door opened at the house of the community leader of Chelm, Gronam Ox, and Zeinvel Ninny entered, carrying a trough full of water. Inside was a large, live carp.

"What is this?" Gronam asked.

"A gift to you from the wise men of Chelm," Zeinvel said. "This is the largest carp ever caught in the Lake of Chelm, and we all decided to give it to you as a token of appreciation for your great wisdom."

"Thank you very much," Gronam Ox replied. "My wife, Yente Pesha, will be delighted. She and I both love carp. I read in a book that eating the brains of a carp increases wisdom, and even though we in Chelm are immensely clever, a little improvement never hurts. But let me have a close look at him. I was told that a carp's tail shows the size of his brain."

Gronam Ox was known to be nearsighted, and when he bent down to the trough to better observe the carp's tail, the carp did something that proved he was not as wise as Gronam thought. He lifted his tail and smacked Gronam across the face.

Gronam Ox was flabbergasted. "Something like this never happened to me before," he exclaimed. "I cannot believe this carp was caught in the Chelm lake. A Chelm carp would know better."

"He's the meanest fish I ever saw in my life," agreed Zeinvel Ninny.

Even though Chelm is a big city, news traveled quickly there. In no time at all the other wise men of Chelm arrived at the house of their leader, Gronam Ox. Treitel Fool came, and Sender Donkey, Shmendrick Numskull, and Dopey Lekisch. Gronam Ox was saying, "I'm not going to eat this fish on the Sabbath. This carp is a fool, and malicious to boot. If I eat him, I could become foolish instead of cleverer."

"Then what shall I do with him?" asked Zeinvel Ninny.

Gronam Ox put a finger to his head as a sign that he was thinking hard. After a while he cried out, "No man or animal in Chelm should slap Gronam Ox. This fish should be punished."

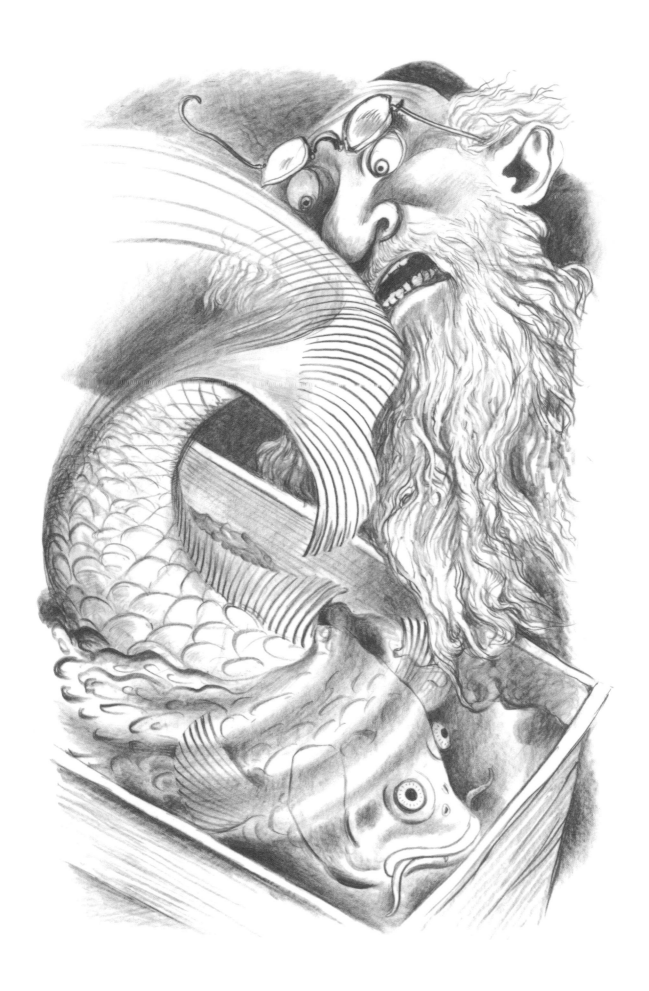

"What kind of punishment shall we give him?" asked Treitel Fool. "All fish are killed anyhow, and one cannot kill a fish twice."

"He shouldn't be killed like other fish," Sender Donkey said. "He should die in a different way to show that no one can smack our beloved sage, Gronam Ox, and get away with it."

"What kind of death?" wondered Shmendrick Numskull. "Shall we perhaps just imprison him?"

"There is no prison in Chelm for fish," said Zeinvel Ninny. "And to build such a prison would take too long."

"Maybe he should be hanged," suggested Dopey Lekisch.

"How do you hang a carp?" Sender Donkey wanted to know. "A creature can be hanged only by its neck, but since a carp has no neck, how will you hang him?"

"My advice is that he should be thrown to the dogs alive," said Treitel Fool.

"It's no good," Gronam Ox answered. "Our Chelm dogs are both smart and modest, but if they eat this carp, they may become as stupid and mean as he is."

"So what should we do?" all the wise men asked.

"This case needs lengthy consideration," Gronam Ox decided. "Let's leave the carp in the trough and ponder the matter as long as is necessary. Being the wisest man in Chelm, I cannot afford to pass a sentence that will not be admired by all the Chelmites."

"If the carp stays in the trough a long time, he may die," Zeinvel Ninny, a former fish dealer, explained. "To keep him alive we must put him into a large tub, and the water has to be changed often. He must also be fed properly."

"You are right, Zeinvel," Gronam Ox told him. "Go and find the largest tub in Chelm and see to it that the carp is kept alive and healthy until the day of judgment. When I reach a decision, you will hear about it."

Of course Gronam's words were the law in Chelm. The five wise men went and found a large tub, filled it with fresh water, and put the criminal carp in it, together with some crumbs of bread, challah, and other tidbits a carp might like to eat. Shlemiel, Gronam's bodyguard, was stationed at the tub to make sure that no greedy Chelmite wife would use the imprisoned carp for gefilte fish.

It just so happened that Gronam Ox had many other decisions to make, and he kept postponing the sentence. The carp seemed not to be impatient. He ate, swam in the tub, became even fatter than he had been, not realizing that a severe sentence hung over his head. Shlemiel changed the water frequently, because he was told that if the carp died, this would be an act of contempt for Gronam Ox and for the Chelm Court of Justice. Yukel the water carrier made a few extra pennies every day by bringing water for the carp. Some of the Chelmites who were in opposition to Gronam Ox spread the gossip that Gronam just couldn't find the right type of punishment for the carp and that he was waiting for the carp to die a natural death. But, as always, a great disappointment awaited them. One morning about half a year later, the sentence became known, and when it was known, Chelm was stunned. The carp had to be drowned.

Gronam Ox had thought up many clever sentences before, but never one as brilliant as this one. Even his enemies were amazed at this shrewd verdict. Drowning is just the kind of death suited to a spiteful carp with a large tail and a small brain.

That day the entire Chelm community gathered at the lake to see the sentence executed. The carp, which had become almost twice as big as he had been before, was brought to the lake in the wagon that carried the worst criminals to their death. The drummers drummed. Trumpets blared. The Chelmite executioner raised the heavy carp and threw it into the lake with a mighty splash.

A great cry rose from the Chelmites. "Down with the treacherous carp! Long live Gronam Ox! Hurrah!"

Gronam was lifted by his admirers and carried home with songs of praise. Some Chelmite girls showered him with flowers. Even Yente Pesha, his wife, who was often critical of Gronam and dared to call him fool, seemed impressed by Gronam's high intelligence.

In Chelm, as everywhere else, there were envious people who found fault with everyone, and they began to say that there was no proof whatsoever that the carp really drowned. Why should a carp drown in lake water? they asked. While hundreds of innocent fish were killed every Friday, they said, that stupid carp lived in comfort for months on the taxpayers' money and then was returned sound and healthy to the lake, where he is laughing at Chelm justice.

But only a few listened to these malicious words. They pointed out that months passed and the carp was never caught again, a sure sign that he was dead. It is true that the carp just might have decided to be careful and to avoid the fisherman's net. But how can a foolish carp who slaps Gronam Ox have such wisdom?

Just the same, to be on the safe side, the wise men of Chelm published a decree that if the nasty carp had refused to be drowned and was caught again, a special jail should be built for him, a pool where he would be kept prisoner for the rest of his life.

The decree was printed in capital letters in the official gazette of Chelm and signed by Gronam Ox and his five sages— Treitel Fool, Sender Donkey, Shmendrick Numskull, Zeinvel Ninny, and Dopey Lekisch.

T. H. WHITE

The Sword in the Stone

In this selection the young King Arthur, known as Wart, is held captive by a witch whose wily black magic is a powerful match for Wart's teacher, the kindly wizard Merlyn.

Every Thursday afternoon, after the last serious arrow had been fired, they were allowed to fit one more nock to their strings and to discharge the arrow straight up into the air. It was partly a gesture of farewell, partly of triumph, and it was beautiful. They did it now as a salute to their first prey.

The Wart watched his arrow go up. The sun was already westing towards evening, and the trees where they were had plunged them into a partial shade. So, as the arrow topped the trees and climbed into sunlight, it began to burn against the evening like the sun itself. Up and up it went, not weaving as it would have done with a snatching loose, but soaring, swimming, aspiring towards heaven, steady, golden, and superb. Just as it had spent its force, just as its ambition had been dimmed by destiny and it was preparing to faint, to turn over, to pour back into the bosom of its mother earth, a terrible portent happened. A gore-crow came flapping wearily before the approaching night. It came, it did not waver, it took the arrow. It flew away, heaving and hoisting, with the arrow in its beak.

Kay was frightened by this, but the Wart was furious. He had loved his arrow's movement, its burning ambition in the sunlight, and, besides, it was his best arrow. It was the only one which was perfectly balanced, sharp, tight-feathered, clean-nocked, and neither warped nor scraped.

"It was a witch," said Kay.

"I don't care if it was ten witches," said the Wart. "I am going to get it back."

"But it went towards the Forest."

"I shall go after it."

"You can go alone, then," said Kay. "I'm not going into the Forest Sauvage, just for a putrid arrow."

"I shall go alone."

"Oh, well," said Kay, "I suppose I shall have to come too, if you're so set on it. And I bet we shall get nobbled by Wat."

"Let him nobble," said the Wart. "I want my arrow."

They went in the Forest at the place where they had last seen the bird of carrion.

In less than five minutes they were in a clearing with a well and a cottage just like Merlyn's.

"Goodness," said Kay, "I never knew there were any cottages so close. I say, let's go back."

"I just want to look at this place," said the Wart. "It's probably a wizard's."

The cottage had a brass plate screwed on the garden gate. It said:

MADAME MIM, B.A. (Dom-Daniel)
PIANOFORTE
NEEDLEWORK
NECROMANCY
No Hawkers, circulars
or Income Tax.
Beware of the Dragon.

The cottage had lace curtains. These stirred ever so slightly, for behind them there was a lady peeping. The gore-crow was standing on the chimney.

"Come on," said Kay. "Oh, do come on. I tell you, she'll never give it us back."

At this point the door of the cottage opened suddenly and the witch was revealed standing in the passage. She was a strikingly beautiful woman of about thirty, with coal-black hair so rich that it had the blue-black of the maggot-pies in it, silky bright eyes, and a general soft air of butter-wouldn't-melt-in-my-mouth. She was sly.

"How do you do, my dears," said Madame Mim. "And what can I do for you today?"

The boys took off their leather caps, and Wart said, "Please, there is a crow sitting on your chimney and I think it has stolen one of my arrows."

"Precisely," said Madame Mim. "I have the arrow within."

"Could I have it back, please?"

"Inevitably," said Madame Mim. "The young gentleman

shall have his arrow on the very instant, in four ticks and ere the bat squeaks thrice.”

“Thank you very much,” said the Wart.

“Step forward,” said Madame Mim. “Honor the threshold. Accept the humble hospitality in the spirit in which it is given.”

“I really do not think we can stay,” said the Wart politely. “I really think we must go. We shall be expected back at home.”

“Sweet expectation,” replied Madame Mim in devout tones.

“Yet you would have thought,” she added, “that the young gentlemen could have found time to honor a poor cottager, out of politeness. Few can believe how we ignoble tenants of the lower classes value a visit from the landlord’s sons.”

“We would like to come in,” said the Wart, “very much. But you see we shall be late already.”

The lady now began to give a sort of simpering whine. “The fare is lowly,” she said. “No doubt it is not what you would be accustomed to eating, and so naturally such highly born ones would not care to partake.”

Kay’s strongly developed feeling for good form gave way at this. He was an aristocratic boy always, and condescended to his inferiors so that they would admire him. Even at the risk of visiting a witch, he was not going to have it said that he had refused to eat a tenant’s food because it was too humble.

“Come on, Wart,” he said. “We needn’t be back before vespers.”

Madame Mim swept them a low curtsey as they crossed the threshold. Then she took them each by the scruff of the neck, lifted them right off the ground with her strong gypsy arms, and shot out of the back door with them almost before they had got in at the front. The Wart caught a hurried glimpse of her parlor and kitchen. The lace curtains, the aspidistra, the lithograph called the Virgin's Choice, the printed text of the Lord's Prayer written backwards and hung upside down, the sea-shell, the needle-case in the shape of a heart with A Present from Camelot written on it, the broomsticks, the cauldrons, and the bottles of dandelion wine. Then they were kicking and struggling in the back yard.

"We thought that the growing sportsmen would care to examine our rabbits," said Madame Mim.

There was, indeed, a row of large rabbit hutches in front of them, but they were empty of rabbits. In one hutch there was a poor ragged old eagle owl, evidently quite miserable and ne-glected, in another a small boy unknown to them, a wittol who could only roll his eyes and burble when the witch came near. In the third there was a molting black cock. A fourth had a mangy goat in it, also black, and two more stood empty.

"Grizzle Greediguts," cried the witch.

"Here, Mother," answered the carrion crow.

With a flop and a squawk it was sitting beside them, its hairy black beak cocked on one side. It was the witch's familiar.

"Open the doors," commanded Madame Mim, "and Greediguts shall have eyes for supper, round and blue."

The gore-crow hastened to obey, with every sign of satisfaction, and pulled back the heavy doors in its strong beak, with three times three. Then the two boys were thrust inside, one into each hutch, and Madame Mim regarded them with unmixed pleasure. The doors had magic locks on them and the witch had made them to open by whispering in their keyholes.

"As nice a brace of young gentlemen," said the witch, "as ever stewed or roast. Fattened on real butcher's meat, I daresay, with milk and all. Now we'll have the big one jugged for Sunday, if I can get a bit of wine to go in the pot, and the little one we'll have on the moon's morn, by jing and by jee, for how can I keep my sharp fork out of him a minute longer it fair gives me the croup."

"Let me out," said Kay hoarsely, "you old witch, or Sir Ector will come for you."

At this Madame Mim could no longer contain her joy. "Hark to the little varmint," she cried, snapping her fingers and doing a bouncing jig before the cages. "Hark to the sweet, audacious, tender little veal. He answers back and threatens us with Sir Ector, on the very brink of the pot. That's how I faint

to tooth them, I do declare, and that's how I will tooth them ere the week be out by Scarmiglione, Belial, Peor, Ciriato Sannuto, and Dr. D."

With this she began bustling about in the back yard, the herb garden, and the scullery, cleaning pots, gathering plants for the stuffing, sharpening knives and cleavers, boiling water, skipping for joy, licking her greedy lips, saying spells, braiding her night-black hair, and singing as she worked.

First she sang the old witch's song:

> *"Black spirits and white, red spirits and gray,*
> *Mingle, mingle, mingle, you that mingle may.*
> > *Here's the blood of a bat,*
> > *Put in that, oh, put in that.*
> > *Here's libbard's bane.*
> > *Put in again.*
> *Mingle, mingle, mingle, you that mingle may."*

Then she sang her work song:

> *"Two spoons of sherry*
> *Three oz. of yeast,*
> *Half a pound of unicorn,*
> *And God bless the feast.*
> *Shake them in a collander,*
> *Bang them to a chop,*
> *Simmer slightly, snip up nicely,*
> *Jump, skip, hop.*
> *Knit one, knot one, purl two together,*
> *Pip one and pop one and pluck the secret feather.*
> *Baste in a mod. oven.*
> *God bless our coven.*

Tra-la-la!
Three toads in a jar.
Te-he-he!
Put in the frog's knee.
Peep out of the lace curtain.
There goes the Toplady girl, she's up to no good
 that's certain.
Oh, what a lovely baby!
How nice it would go with gravy.
Pinch the salt."

Here she pinched it very nastily.

"Turn the malt."

Here she began twiddling round widdershins, in a vulgar
way.

"With a hey-nonny-nonny and I don't mean
 maybe."

At the end of this song, Madame Mim took a sentimental
turn and delivered herself of several hymns, of a blasphemous
nature, and of a tender love lyric which she sang sotto-voce with
trills. It was:

"My love is like a red, red nose
His tail is soft and tawny,
And everywhere my lovely goes
I call him Nick or Horny."

She vanished into the parlor, to lay the table.

Poor Kay was weeping in a corner of the end hutch, lying on his face and paying no attention to anything. Before Madame Mim had finally thrown him in, she had pinched him all over to see if he was fat. She had also slapped him, to see, as the butchers put it, if he was hollow. On top of this, he did not in the least want to be eaten for Sunday dinner and he was miserably furious with the Wart for leading him into such a terrible doom on account of a mere arrow. He had forgotten that it was he who had insisted on entering the fatal cottage.

The Wart sat on his haunches, because the cage was too small for standing up, and examined his prison. The bars were of iron and the gate was iron too. He shook all the bars, one after the other, but they were as firm as rock. There was an iron bowl for water—with no water in it—and some old straw in a corner for lying down. It was verminous.

"Our mistress," said the mangy old goat suddenly from the next pen, "is not very careful of her pets."

He spoke in a low voice, so that nobody could hear, but the carrion crow which had been left on the chimney to spy upon them noticed that they were talking and moved nearer.

"Whisper," said the goat, "if you want to talk."

"Are you one of her familiars?" asked the Wart suspiciously.

The poor creature did not take offense at this, and tried not to look hurt.

"No," he said. "I'm not a familiar. I'm only a mangy old black goat, rather tattered as you see, and kept for sacrifice."

"Will she eat you too?" asked the Wart, rather trembling.

"Not she. I shall be too rank for her sweet tooth, you may be sure. No, she will use my blood for making patterns with on Walpurgis Night.

"It's quite a long way off, you know," continued the goat without self-pity. "For myself I don't mind very much, for I am old. But look at the poor old owl there, that she keeps merely for a sense of possession and generally forgets to feed. That makes my blood boil, that does. It wants to fly, to stretch its wings. At night it just runs round and round and round like a big rat, it gets so restless. Look, it has broken all its soft feathers. For me, it doesn't matter, for I am naturally of a sedentary disposition now that youth has flown, but I call that owl a rare shame. Something ought to be done about it."

The Wart knew that he was probably going to be killed that night, the first to be released out of all that band, but yet he could not help feeling touched at the great-heartedness of this goat. Itself under sentence of death, it could afford to feel strongly about the owl. He wished he were as brave as this.

"If only I could get out," said the Wart. "I know a magician who would soon settle her hash, and rescue us all."

The goat thought about this for some time, nodding its gentle old head with the great cairngorm eyes. Then it said, "As a matter of fact I know how to get you out, only I did not like to mention it before. Put your ear nearer the bars. I know how to get you out, but not your poor friend there who is crying. I didn't like to subject you to a temptation like that. You see, when she whispers to the lock I have heard what she says, but only at the locks on either side of mine. When she gets a cage away she is too soft to be heard. I know the words to release both you and me, and the black cock here too, but not your young friend yonder."

"Why ever haven't you let yourself out before?" asked the Wart, his heart beginning to bound.

"I can't speak them in human speech, you see," said the goat sadly, "and this poor mad boy here, the wittol, he can't speak them either."

"Oh, tell them me."

"You will be safe then, and so would I and the cock be too, if you stayed long enough to let us out. But would you be brave enough to stay, or would you run at once? And what about your friend and the wittol and the old owl?"

"I should run for Merlyn at once," said the Wart. "Oh, at once, and he would come back and kill this old witch in two twos, and then we should all be out."

The goat looked at him deeply, his tired old eyes seeming to ask their way kindly into the bottom of his heart.

"I shall tell you only the words for your own lock," said the goat at last. "The cock and I will stay here with your friend, as hostages for your return."

"Oh, goat," whispered the Wart. "You could have made me say the words to get you out first and then gone your way. Or you could have got the three of us out, starting with yourself to make sure, and left Kay to be eaten. But you are staying with Kay. Oh, goat, I will never forget you, and if I do not get back in time I shall not be able to bear my life."

"We shall have to wait till dark. It will only be a few minutes now."

As the goat spoke, they could see Madame Mim lighting the oil lamp in the parlor. It had a pink glass shade with patterns on it. The crow, which could not see in the dark, came quietly closer, so that at least he ought to be able to hear.

"Goat," said the Wart, in whose heart something strange and terrible had been going on in the dangerous twilight, "put your head closer still. Please, goat, I am not trying to be better than you are, but I have a plan. I think it is I who had better stay as hostage and you had better go. You are black and will not be seen in the night. You have four legs and can run much faster than I. Let you go with a message for Merlyn. I will whisper you out, and I will stay."

He was hardly able to say the last sentence, for he knew that Madame Mim might come for him at any moment now, and if she came before Merlyn it would be his death warrant. But he did say it, pushing the words out as if he were breathing against water, for he knew that if he himself were gone when Madame came for him, she would certainly eat Kay at once.

"Master," said the goat without further words, and it put one leg out and laid its double-knobbed forehead on the ground in the salute which is given to royalty. Then it kissed his hand as a friend.

"Quick," said the Wart, "give me one of your hoofs through the bars and I will scratch a message on it with one of my arrows."

It was difficult to know what message to write on such a small space with such a clumsy implement. In the end he just wrote *Kay*. He did not use his own name because he thought Kay more important, and that they would come quicker for him.

"Do you know the way?" he asked.

"My grandam used to live at the castle."

"What are the words?"

"Mine," said the goat, "are rather upsetting."

"What are they?"

"Well," said the goat, "you must say: Let Good Digestion Wait on Appetite."

"Oh, goat," said the Wart in a broken voice. "How horrible. But run quickly, goat, and come back safely, goat, and oh, goat, give me one more kiss for company before you go." The goat refused to kiss him. It gave him the Emperor's salute, of both feet, and bounded away into the darkness as soon as he had said the words.

Unfortunately, although they had whispered too carefully for the crow to hear their speech, the release words had had to be said rather loudly to reach the next-door keyhole, and the door had creaked.

"Mother, Mother!" screamed the crow. "The rabbits are escaping."

Instantly Madame Mim was framed in the lighted doorway of the kitchen.

"What is it, my Grizzle?" she cried. "What ails us, my halcyon tit?"

"The rabbits are escaping," shrieked the crow again.

The witch ran out, but too late to catch the goat or even to see him, and began examining the locks at once by the light of her fingers. She held these up in the air and a blue flame burned at the tip of each.

"One little boy safe," counted Madame Mim, "and sobbing for his dinner. Two little boys safe, and neither getting thinner. One mangy goat gone, and who cares a fiddle? For the owl and the cock are left, and the wittol in the middle."

"Still," added Madame Mim, "it's a caution how he got out, a proper caution, that it is."

"He was whispering to the little boy," sneaked the crow, "whispering for the last half-hour together."

224

"Indeed?" said the witch. "Whispering to the little dinner, hey? And much good may it do him. What about a sage stuffing, boy, hey? And what were you doing, my Greediguts, to let them carry on like that? No dinner for you, my little painted bird of paradise, so you may just flap off to any old tree and roost."

"Oh, Mother," whined the crow. "I was only adoing of my duty."

"Flap off," cried Madame Mim. "Flap off, and go broody if you like."

The poor crow hung its head and crept off to the other end of the roof, sneering to itself.

"Now, my juicy toothful," said the witch, turning to the Wart and opening his door with the proper whisper of Enough-Is-As-Good-As-a-Feast, "we think the cauldron simmers and the oven is mod. How will my tender suckling pig enjoy a little popping lard instead of the clandestine whisper?"

The Wart ran about in his cage as much as he could, and gave as much trouble as possible in being caught, in order to save even a little time for the coming of Merlyn.

"Let go of me, you beast," he cried. "Let go of me, you foul hag, or I'll bite your fingers."

"How the creature scratches," said Madame Mim. "Bless us, how he wriggles and kicks, just for being a pagan's dinner."

"Don't you dare kill me," cried the Wart, now hanging by one leg. "Don't you dare to lay a finger on me, or you'll be sorry for it."

"The lamb," said Madame Mim. "The partridge with a plump breast, how he does squeak.

"And then there's the cruel old custom," continued the witch, carrying him into the lamplight of the kitchen where a new sheet was laid on the floor, "of plucking a poor chicken before it is dead. The feathers come out cleaner so. Nobody could be so cruel as to do that nowadays, by Nothing or by Never, but of course a little boy doesn't feel any pain. Their clothes come off nicer if you take them off alive, and who would dream of roasting a little boy in his clothes, to spoil the feast?"

"Murderess," cried the Wart. "You will rue this ere the night is out."

"Cubling," said the witch. "It's a shame to kill him, that it is. Look how his little downy hair stares in the lamplight, and how his poor eyes pop out of his head. Greediguts will be sorry to miss those eyes, so he will. Sometimes one could almost be a vegetarian, when one has to do a deed like this."

The witch laid Wart over her lap, with his head between her knees, and carefully began to take his clothes off with a practiced hand. He kicked and squirmed as much as he could, reckoning that every hindrance would put off the time when he would be actually knocked on the head, and thus increase the time in which the black goat could bring Merlyn to his rescue. During this time the witch sang her plucking song, of:

> "Pull the feather with the skin,
> Not against the grain—o.
> Pluck the soft ones out from in,
> The great with might and main—o.
> Even if he wriggles,
> Never heed his squiggles,
> For mercifully little boys are quite immune to
>   pain—o."

She varied this song with the other kitchen song of the happy cook:

> *"Soft skin for crackling,*
> *Oh, my lovely duckling,*
> *The skewers go here,*
> *And the string goes there,*
> *And such is my scrumptious suckling."*

"You will be sorry for this," cried the Wart, "even if you live to be a thousand."

"He has spoken enough," said Madame Mim. "It is time that we knocked him on the napper.

> *"Hold him by the legs, and*
> *When up goes his head,*
> *Clip him with the palm-edge, and*
> *Then he is dead."*

The dreadful witch now lifted the Wart into the air and prepared to have her will of him; but at that very moment there was a fizzle of summer lightning without any crash and in the nick of time Merlyn was standing on the threshold.

"Ha!" said Merlyn. "Now we shall see what a double-first at Dom-Daniel avails against the private education of my master Bleise."

Madame Mim put the Wart down without looking at him, rose from her chair, and drew herself to her full magnificent height. Her glorious hair began to crackle, and sparks shot out of her flashing eyes. She and Merlyn stood facing each other a full sixty seconds, without a word spoken, and then Madame Mim swept a royal curtsy and Merlyn bowed a frigid bow. He

stood aside to let her go first out of the doorway and then followed her into the garden.

It ought perhaps to be explained, before we go any further, that in those far-off days, when there was actually a college for Witches and Warlocks under the sea at Dom-Daniel and when all wizards were either black or white, there was a good deal of ill-feeling between the different creeds. Quarrels between white and black were settled ceremonially, by means of duels. A wizard's duel was run like this. The two principals would stand opposite each other in some large space free from obstructions, and await the signal to begin. When the signal was given they were at liberty to turn themselves into things. It was rather like the game that can be played by two people with their fists. They say One, Two, Three, and at Three they either stick out two fingers for scissors, or the flat palm for paper, or the clenched fist for stone. If your hand becomes paper when your opponent's becomes scissors, then he cuts you and wins; but if yours has turned into stone, his scissors are blunted, and the win is yours. The object of the wizard in the duel was to turn himself into some kind of animal, vegetable, or mineral which would destroy the particular animal, vegetable, or mineral which had been selected by his opponent. Sometimes it went on for hours.

Merlyn had Archimedes for his second, Madame Mim had the gore-crow for hers, while Hecate, who always had to be present at these affairs in order to keep them regular, sat on the top of a stepladder in the middle, to umpire. She was a cold, shining, muscular lady, the color of moonlight. Merlyn and Madame Mim rolled up their sleeves, gave their surcoats to Hecate to hold, and the latter put on a celluloid eye-shade to watch the battle.

At the first gong Madame Mim immediately turned herself into a dragon. It was the accepted opening move and Merlyn ought to have replied by being a thunderstorm or something like that. Instead, he caused a great deal of preliminary confusion by becoming a field mouse, which was quite invisible in the grass, and nibbled Madame Mim's tail, as she stared about in all directions, for about five minutes before she noticed him. But when she did notice the nibbling, she was a furious cat in two flicks.

Wart held his breath to see what the mouse would become next—he thought perhaps a tiger which could kill the cat—but Merlyn merely became another cat. He stood opposite her and made faces. This most irregular procedure put Madame Mim quite out of her stride, and it took her more than a minute to regain her bearings and become a dog. Even as she became it, Merlyn was another dog standing opposite her, of the same sort.

"Oh, well played, sir!" cried the Wart, beginning to see the plan.

Madame Mim was furious. She felt herself out of her depth against these unusual stone-walling tactics and experienced an internal struggle not to lose her temper. She knew that if she did lose it she would lose her judgment, and the battle as well. She did some quick thinking. If whenever she turned herself into a menacing animal, Merlyn was merely going to turn into the same kind, the thing would become either a mere dog-fight or stalemate. She had better alter her own tactics and give Merlyn a surprise.

At this moment the gong went for the end of the first round. The combatants retired into their respective corners and their seconds cooled them by flapping their wings, while Archimedes gave Merlyn a little massage by nibbling with his beak.

"Second round," commanded Hecate. "Seconds out of the ring. . . . Time!"

Clang went the gong, and the two desperate wizards stood face to face.

Madame Mim had gone on plotting during her rest. She had decided to try a new tack by leaving the offensive to Merlyn, beginning by assuming a defensive shape herself. She turned into a spreading oak.

Merlyn stood baffled under the oak for a few seconds. Then he most cheekily—and, as it turned out, rashly—became a powdery little blue-tit, which flew up and sat perkily on Madame Mim's branches. You could see the oak boiling with indignation for a moment; but then its rage became icy cold, and the poor little blue-tit was sitting not on an oak, but on a snake. The snake's mouth was open, and the bird was actually perching on its jaws. As the jaws clashed together, but only in the nick of time, the bird whizzed off as a gnat into the safe air. Madame Mim had got it on the run, however, and the speed of the contest now became bewildering. The quicker the attacker could assume a form, the less time the fugitive had to think of a form which would elude it, and now the changes were as quick as thought. The gnat was scarcely in the air when the snake had turned into a toad whose curious tongue, rooted at the front instead of the back of the jaw, was already unrolling in the flick which would snap it in. The gnat, flustered by the sore pursuit, was bounced into an offensive role, and the hard-pressed Merlyn now stood before the toad in the shape of a mollern which could attack it. But Madame Mim was in her element. The game was going according to the normal rules now, and in less than an eye's blink the toad had turned into a peregrine falcon which was diving at two hundred and fifty miles an hour upon the heron's back. Poor Merlyn, beginning to lose his nerve, turned wildly into an elephant—this move usually won a little breathing space—but Madame Mim, relentless, changed from the falcon into an aullay on the instant. An aullay was as much bigger than an elephant as an elephant is larger than a sheep. It was a sort of horse with an elephant's trunk. Madame Mim raised this trunk in the air, gave a shriek like a railway engine, and rushed upon her panting foe. In a flick Merlyn had disappeared.

"One," said Hecate. "Two. Three. Four. Five. Six. Seven. Eight. Nine . . ."

But before the fatal Ten which would have counted him out, Merlyn reappeared in a bed of nettles, mopping his brow. He had been standing among them as a nettle.

The aullay saw no reason to change its shape. It rushed upon the man before it with another piercing scream. Merlyn vanished again just as the thrashing trunk descended, and all stood still a moment, looking about them, wondering where he would step out next.

"One," began Hecate again, but even as she proceeded with her counting, strange things began to happen. The aullay got hiccoughs, turned red, swelled visibly, began whooping, came out in spots, staggered three times, rolled its eyes, fell rumbling to the ground. It groaned, kicked, and said Farewell. The Wart cheered, Archimedes hooted till he cried, the gore-crow fell down dead, and Hecate, on the top of her ladder, clapped so much that she nearly tumbled off. It was a master stroke.

The ingenious magician had turned himself successively into the microbes, not yet discovered, of hiccoughs, scarlet fever, mumps, whooping cough, measles, and heat spots, and from a complication of all these complaints the infamous Madame Mim had immediately expired.

ROBERT NEWTON PECK
Soup

Soup was my best pal.

His real and righteous name was Luther Wesley Vinson, but nobody called him Luther. He didn't like it. I called him Luther just once, which prompted Soup to break me of a very bad habit before it really got formed. As soon as the swelling went out of my lip, I called him Soup instead of Thoop.

He first discouraged his mother of the practice of calling him Luther. (Using a different method, of course.) She used to call him home to mealtime by yelling, "Luther!" But he never answered to the name. He'd rather miss supper. When his mother got wise, she'd stand out on their back porch, cup her hands to her mouth, and yell, "Soup's on!"

From a distance (their farm was uproad next to ours) all you could hear was "Soup." And that was how the kids who were playing ball in the pasture started thinking his name was Soup, because he answered to it.

When it came to getting the two of us in trouble, Soup was a regular genius. He liked to whip apples. But that was nothing new. Every kid did. The apples had to be small and green and hard, about the size of a golf ball. The whip had to be about four to five foot long, with a point on the small end that you'd whittle sharp with your jackknife. You held the apple close to your chest with your left hand and pushed the pointed stick into the apple, but not so far as it'd come out the yonder side. No matter how careful you speared the apple, a few drops of juice would squirt on your shirt. They dried to small, tiny brown spots that never even came out in the wash.

Sassafras made the best whips. You could swing a sassafras whip through the air so fast it would whistle. The apple would fly off, and you'd think it would never come down. To whip an apple was sport enough for most of us, but not for old Soup.

"Watch this," he said.

"What?" I said.

We were up in the apple orchard on a hillside that over-looked town. Below us was the Baptist church.

"I bet I can hit the Baptist church."

"You better not, Soup."

"Why not?"

"We'll really catch it."

"No we won't. And what's more, I bet this apple can hit the bell in the belltower and make it ring."

"Aw, it won't go that far."

"Oh, no?"

Soup whipped his apple, and I was right. It landed far short of the Baptist church.

"Watch me," I said. And with my next throw I almost hit the church roof.

"My turn," said Soup.

I'll have to admit that Soup put all he had into his next throw. The whip made a whistle that would've called a dead dog. That old apple took off like it'd been shot out of a gun, made a big arc through the sky, and for a few long seconds I thought we'd hear that old bell ring for sure.

But we never heard the sounding brass. What we heard was the tinkling cymbal of a broken window. Breaking a pane of plain old glass wasn't stylish enough for Soup. It had to be stained glass. Even the sound of that stained glass shattering had color in it. I just stood there looking at that tiny little black star of emptiness that was once a window pane. It was like somebody busted my heart.

"No," I said, in almost a whisper.

I wanted the glass to fly up into place again, like it never happened. So that the little black star would erase away like a bad dream. But there it was and there it stayed.

"No," said Soup.

My feet were stuck to the ground like I was standing in twin buckets of mortar. I couldn't run. Not even when a lady ran out of the side door of the church and pointed up at us. Even though she was far below, it felt like her finger took a stab right into my chest. It was a pain, just like when you get stuck with the tip of a sword.

To make matters worse, it was Mrs. Stetson.

My family wasn't Baptist. But I guess that she knew Mama

and Aunt Carrie real well, because she came to call almost every week. Religion was her favorite subject. You'd be hard put to find a soul who knew more about God than Mrs. Stetson. She was a walking, talking Bible, which she could quote chapter and verse. Get her started and it went on like rain. Forty days and forty nights. Just to be in the same room with Mrs. Stetson was like being caught in a downpour. She sure could drench a body with scripture.

But what she was saying now was far from holy. And if there was anything Mrs. Stetson was poor at, it was talking as she climbed full-speed up a steep hill. By the time she reached me, she was so out of breath from the uphill scolding that she couldn't say a word.

I looked around for Soup, but he was gone. Good old Soup. So there I stood, with a sassafras stick in my hand and apple-juice spots on the front of my shirt. Still wet. The mortar in my shoes had now hardened into stone. My ears were ringing with a *tinkle tinkle tinkle* of smashing glass that wouldn't seem to stop.

"You!" she said.

"Me?"

Her eyes burned with the wrath of the Old Testament. It was plain to behold that Mrs. Stetson believed that you had to smite transgressors so that the ground ran red with their blood until the multitudes were sore afraid. Especially sore. But if anybody ever looked sore, it was Mrs. Stetson.

"Robert Peck!" she said in full voice.

Her big old hands shot out and grabbed my face and my hair. She shook me hard enough to shake off one of my shoes. Then after she stopped shaking me, she twisted my head around so my nose was pointing right at the little black star of that broken window pane.

"Just look what you did!" said Mrs. Stetson. "Look me in the eye and tell the truth. Do you dare say you didn't?"

"I didn't."

This was not the response that she expected. I guess what she really sought was an outburst of guilt, a tear-soaked plea to ask for the forgiveness of God and Mrs. Stetson—perhaps not in that order of importance.

"I didn't. Honest, Mrs. Stetson. I didn't throw an apple that far. Look how far it is."

"You *did* do it. I saw you do it. And here's the apple you did it with." She had a pierced apple in one hand and my switch in the other, and I knew I was a goner.

"But I couldn't hit the church from way up here. Nobody could."

"Bosh! Even a fool knows how far an apple will pitch from a stick. Watch."

You won't believe what I saw. Mrs. Stetson somehow let go of her senses. She pushed an apple on a stick, and before I could grab her arm, her temper bested reason. Whissshh! You never saw a worse throw in your life, not if you stood up in that old orchard from now until Judgment. Her apple never even headed in the direction of the Baptist church. Nowhere near. But you couldn't say that apple didn't have any steam to it. No, sir. It flew off her stick (my stick) like a rifle ball, going east by northeast, and finally tipped over a flower pot with a geranium in it outside old Haskin's shack window. And the pot cracked the glass.

Crash-tinkle!

Out came old Mr. Haskin with blood in his eye. His language would have made Satan himself cover his ears. Not real fancy swearing, just a long string of old favorites. He pointed at Mrs. Stetson and me, then he started uphill and coming our way fast.

"Run!" yelled Mrs. Stetson. "That man's a degenerate."

We ran, Mrs. Stetson and I. She had on two shoes and I wore one, which evened the speed a bit, and we ran as if Hell was a step behind. We ran until we could no longer hear the terrible things that old Haskin shouted he would do to Mrs. Stetson the next time she came near his rotten old shack. We didn't stop running, Mrs. Stetson and I, until we darted into Frank Rooker's garage and had bolted the door.

But as we ran in, Soup ran out, after taking one look at Mrs. Stetson. Out the side door he shot, into the arms of Mr. Haskin. Soup still had his switch in hand, and his shirt front was smelled and spotted with apple juice, which was enough evidence for old Haskin. Borrowing the sassafras switch, the old man gave Soup a fine smarting. I'll have to admit it sure must have been a sight to see.

From where Mrs. Stetson and I stood panting, we didn't see it. But we heard it all. Thinking I'd be next, I even winced for poor Soup with every blow. Best of all, we heard him confess up to breaking the window, even though it wasn't the same glass he got thrashed for. In a way, it really was justice.

Mrs. Stetson was right. There really is a God.

FRANK B. GILBRETH and ERNESTINE G. CAREY
Cheaper by the Dozen

It's never dull when you grow up with a dozen freckle-faced brothers and sisters. The authors of this selection—two of the twelve Gilbreth kids— know that family life is not only cheaper but funnier by the dozen.

Dad acquired the *Rena* to reward us for learning to swim. She was a catboat, twenty feet long and almost as wide. She was docile, dignified, and ancient.

Before we were allowed aboard the *Rena*, Dad delivered a series of lectures about navigation, tides, the magnetic compass, seamanship, rope-splicing, right-of-way, and nautical terminology. Radar still had not been invented. It is doubtful if, outside the Naval Academy at Annapolis, any group of Americans ever received a more thorough indoctrination before setting foot on a catboat.

Next followed a series of dry runs, on the front porch of *The Shoe*. Dad, sitting in a chair and holding a walking stick as if it were a tiller, would bark out orders while maneuvering his imaginary craft around a tricky harbor.

We'd sit in line on the floor alongside of him, pretending we were holding down the windward rail. Dad would rub imaginary spray out of his eyes, and scan the horizon for possible sperm whale, Flying Dutchmen, or floating ambergris.

"Great Point Light off the larboard bow," he'd bark. "Haul in the sheet and we'll try to clear her on this tack."

He'd ease the handle of the cane over toward the imaginary leeward rail, and two of us would haul in an imaginary rope.

"Steady as she goes," Dad would command. "Make her fast."

We'd make believe twist the rope around a cleet.

"Coming about," he'd shout. "Low bridge. Ready about, hard a'lee."

This time he'd push the cane handle all the way over toward the leeward side. We'd duck our heads and then scramble across the porch to man the opposite rail.

"Now we'll come up and pick up our mooring. You do that at the end of every sail. Good sailors always make the mooring on the first try. Landlubbers sometimes have to go around three or four times before they can catch it."

He'd stand up in the stern, the better to squint at the imaginary mooring.

"Now. Let go your sheet, Bill. Stand by the centerboard, Mart. Up on the bow with the boat hook, Anne and Ernestine, and mind you grab that mooring. Stand by the throat, Frank. Stand by the peak, Fred. . . ."

We'd scurry around the porch going through our duties, until at last Dad was satisfied his new crew was ready for the high seas.

Dad was never happier than when aboard the *Rena*. From the moment he climbed into our dory to row out to *Rena's* mooring, his personality changed. On the *Rena*, we were no longer his flesh and blood, but a crew of landlubberly scum shanghaied from the taverns and fleshpots of many exotic ports. *Rena* was no scow-like catboat, but a sleek four-master, bound around the Horn with a bone in her teeth in search of rare spices and the priceless treasure of the Indies. He insisted that we address him as Captain, instead of Daddy, and every remark must needs be civil and end with a "sir."

"It's just like when he was in the Army," Ernestine whispered. "Remember those military haircuts for Frank and Bill, and all that business of snapping to attention and learning to salute, and the kitchen police?"

"Avast there, you swabs," Dad hollered. "No mutinous whispering on the poop deck!"

Anne, being the oldest, was proclaimed first mate of the *Rena*. Ernestine was second mate, Martha third, and Frank fourth. All the younger children were able-bodied seamen who, presumably, ate hardtack and bunked before the mast.

"Seems to be blowing up, mister," Dad said to Anne. "I'll have a reef in that mains'il."

"Aye, aye, sir."

"The *Rena's* just got one sail, Daddy," Lill said. "Is that the mains'il?"

"Quiet, you landlubber, or you'll get the merrie rope's end. Of course it's the mains'il."

The merrie rope's end was no idle threat. Able-bodied seamen or mates who failed to leap when Dad barked an order did in fact receive a flogging with a piece of rope. It hurt, too.

Dad's mood was contagious, and soon the mates were as dogmatic and as full of invective as he, when dealing with the sneaking pickpockets and rum-palsied derelicts who were their subordinates. And, somehow, Dad passed along to us the illusion that placid old *Rena* was a taut ship.

"I'll have those halliards coiled," he told Anne.

"Aye, aye, sir. Come on you swabs. Look alive now, or shiver my timbers if I don't keel haul the lot of you."

Sometimes, without warning, Dad would start to bellow out tuneless chanties about the fifteen men on a dead man's chest and, especially, one that went, "He said heave her to, she replied make it three."

If there had been any irons aboard, they would have been occupied by the fumbling landlubber or scurvy swab who forgot his duties and made Dad miss the mooring. Dad felt that to have to make a second try for the mooring was the supreme humiliation, and that fellow yachtsmen and professional sea captains all along the waterfront were splitting their sides laughing at him. He'd drop the tiller, grow red in the face, and advance rope in hand on the offender. More than once, the scurvy swab made a panic-stricken dive over the side, preferring to swim ashore, where he would cope ultimately with Dad, instead of meeting the captain on the latter's own quarterdeck.

On one occasion, when Dad blamed missing a mooring on general inefficiency and picked up a merrie rope's end to inflict merrie mass punishment, the entire crew leaped simultaneously over the side in an unrehearsed abandon-ship maneuver. Only the captain remained at the helm, from which vantage point he hurled threatening reminders about the danger of sharks and the penalties of mutiny. On that occasion, he brought *Rena* up to the mooring by himself, without any trouble, thus proving something we had long suspected—that he didn't really need our help at all, but enjoyed teaching us and having a crew to order around.

Through the years, old *Rena* remained phlegmatic, paying no apparent attention to the bedlam which had intruded into her twilight years. She was too old a seadog to learn new tricks.

Only once, just for a second, did she display any sign of temperament. It was after a long sail. A fog had come up, and *Rena* was as clammy as a shower curtain. We had missed the mooring on the first go-round, and the captain was in an ugly mood. We made the mooring all right on the second try. The captain, as was his custom, was standing in the stern, merrie rope in hand, shouting orders about lowering the sail. Just before the sail came down, a squall hit *Rena*, and she retaliated by whipping her boom savagely across the hull. The captain saw it coming, but didn't have time to duck. The boom caught him on the side of the head with a terrific clout, a blow hard enough to lift him off his feet and tumble him, stomach first, into the water.

The captain didn't come up for almost a minute. The crew, while losing little love for their captain, became frightened for their Daddy. We were just about to dive in after him when a pair of feet emerged from the water and the toes wiggled. We knew everything was all right then. The feet disappeared, and a few moments later Dad came up head first. His nose was bleeding, but he was grinning and didn't forget to spit the fine stream of water through his front teeth.

"The bird they call the elephant," he whispered weakly, and he was Dad then. But not for long. As soon as his head cleared and his strength came back, he was the captain again.

"All right, you red lobsters, avast there," he bellowed. "Throw your captain a line and help haul me aboard. Or, shiver my timbers, I'll take a belaying pin to the swab who lowered the boom on me."

LOUISE FITZHUGH
Harriet the Spy

Harriet isn't thrilled at the idea of being an onion in the school Christmas pageant. But she rises to the occasion with her usual pluck and humor.

Miss Elson stood in the middle of the room and called for order. No one paid the slightest bit of attention, so she hit the blackboard with the eraser which sent up a cloud of smoke, making her sneeze and everyone else laugh. Then she grew very stern and stared a long time at a spot somewhere down the middle aisle. That always worked.

"Now, children," she began when there was silence, "today is the day to plan our Christmas pageant. First, let's have some ideas from the floor about what we would like to do. I don't think I need bother explaining what this day means to us. There is only one new child here who might wonder." The Boy with the Purple Socks looked horribly embarrassed. "And I think I can simplify this by saying that at the Christmas pageant we get a chance to show the parents what we have been learning. Now each one hold up your hand when you have a suggestion."

Sport's arm shot up. "What about pirates?"

"Well, that's a thought. I'll write that down, Simon, but I think I heard something about the fourth grade being pirates. Next?"

Marion Hawthorne stood up. Harriet and Sport looked at each other with pained expressions. Marion said, "I think, Miss Elson, that we should do a spectacular of the Trojan War. That would show everyone exactly what we have been learning." She sat down again.

Miss Elson smiled. "That's a lovely idea, Marion. I shall certainly write that down." Harriet, Sport, and Janie groaned loudly. Janie stood up. "Miss Elson. Don't you think there will be certain difficulties about building a Trojan horse, much less getting us all in there?"

"Well, I don't think we'll go that far in realism, Janie. This is still open for discussion anyway, so let's hear the other ideas before we discuss the details. I don't know how big a spectacular we could have in the time allotted us. Anyway, I think I should remind you that we are not supposed to give a play. The sixth grade is supposed to dance. We are due in the gymnasium in thirty minutes to discuss this dance with Miss Berry, the dance teacher, then be measured for costumes by Miss Dodge. Now you know that once the subject is chosen you all improvise your dances. But this year you will be allowed to choose your subject, whereas always before Miss Berry has chosen it."

"SOLDIERS," screamed Sport.

"Now, not out of turn, Simon. I'll go down the line and each one gets a chance." Miss Elson then called the role. "Andrews?" she said, and Carrie got up and said that she thought it would be nice to have a dance about Dr. Kildare and Ben Casey. Miss Elson wrote it down. There was a great deal of whispering around the room as people started trying to get their gang to agree on something.

"Gibbs?"

"I think that a dance about the Curies discovering radium would be nice. We could all be particles except me and Sport, and we could be Monsieur and Madame Curie."

"Hansen?"

Beth Ellen shot a terrified glance at Marion Hawthorne, who had been sending her a barrage of notes. Finally she said softly, "I think we should all be things you eat at Christmas dinner."

"Hawthorne?"

Marion stood up. "I think that's an excellent suggestion on Beth Ellen Hansen's part. I think we should be Christmas dinner too."

"Hennessey?"

Rachel stood up. "I agree with Marion and Beth Ellen. I think that's a good idea."

"Peters?"

Laura Peters was terribly shy, so shy that she smiled at everybody all the time, as though they were about to hit her. "I think that's a good idea too," she quavered, and sank gratefully back into her seat.

"Matthews?"

The Boy with the Purple Socks stood up and said in an offhand way, "Why not? I'd just as soon be a Christmas dinner as anything else."

"Rocque?"

Simon looked at Harriet. She knew what that look meant. She was becoming aware of the same thing. They were surrounded. They should have gotten together and now it was too late. In a minute they would all be assigned to things like giblet gravy. Simon stood up. "I don't know why we don't do the Trojan War like Marion Hawthorne said first. I would a whole lot rather be a soldier than some carrots and peas."

Very clever, thought Harriet. Maybe Marion would consent to her own idea. How bright Sport is, she thought.

"Welsch?"

"I think Sport's absolutely right" and sat down, intercepting a glare from Marion Hawthorne as she did so. Uh-oh, thought Harriet, she's on to us.

"Whitehead?"

Pinky's was the only name left. Sport threw a pencil right in his face. At first Harriet couldn't see why. Then she saw Pinky look at Sport, then stand up and say sadly, "I agree with Harriet and Simon."

Well, thought Harriet, that's three against the world. Too bad Janie had to be in such a hurry about the Curies.

There was a vote but they knew they had lost even before it happened.

Miss Elson said, "I think that's a lovely idea. Now we can have a little discussion with Miss Berry about which parts of the dinner we will take, and then you can start making up your dances at home. Now let's go to the gym."

Everyone but Marion Hawthorne and Rachel Hennessey looked terribly disgruntled. They all got up and filed after Miss

Elson out of the classroom, down the stairs, into the courtyard, through the courtyard with the little patch of green called the back lawn, and into the gymnasium, where a scene of utter pandemonium greeted them.

It was obvious that everyone in the school was in the gym. There were all sizes and shapes of girls from little ones to older ones just about to graduate. Miss Berry was screeching frantically, and Miss Dodge was measuring so fast she looked as though she might fly right out the window. Hairpins were falling out and her glasses were askew as she whipped through waist after waist, hip after hip. Miss Berry's leotards looked baggy.

Sport looked around wildly. "I've never been so terrified in my life. Look at all these girls." He began to edge his way toward Pinky Whitehead and The Boy with the Purple Socks.

Harriet grabbed him by the collar. "You stay right here. Suppose something happens and we have to have partners." She pushed her face close to his. He began to sweat nervously but stayed next to her after that.

"Now, children, sixth grade over here, please." Miss Elson was gesturing frantically.

Marion Hawthorne looked around pompously at everyone who didn't move instantly. She always seemed to be laboring under the impression that she was Miss Elson's understudy. "Come along there, Harriet," she said imperiously. Harriet had a sudden vision of Marion grown up, and decided she wouldn't look a bit different, just taller and more pinched.

"Boy, does she tee me off," said Sport, digging his hands in his pockets and his sneakers against the floor as though he would never move.

"Simon." Miss Elson spoke quite sharply, and Sport jumped a mile. "Simon, Harriet, Jane, come along now." They moved. "Now we'll stand here and wait our turn with Miss Berry and I don't want any talking. The din in this place is unbearable."

"Isn't it awful?" said Marion Hawthorne in a falsetto.

Harriet thought, Marion Hawthorne is going to grow up and play bridge a lot.

Pinky Whitehead looked as though he might faint. He ran to Miss Elson frantically and whispered something in her ear. She looked down at him. "Oh, Pinky, can't you wait?"

"No," said Pinky loudly.

"But it's so far!"

Pinky shook his head again, was dismissed by Miss Elson, and ran out. Sport laughed. There weren't any bathrooms for boys in the gym.

"Thought he'd never leave," said Janie. She had gotten this from her mother.

Harriet looked at Beth Ellen staring into space. Harriet was under the impression that Beth Ellen had a mother in an insane asylum, because Mrs. Welsch had once said, "That poor child. Her mother is always at Biarritz."

"All right, children, Miss Berry is ready now." They

marched over with flat feet like prisoners. Harriet felt like Sergeant York.

Miss Berry was in her usual state of hysteria. Her hair was pulled into a wispy ponytail, as though it were pulling her eyes back.

She looked at them wildly. "Sixth grade, yes, sixth grade, let's see. What have you decided? Well? What have you decided?"

Marion Hawthorne spoke for them, naturally. "We've decided to be a whole Christmas dinner," she said brightly.

"Lovely, lovely. Now let's see, vegetables first, vegetables . . ." Sport started to sprint for the door. Miss Elson pulled him back by the ear. Pinky Whitehead arrived back. Miss Berry turned to him, enchanted. "*You* will make a *wonderful* stalk of celery."

"What?" said Pinky stupidly.

"And *you*"—she pointed to Harriet—"are an ONION."

This was too much. "I refuse, I absolutely REFUSE to be an onion." She stood her ground. She could hear Sport whispering his support behind her. Her ears began to burn as they all turned and looked at her. It was the first time she had ever really refused to do anything.

"Oh, dear." Miss Berry looked as though she might run out the door.

"Harriet, that's ridiculous. An onion is a beautiful thing. Have you ever really looked at an onion?" Miss Elson was losing all touch with reality.

"I will NOT do it."

"Harriet, that's enough. We won't have any more of this impudence. You ARE an onion."

"I am not."

"Harriet, that is QUITE enough."

"I won't do it. I quit."

Sport was pulling at her sleeve. He whispered frantically, "You can't quit. This is a SCHOOL." But it was too late. A roar of laughter went up from the group. Even that mild thing, Beth Ellen, was laughing her head off. Harriet felt her face turning red.

Miss Berry seemed to come back to life. "Now, children. I think it would be nice to take each thing from its inception to the time it arrives on the table. We must have some more vegetables. You, there"—she pointed to Janie—"you're squash. And you"—she pointed to Beth Ellen—"are a pea." Beth Ellen looked as though tears were close. "You two"—she pointed to Marion Hawthorne and Rachel Hennessey—"can be the gravy. . . ." At this Harriet, Sport, and Janie broke into hysterical peals of laughter and had to be quieted by Miss Elson before Miss Berry could continue. "I don't see what's funny. We have to have gravy. You"—she pointed to Sport—"and you"—she pointed to Pinky Whitehead—"are the turkey." "Well, of all the . . ." began Sport and was shushed by Miss Elson.

After she had made The Boy with the Purple Socks into a bowl of cranberries, she turned to the class. "Now all the vegetables, listen to me," said Miss Berry, planting her feet firmly in the fifth position. Harriet made a mental note to make a note of the fact that Miss Berry always wore, even on the street, those flat, mouse-gray practice shoes. They were always terribly old ones with the cross bar curling away from the arch.

". . . I want you to feel—to the very best of your endeavor—I want you to feel that one morning you *woke up* as one of these vegetables, one of these *dear* vegetables, nestling in the earth, warm in the heat and power and magic of growth, or

striving tall above the ground, pushing through, bit by bit in the miracle of birth, waiting for that glorious moment when you will be . . ."

"Eaten," Harriet whispered to Sport.

". . . once and for all, your essential and beautiful self, full-grown, radiant." Miss Berry's eyes were beginning to glaze. One arm was outstretched toward the skylight; half of her hair had fallen over one ear. She held the pose in silence.

Miss Elson coughed. It was a things-are-getting-altogether-out-of-hand cough.

Miss Berry jumped. She looked as though she had just come up out of a subway and didn't know east from west. She gave an embarrassed titter, then started afresh. "We'll start with the tenderest moment of these little vegetables, for you know, children, this dance has a story, a story, a lovely story." She trilled a bit of laughter to let them know she was still there. "It starts, as do all stories, with the moment of conception." She looked around in a delighted way. Miss Elson turned pale.

"It starts, naturally, with the farmer—"

"Hey, I want to be the farmer," Sport yelled.

"Do not say 'hey' to a teacher." Miss Elson was losing patience.

"Oh, but, dear boy, one of the older girls will be the farmer. A farmer must be taller, after all, than vegetables. Vegetables are very *short*." She looked annoyed that he didn't know this. Sport turned away in disgust.

"Well, the farmer comes in on this lovely morning when the ground is freshly broken, open and yielding, waiting to receive. When he enters, you will all be piled in a corner like seed waiting to be planted. You will just lie there in lumps like this—" and she fell abruptly to the ground. She lay there like a heap of old clothes.

"Come on, let's split; she's gone." Sport turned to go.

"Miss Berry, I think they've got the position," said Miss Elson loudly. Miss Berry turned one inquiring eye over her shoulder to face a royal snub from Miss Elson. She scrambled to her feet.

"All right, children"—she was suddenly crisp—"I want you to start improvising your dances, and I will see what you've done next dance class." The change in her was so remarkable that the children all stared in silence. "Please file over there and be fitted." She turned her back. It was all so swift that Miss Elson stood gaping a minute before she started to herd them toward the costume corner. They all looked back curiously at Miss Berry, who stood, feet planted flatly, her misunderstood nose high in the air.

The costume corner looked like Macy's on sale day. Quantities of tulle flew through the air.

Sport wilted. "Boy, this is a scene I *really* can't make."

It *was* dreary. Harriet remembered it from last year as a long wait with your feet hurting while a terribly flustered Miss Dodge measured you in a sweaty way and, likely as not, stuck you full of pins.

"One day," said Janie, "I am going to come in here with a vial and blow this place sky-high."

The three of them stood glumly, staring at the tulle.

"How do you practice being an onion?" Harriet looked over at Miss Berry, who was falling into another pile of rags on the floor. Evidently all the dances were the same.

Sport got an evil look. "I think I'll scream as loud as I can when she measures me."

Janie's turn came. "Here goes nothing," she said loudly. Miss Dodge blinked her giant eyes behind her glasses, fluttered her tape measure, and dropped several pins from her mouth.

GARRISON KEILLOR
Lake Wobegon Days

I liked Mrs. Meiers a lot, though. She was a plump lady with bags of fat on her arms that danced when she wrote on the board: we named them Hoppy and Bob. That gave her a good mark for friendliness in my book, whereas Miss Conway of fourth grade struck me as suspiciously thin. What was her problem? Nerves, I suppose. She bit her lips and squinted and snaked her skinny hand into her dress to shore up a strap, and she was easily startled by loud noises. Two or three times a day, Paul or Jim or Lance would let go with a book, dropping it flat for maximum whack, and yell, "Sorry, Miss Conway!" as the poor woman jerked like a fish on the line. It could be done by slamming a door or dropping the window, too, or even scraping a chair, and once a loud slam made *her* drop a stack of books, which gave us a double jerk. It worked better if we were very quiet before the noise. Often, the class would be so quiet, our little heads bent over our work, that she would look up and congratulate us on our excellent behavior, and when she looked back down at her book, *wham!* and she did the best jerk we had ever seen. There were five classes of spasms: The Jerk, The Jump, The High Jump, The Pants Jump, and The Loopdeloop, and we knew when she was prime for a big one. It was after we had put her through a hard morning workout, including several good jumps, and a noisy lunch period, and she had lectured us in her thin weepy voice, then we knew she was all wound up for the Loopdeloop. All it required was an extra effort: *throwing* a dictionary flat at the floor or dropping the globe, which sounded like a car crash.

We thought about possibly driving Miss Conway to a nervous breakdown, an event we were curious about because our mothers spoke of it often. "You're driving me to a nervous breakdown!" they'd yell, but then, to prevent one, they'd grab us and shake us silly. Miss Conway seemed a better candidate. We speculated about what a breakdown might include—some good jumps for sure, maybe a couple hundred, and talking gibberish with spit running down her chin.

Miss Conway's nervous breakdown was prevented by Mrs. Meiers, who got wind of it from one of the girls—Darla, I think. Mrs. Meiers sat us boys down after lunch period and said that if she heard any more loud noises from Room 4, she would keep us after school for a half hour. "Why not the girls?" Lance asked. "Because I know that you boys can accept responsibility,"

Mrs. Meiers said. And that was the end of the jumps, except for one accidental jump when a leg gave way under the table that held Mr. Bugs the rabbit in his big cage. Miss Conway screamed and left the room, Mrs. Meiers stalked in, and we boys sat in Room 3 from 3:00 to 3:45 with our hands folded on our desks, and remembered that last Loopdeloop, how satisfying it was, and also how sad it was, being the last. Miss Conway had made some great jumps.

MARY RODGERS
Freaky Friday

Have you ever wondered what it would be like if you and your mother changed places? You're the one who makes breakfast for Daddy; she's the one who goes to school. That's exactly what happens to Annabel Andrews one freaky Friday.

Breakfast went off not too badly, considering it was my first. Luckily, Daddy asked for fried (I learned how to do that a couple of years ago), so I made fried, and toast. I also made a small mistake.

"Sorry about the instant, Daddy, but we're all out of regular," I said, giving him a nice friendly kiss on the cheek.

"*Daddy!* Since when did you start calling me Daddy? You never did that before," he said.

"No, and I won't again, Bill, dear," I said, relieved at least that he wasn't going to make a scene about the coffee. I ran back into the kitchen to find out what Ape Face wanted.

"What'll it be for you, lover boy?" I asked, crossing my arms and giving him the hairy eyeball. Just watch him ask for scrambled!

"Could I have scrambled, Mommy, please?" What did I tell you!

"No, you can't," I said, very briskly. "I don't have time to wash two pans. It's fried or nothing."

"But I don't like fried," he said. (You know, she spoils him rotten, but not me!)

"Then eat cold cereal," I said, slapping down a box of Sugar Coated Snappy Krackles in front of him.

"But these are Annabel's. She bought them with her own money to eat when she watches television. She'll kill me if I eat up her cereal," he said anxiously. What a worrywart.

"Listen, Ben," I said very slowly and carefully. "Annabel *wants* you to eat her Sugar Coated Snappy Krackles. So eat 'em. NOW!" He jumped and started to eat.

Speaking of Annabel reminded me that I hadn't seen myself yet and she was going to be late for school if she didn't hurry. Me, she, I, her? I was getting very mixed up. I also wondered, as I stood outside the door to her room, what—who—I was going to find in there. Was it going to be Annabel's body with Annabel's mind in it, but I wouldn't know what the mind was thinking? Or was it going to be Annabel's body with Ma's mind in it, which would certainly be a more tidy arrangement?

Whoever-it-was was lying on her stomach on the bed, waving her feet in the air and reading a comic book. It certainly looked like Annabel. It looked like her room, too. There were all kinds of clothes dribbling out of drawers and hanging around on the floor. And one sneaker hanging around on a lamp.

"Uh, hi there," I said cautiously.

"Phloomph," it said. It seemed to be eating something.

"How about a nice hot cup of instant?" I suggested.

With that, whoever-it-was sat up in a hurry, turned around, and stared at me with its mouth wide open. It had not swallowed what was in its mouth. A marshmallow. Since I have never in my entire life seen my mother eating a marshmallow, I began to have a sneaking hunch that this was not my mother. It gulped and swallowed.

"A nice hot cup of *instant*?" it repeated. "What are you? Crazy? You know I don't drink that stuff."

It was Annabel all right. No doubt about it. Outside of the fact that Ma doesn't eat marshmallows and I do, there is the fact that if it was really Ma, she wouldn't ask me if I was crazy because she'd know I was Annabel thinking she was Ma. But if *she* was really Annabel too, no wonder she thought I was crazy. Any mother who asks her daughter if she wants a nice hot cup of instant has to be crazy.

"I was talking about a nice hot cup of instant oatmeal," I said in my haughtiest voice, "and I'll thank you not to eat marshmallows before breakfast. It spoils your appetite."

"What appetite?" she said. "I never have any appetite for all that vomitizing stuff you pile into me. Besides, I'm full up on marshmallows." She patted her stomach.

I decided to give in because it was getting too late to argue.

"OK, Annabel, forget breakfast, just get yourself dressed."

"But I can't get dressed," she complained. "I can't get dressed till I find my blue tights and I don't see where they are." I didn't see where they were either but I found some red ones in between Book *B* and Book *S* of the Junior Britannica. (In my library, *S* comes after *B*, and *L* follows that.)

"Why don't you wear red? Red would be nice," I suggested in Ma's most reasonable voice. I should have known better.

"No," she said, crossly, "I want blue." I looked around wildly, trying to remember where I'd put them last night. They were in the wastebasket.

"You are a living doll," she said, blowing me several ballerina kisses. "How can I possibly sank you for zis enormous favor you do for me?" She'd gone into her French routine.

What a nut! At least she was in a good mood again. The thing about Annabel is that she usually changes her moods quickly and often. Today, I wasn't going to know what to expect, or when. What was going on in her head right now, I wondered. Maybe she was thinking about her homework and McGuirk the Jerk. If she wasn't, she should be!

"Annabel, what are you going to tell Miss McGuirk?" I asked.

"About what?" she said.

"About the English composition," I said.

"You mean the English composition I was behind on?" she asked.

"Uh-huh," I said.

"Oh, I handed that in early last week," she said, looking me right in the eye. You want somebody to believe you, you always look 'em right in the eye. It's a slick trick of mine . . . works every time.

"Good girl," I said, because that's what Ma would've said. And anyway, what did I care what went on in school? That was her problem, not mine.

Ape Face stood in the doorway, jacket on, earmuffs on, and a big, gooney smile all over his dumb face. Every day he's ready ahead of time, just to show me up, the fink!

"I'm all ready, Mommy, and I walked Max," he said in his dumb voice. "He did a big thing and two little things. Annabel better hurry or we're going to miss the bus."

"If we do, it's because you're standing in my way," she snarled. "Get out of here, Ape Face, and don't talk to me."

"I wasn't."

"You are now! And don't!" she said, throwing on the rest of her clothes.

"I'm not!" he said.

"Ape Face, *shut up!*" she said. To tell the truth, both of them were getting on my nerves. I tried to remember what Ma did with us in the morning.

"All right, all right, all right, you two, that's enough of that," I said, pushing them to the front door. So far, so good.

"And Annabel, I've told you a million times, don't call him Ape Face; his name is Ben." Even better! I was beginning to sound more like Ma than Ma does.

"Bye-bye, darlings, have a nice day," I said, holding the door open for them. But Ape Face just stood there. What was he waiting for, I wondered? Then a grotesque thought came to me. He was waiting to be kissed and I was going to have to do it. So I did—as quickly as possible. Actually, it wasn't too bad. He smelled kind of nice. But I hoped he didn't expect it again at lunchtime. Annabel didn't expect it at all, she never does. Just as well. I would have felt funny kissing myself good-bye.

DELIA EPHRON

How to Hang Up
the Telephone

G ood-bye."
    " 'Bye."
   "Are you still there?"
   "Are you?"
   "Yeah. Why didn't you hang up?"
   "Why didn't you?"
   "I was waiting for you."
   "I was waiting for *you*. You go first."
   "No, you first."

"No, you first."

"No, you first."

"OK, I know. I'll count to three and we'll both hang up at the same time. Ready? One, two, three, 'bye."

" 'Bye." . . .

"Are you still there?"

"Yeah."

"Why didn't you?"

"What do you mean, me?"

"OK, do it again. This time for real. One, two, two and a half, two and three quarters, three. 'Bye."

" 'Bye."

"Hello."

"Hello."

"Are you still there?"

"Yeah."

BEVERLY KELLER

No Beasts! No Children!

Mother has left; the twins—Antony and Aida—are acting strangely and won't talk; and Dad is being harassed by their grouchy neighbor, Mr. Troup. But even though life is no barrel of laughs for young Desdemona right now, this selection in which Antony finds a doll at a garage sale is very funny.

Antony stepped between them, holding a thing by its neck. Its head was made of china, the scalp dotted with tiny holes but bare of hair. Its one blue eye rolled around like a demented ghoul's, the rubber band that kept it in the head visible through the empty socket. Between its simpering parted lips were a few tiny teeth and more broken ones. This head was sewed onto a dirty gray cloth body which hung limp and lumpy from my brother's fist. Looking at Father, Antony lifted it higher.

"It's a doll," Father said absently. "At least, it was."

"He wants it," I said.

"You don't want that," Father told him.

"If you're not going to buy it, put it down," Mr. Troup snapped at Antony.

Antony clutched the doll to his chest.

"You'd better be careful," I warned Mr. Troup. "He takes his clothes off when he's insulted."

"You don't want that old thing," Father told Antony again.

Antony squeezed his eyes shut until his face purpled.

"I knew you just came to make trouble," Mr. Troup accused Father. "If you're too cheap to buy your own son a miserable two-bit doll . . ."

"I can buy my son any miserable two-bit doll he wants."

Antony opened his eyes to follow the argument.

"All right. How much is your miserable two-bit doll?" Father took out his wallet.

"Ten dollars."

"You're out of your mind."

"That doll is a genuine antique. It belonged to Patty's great-grandmother."

"She didn't take very good care of it," I noted.

"Ten cents," Father said.

"Eight dollars," snapped Mr. Troup.

Antony looked from one to the other, his mouth open so he wouldn't lose time if he decided to scream. Father and Mr. Troup yelled numbers at each other. Finally Father handed Mr. Troup a dollar and told him he was a bandit.

Aida grabbed Father's sleeve and held up a book.

"I am not going to pay one cent for *A Guide to Sewage Treatment in Rural Areas*." Shoving the book at Mr. Troup,

Father seized Aida by the hand and stalked out of the garage.

"At least no son of mine ever played with dolls," Mr. Troup yelled after us.

Father took us downtown and bought Aida a picture book. She wouldn't look at it.

He offered to trade Antony any toy on the counter for the doll. Antony clutched it tighter.

Father bought me a puzzle and took us for sodas.

Aida stared at the table, tears running down her face. Antony patted the doll's grimy ear.

"Do you ever have days when you feel like a total failure?" Father asked me.

"A lot." I felt closer to him than I had for a long time.

When we got home, Aunt was repairing the front fence. "Ugh. What's that?" she greeted us.

"Pat Troup's great-grandmother's doll," I said.

Antony held it up for her to admire. "Poor thing," she murmured. Then she smiled at me. "Aren't you glad you went to the garage sale? I knew it would be fun."

"Antony gives me the creeps," I told Aunt. "He and Poor Thing."

"Poor Thing?"

"That doll. It *dangles* as if all its bones are missing."

"I don't believe dolls have bones."

"You know what I mean. That vacant eye, and the other rolling around, and all the holes in its scalp."

"Think of them as hair roots. That doll probably had a beautiful head of real human hair. Each strand was knotted and drawn through a hole. It was a marvelous doll in its day."

"Well, it's a horrible sight in our day. And Antony carries it everywhere."

"Boys need to love things as much as girls do."

"I know, but it's driving my father crazy."

"Your father isn't silly enough to think that only girls should play with dolls."

"Maybe. But it makes him nervous."

Father's voice came from out back. "How about a game of catch?"

I looked out the window. Antony was sitting in the sandbox rocking Poor Thing. Aida put down a pail and ran to Father.

"Hey, son! How about a game of keep-away?" Father called.

Antony fed Poor Thing a little sand and wiped her mouth.

"Race you to the corner, boy!" Father challenged.

Aida hunkered down for the signal. Antony peered into Poor Thing's eye socket.

"Anybody want to go house hunting?" Father asked. I could tell he didn't mean me.

Antony dragged Poor Thing past him, to our room.

"Your father is trying to relate to you," Aunt told him.

Shaking the sand out of Poor Thing's head, Antony put her in the box he'd fixed for a crib.

When Father got home from house hunting, Aunt tried to relate to him. "It's important for boys to be loving and gentle, Mark."

"I know that. But it's such a horrible creature, and he never leaves it alone."

This was true. Antony took Poor Thing everywhere. People in stores smiled at him in a pitying way, as if he were the Poor Little Match Wretch . . . or they looked nervous, as if Poor Thing might spread whatever ghastly misfortunes she'd survived.

Finally, Aunt said, "We could do something about that doll."

Antony clutched it tight.

"Wouldn't you like her clean and with two eyes?"

He shook his head and hugged the doll harder.

"Think how lovely she'd be with hair," Aunt cajoled.

He backed toward the door, watching Aunt as if she might go into a doll-napping frenzy at any moment.

"If we could leave her at the doll hospital for just a day . . ." Aunt murmured.

Antony paused.

"She could have an operation. When she comes home, we can take her temperature and pulse." She went on as if that doll would make medical history. Antony didn't have a chance.

When she won, Aunt telephoned the doll hospital and said it was an emergency.

The next morning, Antony wrapped Poor Thing in a dish towel and whitened her face with chalk. When the captain arrived, Antony, grim but game, carried the patient to the car.

I offered to play catch with Father, but he had to get ready for work.

Aida and I shot baskets. After she made two in a row, I went in to tell Father, but he said, "Got to run."

A little while later, the captain drove up with Aunt, Antony, and Poor Thing, who looked just the same.

"The hospital turned her away," Aunt explained. "They said there was no hope."

PATRICK F. McMANUS
The Skunk Ladder

My friend Crazy Eddie Muldoon and I were sitting on the Muldoon corral fence one summer afternoon, trying to think of something to do. This was shortly after I had nearly drowned in the creek while testing Eddie's deep-sea diving apparatus, and after we had crashed in our homemade plane during takeoff from the roof of the Muldoon barn, and after our submarine had failed to surface with us in the pond, but before Mr. Muldoon started being treated by old Doc Mosby for a mysterious nervous condition. I recall mentioning to Eddie that

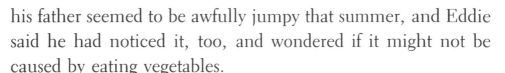

his father seemed to be awfully jumpy that summer, and Eddie said he had noticed it, too, and wondered if it might not be caused by eating vegetables.

Even as we sat on the fence, Mr. Muldoon came by on his tractor and stopped to study us suspiciously. "What are you two up to now?" he demanded.

"Nothin', Pa," Crazy Eddie said. "Just trying to think of something to do."

Mr. Muldoon shuddered. "Well, when you think of it, you let me know before you start to do it, you hear?"

"Sure, Pa," Eddie said. "I guess what we'll do is go dig in the dirt. We've been talkin' about doin' that."

"Okay," said Mr. Muldoon, shifting his tractor into gear. "Just don't build nothin'!" Then he drove off.

"What kind of hole are we going to dig?" I asked Eddie.

He stared off into space, his face enveloped in that dreamy expression that always accompanied one of his wondrous new ideas. "A big hole," he said. "A real big hole."

Digging the hole occupied us for most of a week. One of the problems with digging a big hole is that it is difficult to know when it is big enough and deep enough. There are basically two kinds of holes dug in the ground: (1) applied holes, such as for posts, wells, mines, etc., and (2) holes for holes' sake. Eddie and I were digging one of the latter. Eventually, the hole was so deep we could barely heave shovelfuls of dirt up over its sides. At that point, Eddie judged it to be finished.

Since Eddie had insisted that we keep the sides of the hole squared up, we had to pull ourselves out of it on a rope, one end of which was tied to a pile of stumps nearby. The stump pile also served to screen our digging activities from the view of Mr. Muldoon, who was cutting hay in a field on the far side of the farm. As Eddie often pointed out, any kind of engineering feat should be screened from the eyes of the engineer's parents. That way you could concentrate on your work and didn't have to be answering a lot of dumb questions all the time.

We were immensely proud of the hole, and I still don't believe I've ever seen a nicer one. It was so nice, in fact, that Eddie abandoned his view of it as purely an aesthetically pleasing hole and began trying to think of it as practical.

"You know what we could do with this hole?" he said. "We could make a wild animal trap out of it, you know, like Frank Buck does in Africa. We could cover it up with branches and leaves and grass, and wild animals would come along and fall into it. Then we could tame them and teach them to do tricks."

Eddie fairly glowed with enthusiasm as his idea began to take shape. "And then we could start our own circus," he went on. "We could charge people to see our animals do tricks. We might even get rich. Gosh, I bet we could catch a deer or an elk or a bear or a mountain lion or . . ."

"One of your father's cows," I put in.

Eddie's glow of enthusiasm faded. "Yeah," he said. "I never thought of that."

Both of us stood there silently for a moment, thinking of Mr. Muldoon staring down into the hole at one of his milk cows. It was unpleasant to think about.

"Tomorrow we'd better fill the hole back in," Eddie said.

"How about tonight? Maybe a cow will fall in tonight."

Eddie pondered this possibility for a moment. "I got it," he said. "There's a big ol' door out behind the barn. We'll drag that down here and put it over the hole." And that is what we did, before knocking off work for the day, secure in the knowledge that the door would save us from the uncomfortable experience of watching his father undergo one of his fits of hysteria.

Early the next morning, Eddie and I headed for the big

hole, prepared to start the tedious task of undigging it. As we approached the excavation, a familiar odor reached our nostrils.

"Must be a skunk around here someplace," Eddie said.

"Maybe it's in the hole," I said.

"Couldn't be. We covered it with the door."

Nevertheless, the skunk was in the hole. He had apparently found an open space under the door, slipped in for a look around, and plummeted the eight feet or more to the bottom of the hole. Oddly, he did not seem to be frightened of us. Even stranger, for we did not know that skunks were great diggers, he had hollowed out a huge cavern under one side, in an attempt to dig his way out of the hole.

"We can't fill in the hole with the skunk in there," I said. "How are we going to get him out?"

"Maybe one of us could drop down in the hole, grab him real quick before he sprays, and then throw him out," Eddie said. "I'll yell real loud so he'll look at me and won't notice when you jump in and grab him and . . ."

"I don't like that idea," I said. "Think of something else."

"I got it!" Eddie exclaimed, snapping his fingers. "We'll go up to my dad's shop and build a ladder. Then we'll stick it down the hole and hide someplace while he climbs the ladder. A skunk should be able to figure out how to climb a ladder."

Eddie and I were working on the ladder when his father walked into the shop. "I thought I told you not to build anything," he growled. "What's that?"

"Just a skunk ladder," Crazy Eddie said.

"Oh," his father said. "Well, don't build nothin' else unless you tell me first."

Eddie and I went back out to the hole and stuck the ladder in it. The skunk showed no inclination to climb it, choosing instead to hide in the cavern it had hollowed out. Just then we heard Eddie's father yelling at us: "What did you mean, *skunk ladder?*" We peeked out around the stump pile, and there was Mr. Muldoon striding across the pasture toward us.

"Quick," said Eddie. "Help me put the door back over the hole!"

We threw the door over the hole, neatly hiding it from view. Before we could think of a good explanation for a big pile of dirt out in a corner of the pasture, Mr. Muldoon charged up.

"Now what?" he cried. "Where did that dirt come from? What's my door doing out here?"

He reached down and grabbed the edge of the door.

"Stop, Pa, don't!" Eddie yelled, rushing forward.

From that point on, the actions of the parties involved all blurred together. It is difficult to recall the exact sequence of action, but I will try.

Mr. Muldoon grabbed the door and flipped it off the hole. Then he said, "Smells like a skun . . ." at which time he shot out of sight, leaving his straw hat suspended in the air for perhaps a quarter of a second. (Later, I deduced that Mr. Muldoon had stepped on the edge of the hole, beneath which the skunk had hollowed out its cavern.) A cloud of dust puffed up out of the hole when Mr. Muldoon hit the bottom. Then he yelled several serious swear words with the word "SKUNK!" mixed in with them. Next there were a lot of earthy scrabbling sounds, and Mr. Muldoon came clawing his way up the side of the hole, but the dirt gave way and he fell back in, saying something like "Ooofff!" It is important, perhaps, to realize that all the activity so far had taken place in a span of no more than four seconds. Eddie had meanwhile charged forward, yelling, "Pa, Pa, don't hurt him!" He was standing at the top of the ladder when the skunk rushed up that contrivance and emerged from the cloud of dust. Startled, and not wanting the skunk to reverse ends and

spray him, Eddie grabbed the little animal by the head. The skunk started scratching and biting, so Eddie threw it back down in the hole, where its arrival was followed by a savage bellow from Mr. Muldoon, who, to our surprise, then came racing up the skunk ladder himself.

This was the signal for Eddie and me to start running, which we did, and we continued running until the thunderous sounds of Mr. Muldoon's clodhopper boots faded behind us, and still we ran on, finally outdistancing even the nostril-searing smell of Eddie's father.

Eddie eventually made his way home and placed himself under the protective custody of his mother, until Mr. Muldoon's rage subsided into the odd little facial tic that was to remain with him for several months.

In the ruckus at the skunk ladder, Eddie had been hit in the face with a slight charge of skunk spray. Worried at first that the spray might have affected his brain, Mr. and Mrs. Muldoon finally assumed there would be no lasting ill effects. Twenty years later, however, Crazy Eddie became a Ph.D. in chemistry.

LARRY CALLEN
Fifteen Minutes

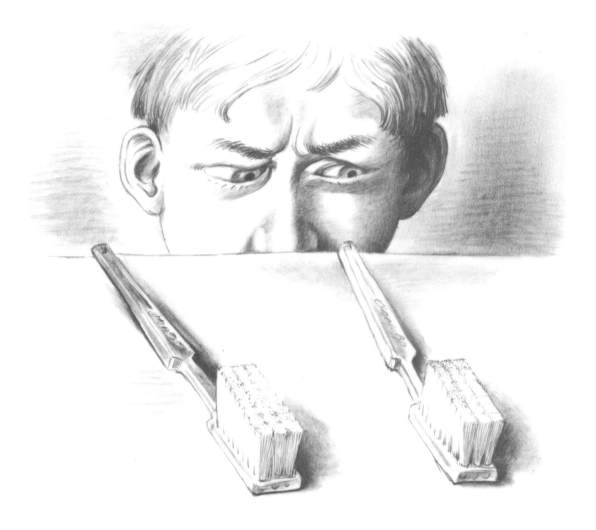

Y ou've got fifteen minutes to make up your mind," Mom said. She put the red toothbrush and the green toothbrush on the table, side by side. "If you haven't decided by the time Violet gets here, I'll do the deciding."

My old toothbrush had been yellow, and its bristles were soft and bent. These two looked pretty good. Maybe the red would be best. I sat down at the table and studied them.

Two minutes later Violet Deever walked in, big smile on her face like she owned the world.

"What're you doing?" she asked.

"Nothing."

She saw the toothbrushes on the table. She reached for one, but I pushed her hand away.

"Pat, stop that," she said. "I asked your mother to buy me a toothbrush. One of those is mine."

Mom heard her and shouted from the kitchen that I had asked first so I had first choice.

"Twelve minutes left to decide, Pat."

"Oh," said Deever. She sat down on the other side of the table and studied the toothbrushes.

"They're both nice, aren't they?" she asked. "You know which one you're going to take yet?"

"Whichever one I want," I said. I wasn't going to have her trying to make me take the one *she* didn't want.

"Maybe you ought to take the red one," she said, touching the end of the red handle. "It's very nice. The bristles look very straight."

Then a sly look crossed her face and I knew she was playing one of her games again. She was going to try and trick me. Well, this time I wasn't going to be tricked. This time I would do the tricking.

"Deever, don't touch them. Mom said I had first choice, and that means first touching, too."

I looked closely at the green one. If she wanted me to take the red one, she must've seen something special about the green one. Or maybe she just liked the color best.

The green one looked a little bit longer than the red one. But maybe it was just where I was sitting. I moved them closer together to compare size.

"It doesn't seem right that you can touch them and I can't," she said. "One of them is going to be mine, isn't it? Well, I

284

don't want you touching my toothbrush. A toothbrush is a very personal thing, Pat. People don't go around touching other people's toothbrushes."

All her talk was getting in the way of my deciding which one I wanted.

"Mom, make Violet stop talking. I can't think when she is talking."

Deever looked at her wristwatch. "You've got only ten more minutes to decide, Pat."

Now she was really trying to get me confused.

"Mom, do I really have only ten more minutes?"

But Mom didn't answer, and Deever smiled and pointed to her watch. Then she drew a little circle around the red toothbrush with her finger. She didn't say a word, but she might as well have.

I looked at the toothbrushes and then I looked at her. She kept telling me the red one was best. She wanted me to think she wanted the green one. But suppose it was one of her tricks? Maybe it was the red one she wanted. Well, two could play at that game.

"I haven't really decided yet, but I think that I might just take the green one," I said.

The expression on her face didn't change a whit. Not an eyelid flickered. She stared me in the eye, daring me to guess what she was thinking.

"You have nine minutes left, Pat," she said.

But I wasn't going to be rushed into anything. I stood up and went to the kitchen for a glass of water. Mom was slicing tomatoes and cucumbers and celery for a salad.

"Mom, do I *have* to decide in fifteen minutes?"

"Decide about what, dear?"

"Aw, Mom. You know. The toothbrush. Violet is sitting

right there, trying to get me to take the one she doesn't want."

Now Mom was washing lettuce at the sink.

"I can't see what difference the color of a toothbrush makes, Pat. Just pick one and be done with it."

But she didn't understand. I went back into the dining room. And I saw right away that Deever had moved both brushes. The green one had been closest to where I was sitting. Now the red one was closest.

"A fly lit on it," she said.

"What?"

"I wouldn't take the green one if I were you, Pat. While you were gone a fly lit on it. Maybe it laid some eggs. How would you like brushing your teeth with a bunch of fly eggs?"

"I'm not listening to that kind of stuff, Deever. I'm picking the one I want. Not the one you *don't* want."

"Know what color fly eggs are, Pat?"

I was looking at the toothbrushes. The bristles of both were snowy white. It looked like there might be a fleck of something on the bristles of the green one, but it surely wasn't fly eggs. Maybe dust is all.

"They are green. That's what color fly eggs are."

I flicked the bristles of the green toothbrush with my finger and whatever was on them disappeared. But if I took the green one, I would wash it with scalding water anyway.

The screen door slammed in the kitchen and I could hear my brother, E.J., asking Mom if he had time to take a shower before dinner. Then he rushed into the dining room. When he saw us, he slowed.

"What are you two doing?" he asked.

"Pat is selecting a toothbrush," said Deever. "He has been at it for exactly seven minutes so far."

E.J. wasn't interested in what we were doing. He kept on

walking. A minute later he came back into the room, holding his own toothbrush.

"Mom," he called, "I think I need a toothbrush worse than anybody. Could I have one of those on the table?"

"I get one," I told him. "Mom says Violet gets the other."

"But if you *could* have one, E.J., which one would you take?" asked Deever.

He stopped at the table and stared down at the two brushes.

"That all the colors there are? Mine is orange. I'd like another orange one."

"Don't you think Pat ought to take the red one?" asked Deever.

E.J. didn't answer. When he had gotten a promise out of Mom to buy him an orange toothbrush, he headed back to the shower.

"I think he secretly wants the red brush, Patrick," said Deever. "But you have first choice."

I'd already wasted more than half of my time and I still didn't know which one I wanted. I like red. It's a bright, kind of loud color. I wouldn't want red clothes, except maybe a tie. Dad's got a red sport coat that he wore one time only, and then swore he would never wear again because everybody kept making jokes about it. But a toothbrush is different. I never heard a toothbrush joke in my whole life.

"Pat, have you ever broken a tooth?" asked Deever.

I was just getting started on my thinking and she got me distracted again.

Mom's not going to fool around. At the end of the fifteen minutes, she's going to decide who gets what color.

"The reason I asked, Pat, is that when you break a tooth, it means a friend will die. I had that happen to me when I was only six years old. It wasn't exactly a person-friend. It was a hamster. But it broke my heart. You know what my hamster's name was, Pat?"

"Deever, will you please let me think?"

She says I ought to take the red one. She knows I'm not going to take the one she wants me to. That means she knows I'll take the green one. And that means she wants the red one. If she just keeps quiet a little bit longer, I'll have this thing puzzled out.

"Red is a very lucky color, Pat. Did you know it can even help you if you have a poor memory? All you have to do is tie a red string around a finger on your left hand—"

"And remember why you tied it there," I snarled. She just wouldn't shut up.

"Mom, what time is it?"

"You have five minutes left, Pat," said Deever. "You are surely taking a long time to make up your mind."

She got up and went into the kitchen. I could hear low voices and laughter. Then she came back, crunching on a celery stick.

She says I should take the red one. But she also knows I won't do it, because she is telling me to do it. But if I'm smart enough to figure that out, then I'll take the red one, and she'll be left with the green one.

Suppose she's figured out that I'll figure it out. Which one does she really want, then?

I was getting confused.

I looked at her. She was still chewing on the celery. Was she trying to say something to me with that green stick? She smiled at me, still chewing.

Maybe I ought to get back to thinking about which one I want, instead of which one she wants. The green one is pretty.

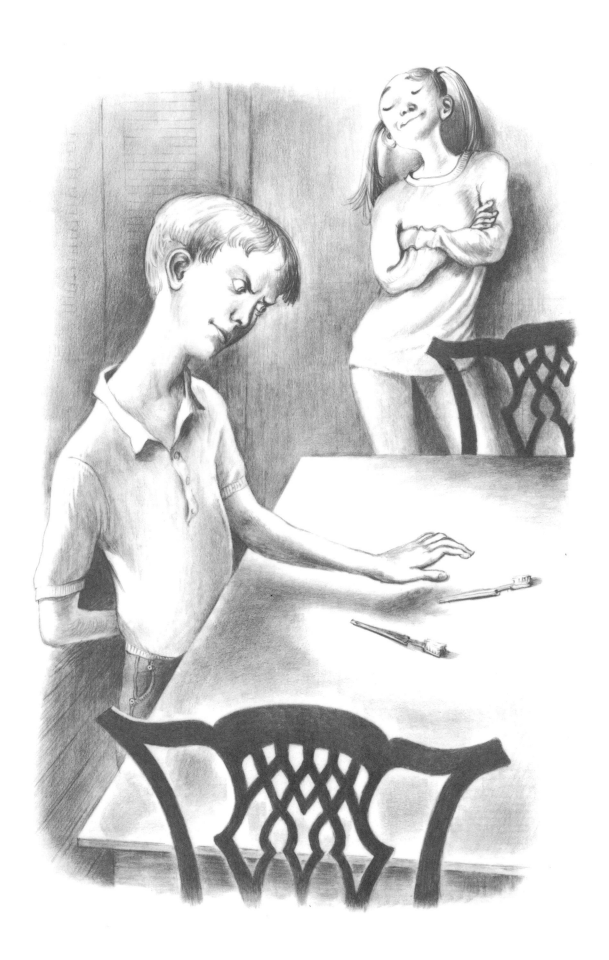

Kind of a grass green. I've got to get that business about fly eggs out of my mind. That's just trickery.

Lots of nice-looking things are green. Lawns are green. Leaves are green. Olives. Emeralds. Watermelons.

Watermelons.

But the sweet part on the inside is red.

"Do you know anything about rotten garbage, Pat? It's ugly and slimy and probably full of fly eggs. Did I ever tell you that once I had a possum for a pet? Possums eat garbage. Did you know that? And they have funny green stuff growing all over their teeth."

I used to like brushing my teeth. Made them feel clean. And I like the taste of toothpaste. They put something in it that tickles your tongue. Sometimes when we run out of toothpaste, I brush with salt, and I even like the taste of that. But I wasn't looking forward to brushing my teeth ever again.

"What time do you think it is, Pat?" she asked.

"All right, Deever. Which one do you *really* want?"

"Oh, I don't have a real preference. I just thought the red one would be nice for you."

I balled my fist. I knew she wasn't going to tell me the truth.

"You're just saying that, right? I'll take the red one, and then you will get the green one, which is the one you really want. I know what you're trying to do, Deever."

She tilted her head, lifted her eyebrows, and kind of sniffed, like she was saying I had a right to my opinion even if I was wrong.

"Ma!" called E.J. from the bathroom. "There's a big green fly in here."

"See there!" said Deever. "I told you so."

Mom came to the rescue with a flyswatter clutched in her

hand. I heard a single *whack!*, and she came walking out with a grin of victory on her face.

"Two minutes to go, Pat," she said as she passed.

"Mom, it's not fair to put all this pressure on me. I haven't had a single minute to think. Deever's been here jabbering away the whole time."

"I'll be back in two minutes," Mom said.

I whirled on Deever. I wanted to yell at her to go away, but she wasn't smiling like she was winning the war or anything. There was a kind of hurt look on her face.

"I thought I had been helping you, Pat," she said.

"Deever, a guy doesn't need help to pick the right color for a toothbrush."

"All right, then. I won't say another word." She sat back in her chair and looked at me. The hurt look stayed on her face. Now she was trying to make me feel guilty.

"One minute!" called Mom.

Which one? Red one? Green one? Ruby one? Emerald one? Somehow I knew she wanted the red one. I just knew it.

I could hear Mom stirring around in the kitchen. She was going to come marching out here any second.

"All right. I've decided," I said.

I stretched my hand out over the toothbrushes. I paused over the red one and looked at Deever's face, but I couldn't tell a thing. Then I moved my hand over the green one. Still nothing.

I scooped my hand down and grabbed the green one, watching her from the corner of my eye. Her face lit up like a Christmas tree.

"Good!" she said.

Now I knew. I dropped the green toothbrush and grabbed the red one. I pulled it close to me. This time I had won.

"Time's up!" yelled Mom.

I grinned at Deever and waited for her smile to fade. But it didn't happen.

She reached out in her dainty way. With two fingers she plucked the green toothbrush from the table.

"Wonderful!" she said. "Green is my favorite color."

MARK TWAIN
Tom Sawyer

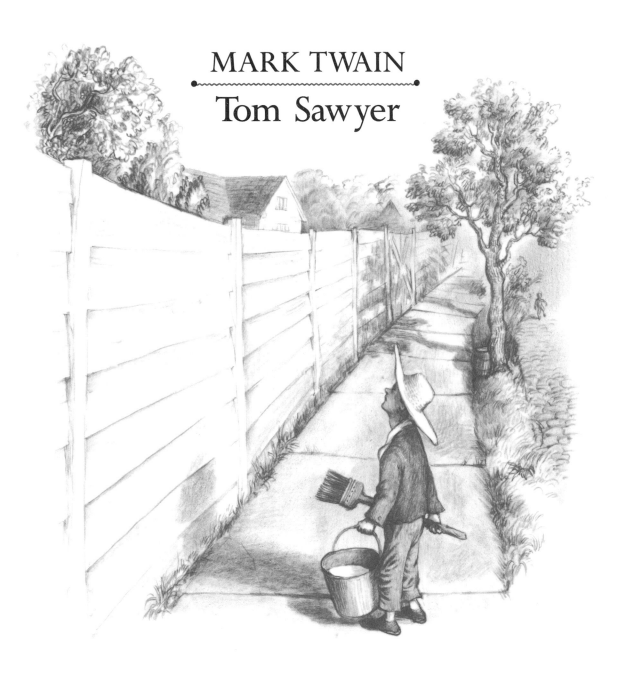

Saturday morning was come, and all the summer world was bright and fresh, and brimming with life. There was a song in every heart; and if the heart was young the music issued at the lips. There was cheer in every face, and a spring in every step. The locust trees were in bloom, and the fragrance of the blossoms filled the air.

Cardiff Hill, beyond the village and above it, was green with vegetation, and it lay just far enough away to seem a Delectable Land, dreamy, reposeful, and inviting.

Tom appeared on the sidewalk with a bucket of whitewash and a long-handled brush. He surveyed the fence, and the gladness went out of nature, and a deep melancholy settled down upon his spirit. Thirty yards of broad fence nine feet high! It seemed to him that life was hollow, and existence but a burden. Sighing, he dipped his brush and passed it along the topmost plank; repeated the operation; did it again; compared the insignificant whitewashed streak with the far-reaching continent of unwhitewashed fence, and sat down on a tree-box, discouraged. Jim came skipping out at the gate with a tin pail, and singing "Buffalo Gals." Bringing water from the town pump had always been hateful work in Tom's eyes before, but now it did not strike him so. He remembered that there was company at the pump. White, mulatto, and Negro boys and girls were always there waiting their turns, resting, trading playthings, quarreling, fighting, skylarking. And he remembered that although the pump was only a hundred and fifty yards off Jim never got back with a bucket of water under an hour; and even then somebody generally had to go after him. Tom said:

"Say, Jim; I'll fetch the water if you'll whitewash some."

Jim shook his head, and said:

"Can't, Ma'rs Tom. Ole missis she tole me I got to go an' git dis water an' not stop foolin' 'roun' wid anybody. She say she spec' Ma'rs Tom gwyne to ax me to whitewash, an' so she tole me go 'long an' 'tend to my own business—she 'lowed *she'd* 'tend to de whitewashin'."

"Oh, never you mind what she said, Jim. That's the way she always talks. Gimme the bucket—I won't be gone only a minute. *She* won't ever know."

"Oh, I dasn't, Ma'rs Tom. Ole missis she'd take an' tar de head off'n me. 'Deed she would."

"*She!* she never licks anybody—whacks 'em over the head

with her thimble, and who cares for that, I'd like to know? She talks awful, but talk don't hurt—anyways, it don't if she don't cry. Jim, I'll give you a marble. I'll give you a white alley!"

Jim began to waver.

"White alley, Jim, and it's a bully tow."

"My, dat's a mighty gay marvel, *I* tell you. But, Ma'rs Tom, I's powerful 'fraid ole missis."

But Jim was only human—this attention was too much for him. He put down his pail, took the white alley. In another minute he was flying down the street with his pail and a tingling rear, Tom was whitewashing with vigor, and Aunt Polly was retiring from the field with a slipper in her hand and triumph in her eye.

But Tom's energy did not last. He began to think of the fun he had planned for this day, and his sorrows multiplied. Soon the free boys would come tripping along on all sorts of delicious expeditions, and they would make a world of fun of him for having to work—the very thought of it burnt him like fire. He got out his worldly wealth and examined it—bits of toys, marbles, and trash; enough to buy an exchange of work maybe, but not enough to buy so much as half an hour of pure freedom. So he returned his straitened means to his pocket, and gave up the idea of trying to buy the boys. At this dark and hopeless moment an inspiration burst upon him. Nothing less than a great, magnificent inspiration. He took up his brush and went tranquilly to work. Ben Rogers hove in sight presently; the very boy of all boys whose ridicule he had been dreading. Ben's gait was the hop, skip, and jump—proof enough that his heart was light and his anticipations high. He was eating an apple, and giving a long melodious whoop at intervals, followed by a deep-toned ding dong dong, ding dong dong, for he was personating a steamboat! As he drew near he slackened speed, took the middle of the street, leaned far over to starboard, and rounded-to ponderously, and with laborious pomp and circumstance, for he was personating the *Big Missouri*, and considered himself to be drawing nine feet of water. He was boat, and captain, and engine-bells combined, so he had to imagine himself standing on his own hurricane-deck giving the orders and executing them.

"Stop her, sir! Ling-a-ling-ling." The headway ran almost out, and he drew up slowly towards the sidewalk. "Ship up to back! Ling-a-ling-ling!" His arms straightened and stiffened down the sides. "Set her back on the stabboard! Ling-a-ling-ling! Chow! ch-chow-wow-chow!" his right hand meantime describing stately circles, for it was representing a forty-foot wheel. "Let her go back on the labboard! Ling-a-ling-ling! Chow-ch-chow-chow!" The left hand began to describe circles.

"Stop the stabboard! Ling-a-ling-ling! Stop the labboard! Come ahead on the stabboard! Stop her! Let your outside turn over slow! Ling-a-ling-ling! Chow-ow-ow! Get out that head-line! Lively, now! Come—out with your spring-line—what're you about there? Take a turn round that stump with the bight of it! Stand by that stage now—let her go! Done with the engines, sir! Ling-a-ling-ling!

" 'Sht! s'sht! sht!" (Trying the gauge-cocks.)

Tom went on whitewashing—paid no attention to the steamer. Ben stared a moment, and then said:

"Hi-yi! You're up a stump, ain't you!"

No answer. Tom surveyed his last touch with the eye of an artist; then he gave his brush another gentle sweep, and surveyed the result as before. Ben ranged up alongside of him. Tom's mouth watered for the apple, but he stuck to his work. Ben said:

"Hello, old chap; you got to work, hey?"

"Why, it's you, Ben! I warn't noticing."

"Say, I'm going in a swimming, I am. Don't you wish you

could? But of course, you'd druther work, wouldn't you? 'Course you would!"

Tom contemplated the boy a bit, and said:

"What do you call work?"

"Why, ain't that work?"

Tom resumed his whitewashing, and answered carelessly:

"Well, maybe it is, and maybe it ain't. All I know is, it suits Tom Sawyer."

"Oh, come now, you don't mean to let on that you like it?"

The brush continued to move.

"Like it? Well, I don't see why I oughtn't to like it. Does a boy get a chance to whitewash a fence every day?"

That put the thing in a new light. Ben stopped nibbling his apple. Tom swept his brush daintily back and forth—stepped back to note the effect—added a touch here and there—criticized the effect again, Ben watching every move, and getting more and more interested, more and more absorbed. Presently he said:

"Say, Tom, let me whitewash a little."

Tom considered; was about to consent; but he altered his mind: "No, no; I reckon it wouldn't hardly do, Ben. You see, Aunt Polly's awful particular about this fence—right here on the street, you know—but if it was the back fence I wouldn't mind, and she wouldn't. Yes, she's awful particular about this fence; it's got to be done very careful; I reckon there ain't one boy in a thousand, maybe two thousand, that can do it the way it's got to be done."

"No—is that so? Oh, come now; lemme just try, only just a little. I'd let you, if you was me, Tom."

"Ben, I'd like to, honest injun; but Aunt Polly—well, Jim wanted to do it, but she wouldn't let him. Sid wanted to do it, but she wouldn't let Sid. Now, don't you see how I am fixed? If you was to tackle this fence, and anything was to happen to it—"

"Oh, shucks; I'll be just as careful. Now lemme try. Say—
I'll give you the core of my apple."

"Well, here. No, Ben; now don't; I'm afeard—"

"I'll give you all of it!"

Tom gave up the brush with reluctance in his face, but
alacrity in his heart. And while the late steamer *Big Missouri*
worked and sweated in the sun, the retired artist sat on a barrel
in the shade close by, dangled his legs, munched his apple, and
planned the slaughter of more innocents. There was no lack of
material; boys happened along every little while; they came to
jeer, but remained to whitewash. By the time Ben was fagged
out, Tom had traded the next chance to Billy Fisher for a kite
in good repair; and when he played out, Johnny Miller bought

in for a dead rat and a string to swing it with; and so on, and so on, hour after hour. And when the middle of the afternoon came, from being a poor poverty-stricken boy in the morning Tom was literally rolling in wealth. He had, besides the things I have mentioned, twelve marbles, part of a jew's harp, a piece of blue bottle-glass to look through, a spool-cannon, a key that wouldn't unlock anything, a fragment of chalk, a glass stopper of a decanter, a tin soldier, a couple of tadpoles, six firecrackers, a kitten with only one eye, a brass doorknob, a dog collar—but no dog—the handle of a knife, four pieces of orange peel, and a dilapidated old window sash. He had had a nice, good, idle time all the while—plenty of company—and the fence had three coats of whitewash on it! If he hadn't run out of whitewash he would have bankrupted every boy in the village.

Tom said to himself that it was not such a hollow world after all. He had discovered a great law of human action, without knowing it, namely, that, in order to make a man or a boy covet a thing, it is only necessary to make the thing difficult to attain. If he had been a great and wise philosopher, like the writer of this book, he would now have comprehended that work consists of whatever a body is obliged to do, and that play consists of whatever a body is not obliged to do. And this would help him to understand why constructing artificial flowers, or performing on a treadmill, is work, whilst rolling ninepins or climbing Mont Blanc is only amusement. There are wealthy gentlemen in England who drive four-horse passenger-coaches twenty or thirty miles on a daily line, in the summer, because the privilege costs them considerable money; but if they were offered wages for the service that would turn it into work, then they would resign.

THOMAS ROCKWELL
How to Eat Fried Worms

Billy makes a bet that he can eat fifteen worms in fifteen days. If he performs this gastronomical feat, he wins a minibike. Here he gets ready to take the first bite.

Six, seven, eight, nine, *ten!*"

Billy was doing push-ups in the deserted horse barn. He wasn't *worried* about eating the first worm. But people were always daring him to do things, and he'd found it was better to look ahead, to try to figure things out, get himself ready. Last winter Alan had dared him to sleep out all night in the igloo they'd built in Tom's backyard. Why not? Billy had thought to himself. What could happen? About midnight, huddled shivering under his blankets in the darkness, he'd begun to wonder if he should give up and go home. His feet felt like aching stones in his boots; even his tongue, inside his mouth, was cold. But half an hour later, as he was stubbornly dancing about outside in the moonlight to warm himself, Tom's dog Martha had come along with six other dogs, all in a pack, and Billy had coaxed them into the igloo and blocked the door with an orange crate, and after the dogs had stopped wrestling and nipping and barking and sniffing around, they'd all gone to sleep in a heap with Billy in the middle, as warm as an onion in a stew.

But he hadn't been able to think of anything special to do to prepare himself for eating a worm, so he was just limbering up in general—push-ups, knee bends, jumping jacks—red-faced, perspiring.

Nearby, on an orange crate, he'd set out bottles of ketchup and Worchestershire sauce, jars of piccalilli and mustard, a box of crackers, salt and pepper shakers, a lemon, a slice of cheese, his mother's tin cinnamon-and-sugar shaker, a box of Kleenex, a jar of maraschino cherries, some horseradish, and a plastic honey bear.

Tom's head appeared around the door.

"Ready?"

Billy scrambled up, brushing back his hair.

"Yeah."

"TA RAHHHHHHHHH!"

Tom flung the door open; Alan marched in carrying a covered silver platter in both hands, Joe slouching along beside him with a napkin over one arm, nodding and smiling obsequiously. Tom dragged another orange crate over beside the first; Alan set the silver platter on it.

"A chair," cried Alan. "A chair for the monshure!"

"Come on," said Billy. "Cut the clowning."

Tom found an old milking stool in one of the horse stalls.

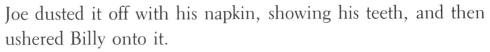

Joe dusted it off with his napkin, showing his teeth, and then ushered Billy onto it.

"Luddies and gintlemin!" shouted Alan. "I prezint my musterpiece: Vurm a la Mud!"

He swept the cover off the platter.

"Awrgh!" cried Billy, recoiling.

The huge night crawler sprawled limply in the center of the platter, brown and steaming.

"Boiled," said Tom. "We boiled it."

Billy stormed about the barn, kicking barrels and posts, arguing. "A night crawler isn't a *worm*! If it was a worm, it'd be called a worm. A night crawler's a night crawler."

Finally Joe ran off to get his father's dictionary:

> *night crawler n:* EARTHWORM; esp: a large earth-
> worm found on the soil surface at night

Billy kicked a barrel. It still wasn't fair; he didn't care what any dictionary said; everybody knew the difference between a night crawler and a worm—look at the thing. Yergh! It was as big as a souvenir pencil from the Empire State Building! Yugh! He poked it with his finger.

Alan said they'd agreed right at the start that he and Joe could choose the worms. If Billy was going to cheat, the bet was off. He got up and started for the door. He guessed he had other things to do besides argue all day with a fink.

So Tom took Billy aside into a horse stall and put his arm around Billy's shoulders and talked to him about George Cunningham's brother's minibike, and how they could ride it on the trail under the power lines behind Odell's farm, up and down the hills, bounding over rocks, rhum-rhum. Sure, it was a big worm, but it'd only be a couple more bites. Did he want to lose a minibike over *two bites*? Slop enough mustard and ketchup and horseradish on it and he wouldn't even taste it.

"Yeah," said Billy. "I could probably eat this one. But I got to eat *fifteen*."

"You can't quit now," said Tom. "Look at them." He nodded at Alan and Joe, waiting beside the orange crates. "They'll tell everybody you were chicken. It'll be all over school. Come on."

He led Billy back to the orange crates, sat him down, tied the napkin around his neck.

Alan flourished the knife and fork.

"Would monshure like eet carved lingthvise or crussvise?"

"Kitchip?" asked Joe, showing his teeth.

"Cut it out," said Tom. "Here." He glopped ketchup and mustard and horseradish on the night crawler, squeezed on a few drops of lemon juice, and salted and peppered it.

Billy closed his eyes and opened his mouth. "Ou woot in."

Tom sliced off the end of the night crawler and forked it up. But just as he was about to poke it into Billy's open mouth, Billy closed his mouth and opened his eyes.

"No, let me do it."

Tom handed him the fork. Billy gazed at the dripping ketchup and mustard, thinking, Awrgh! It's all right talking about eating worms, but *doing* it!?!

Tom whispered in his ear. "Minibike."

"Glug." Billy poked the fork into his mouth, chewed furiously, *gulped!* . . . *gulped!* . . . His eyes crossed, swam, squinched shut. He flapped his arms wildly. And then, opening his eyes, he grinned beatifically up at Tom.

"Superb, Gaston."

Acknowledgments

"The Harps of Heaven" from *The Devil's Storybook* by Natalie Babbitt. Copyright © 1974 by Natalie Babbitt. Reprinted by permission of Farrar, Straus and Giroux, Inc.

"Dribble!" from *Tales of a Fourth Grade Nothing* by Judy Blume. Text copyright © 1972 by Judy Blume. Reprinted by permission of the publisher, E. P. Dutton, a division of New American Library.

Excerpts from *The Midnight Fox* by Betsy Byars. Copyright © 1968 by Betsy Byars. Reprinted by permission of Viking Penguin Inc.

"Fifteen Minutes," from *Who Kidnapped the Sheriff?* by Larry Callen. Copyright © 1985 by Larry Callen. By permission of Little, Brown and Company, in association with Atlantic Monthly Press.

"The Pudding Like a Night on the Sea," from *The Stories Julian Tells*, by Ann Cameron. Copyright © 1981 by Ann Cameron. Reprinted by permission of Pantheon Books, a division of Random House, Inc.

"Beezus' Birthday" from *Beezus and Ramona* by Beverly Cleary. Copyright © 1955 by Beverly Cleary. By permission of William Morrow & Company.

"Formula 86 Delayed Action Mouse-Maker" from *The Witches* by Roald Dahl. Copyright © 1983 by Roald Dahl. Reprinted by permission of Farrar, Straus and Giroux, Inc. and in Canada by Jonathan Cape Ltd.

Excerpt from *Half Magic* by Edward Eager. Copyright 1954 by Harcourt Brace Jovanovich, Inc.; renewed 1982 by Jane Eager. Reprinted by permission of the publisher.

"Prodigy Street" from *Write if You Get Work: The Best of Bob and Ray* by Bob Elliott and Ray Goulding. Copyright © 1975 by Robert B. Elliott and Raymond W. Goulding. Reprinted by permission of Random House, Inc.

Excerpt from *How to Eat Like a Child* by Delia Ephron. Copyright © 1977, 1978 by Delia Ephron. Reprinted by permission of Viking Penguin Inc.

Excerpt from *Understood Betsy* by Dorothy Canfield Fisher. Copyright 1916, 1917, 1944, 1945 by Meredith Corporation. Reprinted by permission of Henry Holt and Company.

Pages 119–128 (text only) from *Harriet the Spy* by Louise Fitzhugh. Copyright © 1964 by Louise Fitzhugh. Reprinted by permission of Harper & Row, Publishers, Inc.

"February," from *McBroom's Almanac* by Sid Fleischman. Text copyright © 1984 by Sid Fleischman. By permission of Little, Brown and Company.

Chapter 12 from *Cheaper by the Dozen* by Frank B. Gilbreth, Jr., and Ernestine Gilbreth Carey (Thomas Y. Crowell). Copyright 1948, © 1963 by Frank Gilbreth, Jr., and Ernestine Gilbreth Carey. Reprinted by permission of Harper & Row, Publishers, Inc.

"Charles" from *Life Among the Savages* by Shirley Jackson. Copyright 1953 by Shirley Jackson. Copyright renewed © 1981 by Laurence Hyman, Barry Hyman, Mrs. Sarah Webster, and Mrs. Joanne Schnurer. Reprinted by permission of Farrar, Straus and Giroux, Inc.

Excerpt from *The Phantom Tollbooth*, by Norton Juster. Copyright © 1961 by Norton Juster. Reprinted by permission of Random House, Inc.

Excerpt from *Lake Wobegon Days*, by Garrison Keillor. Copyright © 1985 by Garrison Keillor. Reprinted by permission of Viking Penguin, Inc.

Excerpt from *No Beasts! No Children!* by Beverly Keller. Copyright © 1983 by Beverly Keller. By permission of Lothrop, Lee & Shepard Books (A Division of William Morrow & Company).

"The Elephant's Child" from *Just So Stories*, by Rudyard Kipling.

Excerpt from *In One Era and Out the Other* by Sam Levenson. Copyright © 1973 by Sam Levenson. Reprinted by permission of Simon & Schuster, Inc.

"The Thought-You-Saiders Cure" from *Mrs. Piggle-Wiggle's Magic* by Betty MacDonald (J. B. Lippincott Co.). Text copyright 1949 by Betty MacDonald. By permission of Harper & Row, Publishers, Inc.

"The Doughnuts" from *Homer Price* by Robert McCloskey. Copyright 1943, renewed © 1971 by Robert McCloskey. Reprinted by permission of Viking Penguin Inc.

"The Skunk Ladder" from *The Grasshopper Trap* by Patrick F. McManus. Copyright © 1985 by Patrick F. McManus. Reprinted by permission of Henry Holt and Company, Inc.

Excerpt from *The Story of the Treasure Seekers*, by E. Nesbit.

Excerpt from *Ghosts I Have Been* by Richard Peck. Copyright © 1977 by Richard Peck. Reprinted by permission of Viking Penguin Inc.

"Apples and Mrs. Stetson," from *Soup*, by Robert Newton Peck. Copyright © 1974 by Robert Newton Peck. Reprinted by permission of Alfred A. Knopf, Inc.

Chapter 4 from *The Best Christmas Pageant Ever* by Barbara Robinson. Text copyright © 1972 by Barbara Robinson. Reprinted by permission of Harper & Row, Publishers, Inc.

Excerpt from *How to Eat Fried Worms* by Thomas Rockwell. Reprinted by permission of Franklin Watts, Inc. Copyright © 1973 by Thomas Rockwell.

Chapter 3 from *Freaky Friday* by Mary Rodgers. Copyright © 1972 by Mary Rodgers. Reprinted by permission of Harper & Row, Publishers, Inc.

PAMELA POLLACK grew up in New York City and went to college and library school at Queens College. For ten years she was a book review editor at *School Library Journal*.

In choosing the pieces for *The Random House Book of Humor*, Pamela Pollack read hundreds of books. She says, "The stories I picked all view life from a funny perspective and each one is different. I chose them because the situations they depict are universal—and because they made me laugh."

Pamela Pollack lives in New York City, where she is an editor of children's books.

PAUL O. ZELINSKY began illustrating books for children ten years ago. Since then he has done fifteen books, including *Hansel and Gretel* and *Rumpelstiltskin*, both of which were Caldecott Honor Books.

For Paul Zelinsky, the challenge of *The Random House Book of Humor* was "to make drawings to suit a really varied group of stories, especially ones that in their original edition had such memorable illustrations."

A graduate of Yale, Paul Zelinsky lives in Brooklyn with his wife and two young children.

the little school
2812 - 116 N. E.
BELLEVUE, WASHINGTON 98004